Twisted Sister

SISTERS OF SIN

TWISTED SISTER

NATALIE M. ROBERTS

FIVE STAR

An imprint of Thomson Gale, a part of The Thomson Corporation

Detroit • New York • San Francisco • New Haven, Conn. • Waterville, Maine • London

This novel is a work of fiction. Names, characters, places and incidents are either the product of the author's imagination, or, if real, used fictitiously.

Set in 11 pt. Plantin.

LIBRARY OF CONGRESS CATALOGING-IN-PUBLICATION DATA

Roberts, Natalie M.
Twisted Sister : sisters of sin / Natalie M. Roberts. — 1st ed.
p. cm.
ISBN-13: 978-1-59414-573-5 (alk. paper)
ISBN-10: 1-59414-573-3 (alk. paper)
1. Police—California—Santa Barbara—Fiction. 2. Santa Barbara (Calif.)—Fiction. 3. Serial murders—Fiction. I. Title.
PS3603.04545T85 2007
813′.6—dc22 2007017645

First Edition. First Printing: October 2007.

Published in 2007 in conjunction with Tekno Books and Ed Gorman.

Printed in the United States of America on permanent paper
10 9 8 7 6 5 4 3 2 1

This one's for my BIGGEST FAN, Carlene.
There, I did it.
Now please don't take me to your cabin . . .

As always, I am deeply indebted to my agent
Karen Solem.

Chapter One

She hated being a victim.

Nothing worse than being prey. *Nails on a chalkboard. The sound of a shovel scraping on cement, making your hair stand up on end and filling your mouth with the taste of metal.*

The man in the old pickup truck driving next to her had been riding even with her burgundy Nissan Sentra for the last seven blocks. His window rolled down, he hooted and hollered, trying to get her attention.

She pretended not to see him, but had already grown tired of the game.

Mustn't be so impatient. These things take time.

Time. Time to make her own rules. She'd practiced and was ready.

She met his stare head on. Instead of being embarrassed and chagrined, like any *decent* person would be, it only encouraged him. He gave her what he must have thought an engaging grin, but since he was missing several teeth, the look was oddly disconcerting—like a sexual overture from a Halloween pumpkin. Did he really think she would respond to his honks and gestures by pulling over and dropping her pants, ready for action?

Since he showed no signs of stopping his ridiculous behavior, she assumed this was, indeed, what he thought.

Had this type of come-on worked for him before? She wondered about the women it might work on. She knew women like that and hated them.

Oh, knock it off. His desperation makes it easier for you. Be patient.

Another two blocks and she'd had enough. It was time to make her move, before she lost it and betrayed herself. She abruptly pulled over to the side of the road.

The man in the truck appeared to be shouting with glee. He swerved over in front of her car, stopping his pickup truck but staying inside.

He was playing hard to get now?

It didn't matter.

She fought back a smile as she wondered what he might be thinking. He probably thought this was a chance encounter, chalked up to his incredible charm and fantastic good looks. He couldn't be more wrong, about both his own assets and her intentions.

She got out of her car and walked forward to the pickup. There was no need to hurry.

She was used to getting attention, and had become comfortable with it. Sometimes, though, they went too far. It was never sincere, anyway—just a way for a man to get sex.

Several men stared at her, their cars slowing as they gawked. She ignored them and continued to the truck.

The pumpkin man, whom she knew to be Jake Higgins, leaned out of his window, trying to be nonchalant. The sweat stains under his armpits betrayed him. He was nervous.

Good, but move slow. Don't want him to run away. Walk up slowly.

She reached the window and stopped, her eyes meeting his.

It had been so easy. Now she was the hunter.

In her blue jeans, white T-shirt and long, flowing blond hair, she was the total picture of a California girl, the ones Jake Higgins always saw in the pages of the girlie magazines he favored. Woody's bookstore had a whole section of them, just filled with babe-o-licious coastal blondes. The one walking toward him now had mile-long legs, and she sauntered toward him, her hips swaying slightly.

"Look at that. She's gorgeous. Hot damn." He spoke softly under his breath, licking his lips nervously.

Jake Higgins couldn't believe his luck. Maybe she was a hooker. Women never pulled over.

His left leg started to jitter and he felt the sweat pouring from his glands. It was hard to stay cool, especially on a sunny early-October day in Southern California.

He'd give it his best shot. When she reached the window, he put on a mask of bravado.

"Hey baby, what's up? You looking for a good time? You found the right guy. Name's Jake." He put his hand out, as if he were going to shake hers, then pulled it back with an embarrassed grin, wiping it on the leg of his faded, hole-ridden jeans.

She stared without speaking. Jake began to feel uneasy, and his left leg started jumping even more. He put a hand on it to try to stop the motion, and squirmed in his seat. Her dark blue eyes seemed to see right through him, to the trash his mother always said he was, and he looked away from the intensity of her stare. Up close, she wasn't as attractive as he'd thought. There was something off about her, he didn't know what. But she was still a looker.

He was grateful when she spoke.

"Does this usually work for you? Do women just pull over on the road and let you have your way with them, and then on you go?"

Her voice was soft and low, almost a throaty growl, and he felt the crotch of his jeans tighten. He laughed and said, "Hell, yeah. Well it worked with you, didn't it? Baby, get in. Let's go for a ride. This is your lucky day."

And mine too, he thought.

She continued to watch him, and he felt the grin on his face turn artificial. It hurt now, holding the muscles in place. His smile started to droop. She didn't move. Why wasn't she jumping eagerly into his truck? Maybe this hadn't really worked.

"Look," he said, suddenly impatient, "you wanna go somewhere and play with Jake? I promise you, baby, you will never forget it. I'll show you the best time you've ever had." He grabbed his crotch and moved it up and down. "You go for a ride with Jake, you'll be beggin' for more."

She moved, breaking the uncomfortable eye contact, and walked around the truck to the passenger side, and then she was in his truck. The roomy cab was now small and hot. A warm flush started in his belly and moved up his chest, heating up in slow degrees until it reached his cheeks, fiery and uncomfortable. His cock hardened at the mere realization that she sat next to him.

He started the truck and pulled into traffic, almost ramming into another car in his eagerness.

It was the middle of the day and he was about to get lucky. He had a hard-on that wouldn't quit and a beautiful woman by his side. The guys at Froggie's Bar were not going to believe this.

"Why don't you pull over in there," she suggested in her soft, sexy voice, pointing to an alley between a grocery store and Woody's bookstore. This was familiar territory for him. They were on his turf now, and he felt his nervousness fade away and an incredible rush replace it.

He turned the steering wheel as she reached over and put her hand between his legs, almost touching his cock.

"Woohoo," he shouted, unable to contain his joy. Nothing like this had ever happened to him before. Jake Higgins had been lying. He always had to persuade women, sometimes with a backhand, to do what he wanted.

Sure, he'd tried. You can't blame a guy for trying. Everyone knew women were always asking for it anyway. Teasing and leading a guy on, and then pulling back and pretending to be shy, nervous, scared. This one was for real. And he had known it all along; known women were just like men. Wait till he told the guys.

As he pulled over into the alley and stopped the truck, he turned to reach for her.

She leaned toward him, the soft hair falling forward as she moved.

He unzipped his pants and his rigid cock burst out of the top. His last pair of clean underwear had been worn two days ago, and he didn't feel like visiting the Laundromat, so there was nothing between the beautiful blonde and . . .

Jake saw the blood spurting up before he realized anything had happened. "What the fu . . . ?" Then he screamed. The pain . . . in his crotch . . . He looked down. "Oh my God, you . . . help me . . . you . . . You cut my fuckin' dick off . . ."

"You won't be needing your dick anymore, Jakie," she said in her sexy, deep voice. "No more fucking for you."

Chapter Two

"It wasn't like I asked him up for sex." Tears streamed down Tessa Morrow's face in big, black rivers of mascara and saline. "I just wanted to have another drink. I liked him."

It was Tuesday night group. Kelsey Waite was frustrated.

The "Man Haters Club of Santa Barbara" certainly was appropriate when Tessa had the floor. Quinn Anderson, Kelsey's lover and new roommate, had given the group that little moniker. Sometimes Kelsey found it irritating he would categorize her group this way. Sometimes, it was just truthful.

Tessa had been with the Women Against Violence group since Kelsey and Alisha Telford founded it over a year ago. Tessa saw the first flier on the hospital bulletin board during one of her many forays into the emergency room. This was her fifth date-rape in as many months.

Kelsey tried to be patient. She knew what it was like to be a victim. It hadn't been long ago she'd found herself at the mercy of a polygamous cult leader who kidnapped her daughter and murdered her neighbor. Kelsey's own father had basically delivered her into the hands of David Stone and the Church of the Lamb of God.

If anyone should be compassionate, it was Kelsey, but she had to really dig deep to find it for Tessa, who lived for melodrama. Kelsey tapped her ever-handy pencil into the palm of her left hand while Tessa sobbed. Her impatience showing, she crossed and uncrossed her legs several times. Tessa didn't seem to notice.

It was Kelsey's turn to run the group, and she was tired of Tessa's attention-stealing tactics. The older, small redhead in the back had just joined them. She looked scared and alone. If Tessa kept up her histrionics, the newcomer might not get a chance to speak.

"All right, Tessa. I'm sorry this happened. You have to stop letting them up into your apartment. Remember what we talked about? Empower yourself. Don't be a victim. Same advice as last time, okay?"

Tessa turned off the tears as if they had been flowing from a faucet.

"Thank you, thank you. We have to stick together."

"Okay, anyone else?" Kelsey looked around the room, her gaze resting for a moment on her subdued partner, Alisha.

Something was up with 'Lisha. She was too quiet, pensive and moody. No time to dwell on it now, though.

"No one else?" When no one spoke up, she looked at the clock. Damn. Tessa had managed to use up the last of the time.

"Okay, well, thanks everybody. Thanks for coming tonight. Please be safe."

The sudden noise of mingling female voices signaled the end of the meeting and beginning of the bonding. In some ways, Kelsey thought, this part was more important than anything else.

A tall blond woman approached her and spoke. "Good job tonight, Kelsey." Dr. Tamara Rowe was a licensed clinical psychologist and on-staff with Santa Barbara Community Hospital. She volunteered her time with the group. She was also the victim of an abusive boyfriend.

"Thanks, Tammy," Kelsey said with a smile. "Now if I could just get Tessa under control . . ."

"No hope there. She lives for this."

"Don't I know it," Kelsey said with a smile.

"How goes the job search?"

"Quinn keeps telling me just to stay home and keep painting. He swears I'm going to make a sale to a gallery any day. I doubt it. My paintings are too dark. Thomas Kincaid I ain't."

"Sure you will. You've got the talent. You just have to believe in yourself. I'm headed out. See you next week."

"Thanks again, Tammy," Kelsey said, making her way through the hospital conference room toward the newcomer. She dodged in and out of groups of three and four women who were chatting.

"Kelsey, I need to talk to you. It's *so* important."

Damn.

"Tessa, can it wait? I need to speak with someone before she leaves."

"But *Kelsey,*" she whined. "It's really important."

"Just a sec, okay? Just a minute."

She pushed past the last group of women and saw the redhead walking out the door. "Hey, wait."

The woman turned slowly. Her eyes were bare of makeup and were red-rimmed. Short and thin, she slouched over, as if the closer she got to the ground, the better were her chances of disappearing. The redhead appeared to be in her forties, although whatever burdens she lugged around with her made her eyes look ancient.

"I'm Kelsey. Sorry to chase you down like this. I just didn't want you to get away without my saying hello."

"I shouldn't have come," the woman said in a voice devoid of life.

"Oh, no, everyone is always welcome here. We're glad you came . . ."

"It was a mistake. I just wanted to see her. It was a mistake." She scrambled down the empty hospital corridor, her shoes making a hollow, eerie noise that echoed off the walls, and out into the murky night.

Chapter Three

Alisha Telford was late.

She hurried into the nurse's lounge, rushed to her locker, and quickly twisted the dial of her combination lock. Tonight was a special night, and she was running behind because of a multiple trauma on the freeway. A long lunch running errands hadn't helped either. She had returned to find the emergency room a mess. A four-car pileup had yielded ten victims—how did six grown men fit into a Geo Metro, anyway?

Alisha was meeting Joe, Kelsey, and Quinn at Cafe Pinot in less than thirty minutes, and she'd hoped to go home to shower and change. Now, she would just have to pull herself together as best as she could. She always kept a clean pair of jeans and a shirt in her locker. Today she thanked her lucky stars the jeans were nearly new and the shirt was the color of blue that matched her eyes and set off the highlights in her blond hair.

She changed in a hurry, ran a brush through her hair, and lipstick over her lush, thick lips. She rarely wore makeup, and had always been grateful for her good skin and flawless complexion. Although Alisha didn't see it herself, she had been told she was a natural beauty. This worked to her advantage right now, since she had very little time and a twenty-minute drive to the restaurant ahead of her.

She dabbed the excess lipstick off with a tissue, ran the brush quickly through her hair again, and gave herself a last once-over in the mirror.

Tonight was the night. Joe was going to propose; she just knew it.

Ready to go, she shoved her dirty uniform into the bottom portion of her locker and slammed it shut, making sure she had her wallet and her keys before she headed out the door. As she walked past the nurse's station, she heard two of her coworkers chatting. Alisha tapped on the counter in greeting, then rushed by, until she heard a snippet of conversation from the two women.

". . . He was stabbed in the dick, can you believe it? Cut it right off. But the main wound was the femoral artery. He bled to death behind Woody's Bookstore. A bum found him this morning. Name was Jake Higgins."

She stopped cold and turned to the women, staring, and Maggie gave her an odd look.

"Everything all right, Alisha?"

"The name. Did you say Jake Higgins?" she asked Maggie.

"Uh, yeah, I was just telling Annie about an ER vic brought in DOA."

"The name was Jake Higgins?"

The two nurses looked at each other, Annie shrugged, and Maggie turned to her. "Yes, Jake Higgins. Alisha, are you all right? You don't look so hot. Is something wrong? You didn't know him, did you?"

A wave of nausea hit Alisha. Her cheeks flushed with warmth, a sharp contrast to the chill in her soul. This could not be happening. Not the same Jake Higgins she knew. Silly. There had to be a whole lot of men named Jake Higgins in this world.

She started to walk again, headed toward her car in the staff parking lot. *It wasn't him.* She'd almost reached her car when she abruptly turned around and headed back to the door and into the ER. She turned left and walked into the triage area. Her shoes made a rapid slap-slap sound on the tile floor as she approached her friend Steve, who was head nurse on duty.

She just wanted to make sure—just to ease her mind. Jake Higgins couldn't be here now, in this hospital. He couldn't.

"Steve, is the stabbing victim still in here? The one who died?"

He looked tired, and rubbed his eyes as he looked at her. "Yeah," he said, motioning to one of the curtains. "Right there, curtain three. Waiting for the morgue guys."

"What was his name?" she asked him in a hushed whisper.

He looked at her in surprise, then reached for a chart in front of him on the counter. "Jacob. Jacob Higgins. Why, Alisha? You know this guy? You're white as a ghost."

She walked to the curtain, pulled it roughly aside, and stepped into the room that held the dead body of Jacob Higgins. Jacob sounded dignified. He didn't deserve it.

Too close to home. Too damn close to home.

Maybe it wasn't him. It couldn't be him. Jake Higgins was scum. He was also nowhere near Santa Barbara Community Hospital, right? The last she'd heard of him, he was headed to Oregon—or so she'd been told.

A sheet, stained with red, draped the corpse. The outline showed the shape beneath was a body. A big, bulky body.

She inhaled deeply and reached out with a shaking hand. It stopped just short of the sheet. She forced herself to continue and pulled the sheet down from the top until it displayed the head, neck and shoulders of the dead man.

A little moan escaped her lips. It was him. He was older, and weathered, but she still would have recognized him anywhere. Life had not been kind to this man, who had treated his body like an amusement park. He had been her horror ride.

He was her father's friend. He raped her when she was only sixteen. He was dead.

Finally, Jake Higgins had gotten just what he deserved. She pulled the sheet down further and the room began to shrink. The whole world closed in, and there was nothing left except her and the body of the man who destroyed her life years before.

The tool he'd used to wreak havoc was missing. Gone. Severed neatly with surgical precision.

She stared.

The game had started. She wasn't ready.

Detective Joe Malone quietly pulled the curtain back and watched Alisha, his current girlfriend, stare at the disfigured and murdered body of his latest assignment. Fear, puzzlement, and disgust all played across her beautiful face, but there was something else. Something akin to—satisfaction?

"Alisha?"

Startled, she jumped, and placed a hand to her chest as she turned to him.

He watched her face change, shades of deception and concealment in her eyes. Joe had been a cop long enough to know something was wrong here; something was off.

"Joe, you're supposed to be at the Cafe. I was just on my way. I just stopped here to . . . to . . ." Alisha was a terrible liar, and Joe knew it. She'd told him so many times. Instead of lying, she just avoided answering; something Joe had tried to point out was a lie in itself.

" 'Lish, what's wrong? Why are you in here?"

"Why are you here?" She stalled for time, answering his question with a question, another tactic she used to avoid talking about things she wasn't comfortable with.

"We got called out on this homicide, me and Quinn. Kelsey's waiting at the restaurant for you. We were going to join you later, if we could. Alisha, why are you in here? Do you know this guy? What's going on?"

A myriad of emotions ran across her face, and Joe watched closely as he waited for an answer. "Alisha?"

"He was my father's friend, a family friend. He . . . I haven't seen him for a lot of years. It's just a shock, that's all. I heard someone say his name when I was leaving . . . and I came to see . . ."

"Oh honey, I'm so sorry," Joe said, enfolding her in his strong arms, sensing some of this was true, but something else was missing. There was a part shc wasn't sharing.

She buried her head in his shirt like a small child, burrowing close, looking for comfort. He put his arms around her and waited.

"Jake Higgins was more than a family friend, Joe," Alisha finally said, her voice muffled in his shirt. She pulled away as he touched her shoulders gently. She looked up into his eyes, and he could see the tears spilling over. He reached down to wipe away the moisture, but she pulled back from him before he could touch her, and turned again to face the body laying on the gurney.

Her breathing was harsh and shallow, and offered a portent of truths to come that were ugly and sinister.

"Jake Higgins was a rapist. He raped me when I was sixteen, and told my dad I seduced him. My father beat me and tried to force me to marry Jake. I refused.

"I'm glad he's dead."

Joe's mouth fell open, and a million bees seemed to be buzzing around his head, filling his ears with fearsome roaring. He shook his head sharply, trying to clear his mind and chase away the loud buzzing.

Alisha turned away from him, avoiding eye contact, her gaze fixed firmly on an invisible spot just above the dead body on the gurney.

He watched her closely, and sensed her discomfort. Her stoic profile revealed nothing now, as though she had put on a mask to cover her anxiety, but her twitching fingers and shuffling feet betrayed her.

He tried to think of the right words to use. He tried to think of *any* words to say. Someone had hurt Alisha very badly in the past: he'd known it for a long time. He just didn't think it was something like this. He saw similar shit every day and he kept himself hardened to it, not letting the filth touch him. Emotionally closed off, his ex-wife called him. She saw it as a character flaw. He saw it as survival. Now it was happening to him.

No, not to him. To someone he loved. Now he understood her strange behavior when he caught her staring at the corpse.

Joe looked at her again and opened his mouth to speak. No words came out.

"I'm sorry. I didn't tell you because . . ." Her quiet, despair-tinged voice pierced his temporary armor of shock, and when he saw the tears fall slowly down her face, the sight spurred him into action. He reached for her just as the color completely left her face and she began to sway.

Joe grabbed her by the shoulders, turned her around, and pushed her out of the death-shrouded room. A single chair had been carried in from the waiting room, and was pushed up against the wall. The garish orange color was out of place in the sterile surroundings, and Joe steered Alisha toward it like a boat to shore.

He pushed her firmly down into the chair, exerting pressure on her shoulders, and she sat upright and still for a moment, looking straight ahead.

Neither of them spoke, and Joe avoided her eyes, worried about what she'd read there. He'd been a cop for so long his emotions rarely reached the surface. His stoicism kept suspects and victims from interpreting his signals and jumping to conclusions; but this was no ordinary victim.

This was the woman he loved, admitting she'd been violated as a teenager by the scum . . .

"You okay?" he asked her, finally managing to get some words out.

He was here at the hospital to investigate a murder. The victim, it turned out, was a sadist and a rapist who had stolen Alisha's innocence. He felt the anger come over him and struggled for composure. He had a murder to solve. He had to try to find justice for the miserable wreck of a man named Jake Higgins.

Joe knew he was no fixer. His ex-wife would attest to that. He couldn't fix Alisha's nightmares and her agonies. And yet, he couldn't leave. He loved her. How could he abandon her now? Tonight, he'd been prepared to ask her to be his wife.

Quinn Anderson walked up behind Joe, and patted him on the shoulder, making him jump. He'd totally forgotten about his partner, who had been standing behind him and obviously heard the whole thing.

"Hey, Jogo, why don't you get a cup of coffee? I'll get a little more information from Alisha. Then she can go meet Kelsey, and we can continue this investigation."

Joe felt lost. He hated hospital coffee. It was almost as bad as police-station coffee. Obediently, as though he had no will of his own, he moved away toward the lounge. He walked only a few feet before stopping. He came back, and leaning down, put his arms around Alisha, hugging her tightly. He was ashamed of himself, ashamed of his reaction, but he needed some time to think. He smiled a weak smile and kissed her on the cheek. Then he turned and walked away.

Joe felt her eyes on him as he left, heard a small sob escape her lips. He just needed a minute to compose himself. Then he could go back and be the strong man she needed.

The one who had a killer to catch.

Quinn reached out and touched Alisha's shoulder and let her

know, without words, she had his support. In the short time she'd known him, they'd become good friends, although he didn't know much about her. Like his lover Kelsey, she had suffered abuse in her past, and she kept her true self locked tightly away from public view.

Quinn watched as her gaze followed Joe, who trudged down the hall toward the break room, his shoulders drooping, his right hand rubbing his left arm. His partner's big, square body housed the soul of a teddy bear, and Quinn knew he'd allowed Alisha to see that side of him. She was lucky.

"Why does life have to be so complicated?" Alisha asked quietly, turning back to him after Joe disappeared inside the door to the break room.

"If I had the answer to that, I'd be on TV making millions, not working as a cop," Quinn answered, even though he knew it had been a rhetorical question. "I have to ask you some questions, Alisha. I'm sure you realize that."

"Yes," she said in a quiet voice, looking down at the floor. She put her hands behind her back and swung her feet under the chair, looking like a child who was about to be reprimanded for stealing a cookie.

"How long has it been?"

"You mean since I saw him last?"

"Yeah."

"Sixteen years. I . . . I heard he left Chapel Grace." She twirled a strand of long, fine blond hair around the end of her index finger. "That's where I'm from."

"What do you mean, you heard?"

"Thomas—my brother—beat him up one night, several years after he attacked me. He waited for him outside a bar. It was really bad, and we ran because the sheriff was—oh shit, the sheriff was Jake's brother. He was also my dad's friend. Tommy and I left town right after that. We've never been back."

"You have a brother?"

"I had a brother."

She said no more, forcing Quinn to prod her to continue.

"Alisha, I hate to do this to you, I do. I can tell you're upset. Can you just tell me what you know about him? I mean in the past few years? How did you hear about him?"

"My darling mother. I wrote to her, asking her to send me my things. I didn't have much, just a few pictures and my diary. I asked her to send it to a P.O. box. I didn't want to see her again, either. She never protected Tommy and me from my father.

"Look, Quinn, I haven't seen Jake Higgins for sixteen years. Honest to God. I'll never forget him, but I haven't seen him."

"I know, Alisha, but how did your mother tell you about Jake?"

Alisha sighed and put her head down onto her hands, covering her eyes and rubbing them fiercely, as if trying to make the images of the past disappear.

"She wrote me a letter, okay? Didn't send me my stuff, my pictures, or my diary. Just wrote a stupid letter and told me to come back. She said Jake was gone to Oregon looking for work. Pretending, just like she always did, that nothing was wrong, nothing had ever happened."

"You mean between you and Jake?"

"No." Alisha pulled her head up and looked at him with a weary expression on her face. She bit her bottom lip and drew blood, making Quinn wince. "Between my father and me."

Quinn felt a twinge of unease, attributing it to the fact he was poking around in a good friend's closet, her skeletons lurking there to shock him. He decided to stop the conversation there. He knew he would have to return to the subject of her father and Jake Higgins, but now wasn't the time.

"Okay. Well, I'm going to talk to the docs here, okay? Snoop around a bit. You go find Joe. Talk. He's a good man, 'Lish. He'll stand by you. Then you go meet Kelsey. She hates being alone."

"I know."

"We're going to have to talk more about this, Alisha." Quinn's voice was quiet, but she winced as though he'd screamed the words at her. She nodded her head, and he walked away after touching her on the shoulder.

Quinn spied the head ER nurse and decided to question him next.

Alisha is hiding something. But what? And God, do I want to know?

He turned his head and saw Alisha still sitting in the chair, head in her hands again, her body a posture of defeat. Women with secrets. First Kelsey, now Alisha. They were turning out to be his specialty.

Chapter Four

The little room stank. It was a pull-your-gut-up-through-your-nose kind of smell. She didn't mind. She'd grown used to it.

The smell came from the latest part. It lingered in the air, attached to invisible atoms and molecules, a scented gruesome reminder, for the part was no longer out in the air decomposing. It had its own little formaldehyde-tinged environment. There were four of them. Four "parts."

Daddy used to call it his "Little Richard." Four Dicks sitting in a row, each of them in its individual mason jar. She giggled.

The first three men had been homeless. Now they were dickless. Two of them died. The third one lived, but would never, ever, be the same. Still, it had been careless, letting him live. She let the anger pull her under for a moment, and then shook it off.

No way, not going to let one disappointment take away her euphoria.

Those first three had been just for practice, anyway. She'd learned from her mistakes, and that was the most important thing.

Thank goodness she learned from her mistakes, because those first men were disgusting. Didn't the homeless ever bathe?

She put a hand to her mouth and giggled again, a coquettish smile on her lush lips, which were covered in the lovely shade of plum spice. She could see her reflection in the broken mirror she'd propped up on a shelf across the room. The shiny fragment was just a piece of a larger mirror that used to take up one entire wall of the room where she'd been raised. Her little altar to the "old times." She admired her long, manicured fingernails, painted in the same shade as her lips, and blew herself a kiss.

The one who'd lived had hurt her. Given her a black eye. That had been hard to explain most places, but not at group. There, the other women coddled her. She'd told them a story about "boyfriend." The one who beat her on a regular basis. They said angry words and made angry faces and urged her to turn him in. Call the cops. Press charges. Urged her, at the least, to leave him.

She promised to do just that. No more boyfriend. Of course, "boyfriend" was nonexistent. She didn't like men. Wouldn't have dreamed of having an actual boyfriend. She was just getting revenge. Revenge for all of them.

It had been so easy to lure Jake Higgins to Santa Barbara. Just a telephone call, really, and a promise that some unfinished business would be completed. He wasn't the brightest man. Didn't suspect a thing; not until he was looking down at his bloody, empty crotch.

Calvin Reynolds was next.

Chapter Five

Joe leaned against the wall of the break room, sipping the motor oil the hospital passed off as coffee. It was strong, and he needed strong. The last few minutes had brought about more than one revelation he was not prepared for, and he couldn't seem to calm down. His heart raced as he thought about Alisha, and a sharp pain hit him. His chest felt tight.

I sure don't need this coffee. Probably pure caffeine.

It definitely wasn't helping with the palpitations or heartburn. The pain and discomfort had been bothering him off and on for the last few weeks, enough so he even made an appointment with his doctor.

His thoughts went back to Alisha, and the tightening and pain got worse.

Joe had spent a long time convincing her to give their relationship a chance. He had fifteen more years of life experience than she did, and a son and daughter from a first marriage. Alisha was young and beautiful, and still had so much ahead of her. At twenty-nine, she was stunning, and he couldn't believe she even gave him the time of day, let alone access into her life.

Alisha spent the first three months of their relationship giving him reasons why it wouldn't work. It became a game of sorts, where she would come up with her reasons, and one by one he discounted them all.

"What's the reason d'jour?" became his standard greeting

whenever he picked her up for dinner, or a movie, or a night on the town.

Tired of making excuses, or at least he assumed so, she finally agreed to try a mutually exclusive relationship.

They had come close to making love more than once, but Alisha always pulled away. Joe knew something had frightened her, something had happened to her in the past, and he didn't push her. She always told him she was amazed at his patience.

Now he understood. As much as he could understand, being a man. Unless it was something else. The look on her face as she stared at Jake Higgins' body—what was that look?

Joe pulled at the neckline of his collar. His tie seemed too tight, and he was hot. *I must really be upset about this Alisha thing.* He was sweating profusely, and a pain gripped his left arm and moved into his back, paralyzing him for a second. He couldn't breathe, and he reached out for something to hold on to. The coffeepot teetered for a second and then fell to the floor, where it shattered into small pieces.

He found himself on the floor beside the coffeepot, writhing in incredible pain. He could feel the wet, hot coffee soaking through his suit jacket.

He was oddly concerned about the horrible mess the coffee had made on the break-room floor, and as his vision began to blur, he randomly thought, *Damn, that stain will ruin this jacket. And I just bought it special for tonight.*

Joe wanted to yell for help, but the sharp knife stabbing into his heart made it hard to breathe. No sound would come out of his mouth.

He slowly reached his right hand into his pocket and pulled out the small black box, clutching it tightly in his hand, then dropping it as pain coursed through his body like a lightning bolt.

He was going to die, he thought, going to die in a hospital, fifty feet away from doctors and nurses who could save his life, and all because he couldn't yell.

Life was ironic.

He looked up to see Alisha pushing through the door. She must have been close.

"Joe!" She ran to him and dropped to the floor. His face contorted with pain, and he gasped as he tried to make words. None came out.

Joe's mouth opened, and closed, his chest heaved, and he clutched his left arm weakly.

Alisha looked down at his side and saw the small black box he'd dropped. She picked it up and opened it, gasping at the half-carat diamond ring inside. She looked back down at him, mouthed an "I love you," and then slipped the ring out of the box and into her pocket.

She threw the box at a wastebasket not far from where she knelt. "Two points."

What was she doing? Joe tried to think. To reason. To . . .

Two points? He was dying, and she was shooting imaginary hoops?

What was she doing?

Alisha knelt back down next to Joe, and a warm smile crossed her face. He gasped to breathe, gray, clammy, dying.

"Help me! Help! In the break room. A heart attack! Get the gurney. *Help!*" She screamed as loud as she could, hearing the hint of hysteria in her voice, acknowledging it. She looked down at dear sweet Joe, and stroked his face, as he watched her, a puzzled expression in his eyes before they lost focus.

She heard shouts and the sound of wheels on tile, and she grabbed at the tie around his neck and loosened it.

Alisha pulled the tie from around his neck and tossed it aside, talking to him while she undid the buttons of his shirt.

"You better not leave me now, Joe Malone, or I'll tell you what. I will make your life miserable. You said you wanted into this relationship, and now, by God, you are in it and you are not getting out of it this easily."

Alisha watched Joe's face, a mixture of puzzlement and anger, and then the agony wiped it all away, and he mouthed something, words she couldn't understand. She leaned closer to him, aware of the footsteps foretelling the approach of the medical team. Steve led the group of medical professionals who filled the break room and he reached down to pull Alisha away. She moved closer to Joe's mouth and heard him say, "Who . . . Why?"

"I love you, too," she yelled, despair kicking in, making her forget all about the ring, thinking about all she'd lost, and then Steve grabbed her shoulders and lifted her to her feet, moving her away from Joe.

"Let them work, 'Lish," he said quietly, holding her back as she fought to return to Joe. Finally, she collapsed in sobs and Steve tried to lead her from the room, but she resisted. The ER team moved swiftly as they picked Joe up and loaded him onto the gurney.

They wasted no time, moving the gurney swiftly out of the break room and down the hall into the cardiac care area of the ER. Alisha followed closely, until a hand stopped her, pulling her back.

"You can't go in there, hon," Steve said. "You're too close to the situation. Please, just stay here."

"I want to help him, I have to help him," she said in anguish, tears rolling down her face. "God, you cannot do this to me. You can't. I have finally found someone, finally found a good man and you cannot take him from me."

A gust of air swooped past them as the automatic doors leading from the hospital into the ER opened. Dr. Mahendra Patel bustled through and rapidly disappeared into the room where Joe was being treated.

Dr. Patel was the best cardiac care surgeon in the Santa Barbara area. Alisha knew if anyone could save Joe, it would be him. She put a hand to her mouth as she watched the room.

After a minute, Alisha walked to one of the chairs at the nurse's station, and fell into it, her head going into her hands and the sobs breaking free from her throat with abandon.

It's always so hard. So hard. Every damned time.

It was like a bad omen, seeing the face and body of Jake Higgins in the ER. Something awful was going to happen. *That* was totally unexpected. Something was wrong here.

She'd seen the face of death in Jake Higgins, and now Joe. It wasn't his time. Why was this happening?

The standard-issue black-and-white clock on the wall appeared to be broken. The second hand moved in slow motion. Five minutes. Ten. Fifteen . . . Dr. Patel came out of the room, still wearing the medical scrubs he donned after entering the room.

Steve, sitting next to Alisha at the nurse's station, jumped up and walked over to the doctor, saying something quietly in his ear and then pointing to Alisha.

Dr. Patel headed over to her, a look of compassion and sadness on his face. She stood quickly, and immediately felt dizzy, the room spinning around her. Alisha felt a hand on her back, and she looked behind her to see Quinn. He had evidently been told what had happened, as his face was grave and shocked.

Dr. Patel approached her, and took her hand. She knew it was bad. Alisha knew it was over.

It wasn't his time, dammit. This isn't fair.

"I am so sorry, Nurse Telford. I understand this man was your fiancé," he said in his clipped and proper English, tinged with the lilt of an Indian accent. She didn't correct him, didn't tell him Joe hadn't proposed yet, didn't tell him about the ring in her pocket. She couldn't speak.

"I'm so sorry." The words uttered so many times in this very emergency room now applied to her, once again, like so many times in her cluttered and violent past. She owned those words; they had always been hers.

She shook herself, trying to clear her head, trying to focus.

"We tried everything," Dr. Patel said. To Alisha's befuddled brain, he sounded as if he stood on the other side of a long tunnel. "He suffered a massive heart attack. There was too much damage. An autopsy will show more, but there was nothing more we could do. Is there someone we can call for you?"

The tears welled in Alisha's eyes, and she started to sob. She felt like an idiot, but she could not control her grief. Quinn put his arms around her, and they hugged each other tightly.

When he let go, Alisha collapsed into a chair.

Quinn turned to Steve and asked him to call the restaurant where Kelsey waited for them.

There would be no celebration tonight.

Chapter Six

Life was funny, thought Kelsey, as she tucked Alisha Telford into Tia's small twin bed and turned out the light. It hadn't been so long ago Alisha had tucked Kelsey's injured body and soul into bed.

It hadn't even been a year since Kelsey's daughter had been kidnapped and her neighbor murdered, both victims of a polygamous cult from Kelsey's past. That adventure had resulted in her being hit by a police car, meeting Alisha in the hospital, and traveling to Utah with Quinn to face down the demons of her past.

In a fight for her very life, and that of her daughter Tia, Kelsey had come out victorious. She'd faced down her nightmares in a manner so direct she knew she would never be the same, yet would always be stronger for the experience. Sometimes she would wake from a tormented sleep, drenched in sweat, not really remembering the vivid dreams that set her heart pounding with the fury of a hurricane, but knowing what they were, all the same.

David Stone, the cult leader, still awaited trial, being held in a rural county jail in central Utah. She was trying to move on, but a very large piece of Kelsey was still in Utah. Her mother sat in a barren room on the fifth floor of LDS Hospital, never speaking, interrupting long silences only long enough to erupt with bone-chilling screams.

Kelsey sighed.

Don't think about it. There's nothing you can do.

Now Alisha was forced to face her tumultuous past and, in addition, had to grieve over the man she had loved. Kelsey had made her take one of the pills Dr. Patel prescribed. Tia would be sleeping with Kelsey tonight, and Quinn had willingly moved to the couch.

He was in shock too, and grieving. So many of the people Kelsey loved were hurting, and she could do nothing to help. It was an odd change for her, and not one she was comfortable with. She'd rather carry the pain herself, because at least she could control it. In others, it became unmanageable, and she had to play a guessing game, only hoping at saying and doing the right thing to make the situation better.

Quinn was distant and quiet, and had said little since bringing Alisha from the hospital to their home.

"Did she argue?" Kelsey had whispered to him, as she watched her friend walk lifelessly from room to room, stopping at each window to look outside, as if expecting Joe to reappear and the whole nightmare to dissipate.

Quinn just shook his head as an answer to Kelsey's question, grabbed a beer from the fridge, twisted the top off, and smacked the bottle down on the oak table. The chair scraped the tiled floor as he moved it out and heaved his body into it. Sitting straight up, his back not touching the chair, he stared off into space, his mouth a straight, grim line.

Kelsey went to him and ran her fingers gently across his furrowed brow, and then she went to Alisha, taking her by the hand and leading her to the living room sofa.

"Let's talk."

But Alisha barely spoke the rest of the night, and she took the sleeping pill without complaint at eight, after picking at a dinner of barbecued chicken and salad, one of her favorite meals.

Now the house was filled with bodies but felt empty, and

Kelsey wandered slowly through her beloved home, touching knickknacks and pictures. Tia as a baby; Kelsey and Alisha clowning on the beach; Joe and Alisha drinking wine and mugging for the camera, a picture taken just the month before.

The small but comfortable cottage she shared with Quinn and her young daughter Tia was located in the Mesa area of Santa Barbara. Kelsey had inherited the two-bedroom, two-bath home from her late Aunt Regina, and she considered herself fortunate to live in the neighborhood. The ocean views were stunning, and the eclectic and charming interior of the house suited Kelsey's inner artist. She wandered into the small den that also served as a family room, and surveyed the contents of the room. She loved the fireplace, which warmed the house on the occasions the temperature dropped. The room also had high ceilings, hardwood floors, and built-in bookshelves. Those bookshelves were now filled with the massive library belonging to Quinn.

Kelsey liked to tease him about being a literary cop. In addition to being a voracious reader, he also wrote poetry and had completed two novels—which he had never submitted anywhere.

"I don't write them for anyone else. I write them for me," Quinn told her when she pressed him.

"Guess I'm lucky I got to read them."

"You are." With that comment, Quinn had ended the conversation. He didn't share his feelings or opinions easily. Kelsey always thought of him as the strong, silent type.

Kelsey could make out the shadow of Quinn's body on the sofa next to the window, reclined on his side facing the back of the couch. She thought she could hear heavy breathing, and reluctantly she left him without saying or doing anything. She wanted so badly just to touch his shoulder blades, or run her fingers down his spine.

As she walked down the hallway, she thought about her

friend. Alisha was the silent type, too. Kelsey knew most of Alisha's story, but few other people did. The woman was a cache of secrets. Kelsey understood. It's why they were such good friends. They had shared past heartache before starting Women Against Violence. The two of them had been spurred to start the Tuesday night group after discovering common ground—they had both been victims, and neither one of them intended to stay that way.

Alisha had no one else. No family or close friends. Kelsey didn't either. They were like sisters.

Kelsey walked into the kitchen and picked up the handset of the cordless phone. She dialed Tamara Rowe's number, leaving a message on the answering machine when Tammy didn't pick up. She'd hoped the psychologist could come and talk to Alisha in the morning. After a quick glance at her watch, she saw it was only nine p.m., and yet the house was silent as though they were all small children, tucked in tightly and visited by the sandman.

Kelsey sat down in one of the rigid kitchen chairs with a thump, and the events of the night played through her head like a horror movie.

She couldn't believe the man who raped Alisha had been murdered and brought to the very hospital where she worked. It had been sixteen years since he had violated Alisha, and she had never gotten over it.

It seemed too great a coincidence, and yet appeared to be totally random.

"Okay, maybe I can believe it. But still . . ."

Joe and Quinn were the investigating detectives. Joe was in love with Alisha. This was just too weird for words. Joe. Joe had been in love with Alisha. Now he was dead.

"Ugh," she said, putting her hands to her tired eyes and rubbing them like a small child. "No more thinking this way. Not tonight."

Kelsey stood up and quietly padded through the hallway, stopping to kiss Quinn goodnight, unable to keep herself away from him, even though she didn't want to bother him. She watched him for a moment, as he tossed and turned on the sofa. She leaned down and kissed his cheek, and lovingly caressed his face. If she had lost Quinn now, after finally finding a man she was safe with, she didn't know how she would bear it.

Quinn didn't speak or open his eyes, so she reluctantly continued on to her bedroom.

Kelsey sighed again deeply as she changed into an oversized t-shirt and slipped into bed beside Tia.

She felt a keening in her heart, and recognized it as loneliness. Loneliness had been her friend for a long time. Kelsey Waite knew an awful lot about grief, and the most important thing she knew was everyone deserved to mourn. Understanding didn't help to explain why she felt as though she were alone on a deserted island, though.

She wanted to go into the living room and lie down next to Quinn, feeling his warmth and reveling in his closeness. She wanted to comfort him, like he had comforted her. But Kelsey couldn't force herself on Quinn. He would come to her when he was ready.

Quinn had spent a lot of time on the phone while she settled Alisha into bed. Several times he had raised his voice, but she couldn't catch the words.

She didn't think she would sleep, but amazingly, she drifted off soon after her head hit the pillow.

Someone close by screamed.

Kelsey jerked awake, and tried to think. The sounds of

anguish came from Tia's room. She struggled to find her way out of bed. She had to save Tia. Disoriented and not fully awake, she rushed out the door. Realization hit her. Tia had been quietly sleeping beside her. She turned back and looked. The little girl was still asleep.

It was Alisha who'd screamed; whose nightmares rang through the small house. At the same time Kelsey came to this awareness, the screams stopped. When she reached the room, she realized Quinn had already come to Alisha's side, and was soothing her.

"It was a bad dream," he said to Kelsey when he realized she stood near him. "She had a bad dream. Can you get her a drink?"

Kelsey was happy to be useful, and she padded to the kitchen to get Alisha a drink of water. She was stunned by the sight of her friend, so withdrawn and grief-stricken, curled into a fetal position on Tia's bed.

Alisha looked almost as tiny and vulnerable as Tia, Kelsey thought, although in reality her friend was quite tall. Grief, no one's good friend, seemed to rob her of her stature, true to its debilitating nature.

She took the water to the bedroom, and looked at her watch. It was one a.m., and Alisha could have another pill. She moved to the nightstand to get a tranquilizer, but Alisha's voice stopped her.

"Please, Kelsey, no. I need to think clearly. I need to grieve, okay? I need to clearly remember everything. I can't do it if I'm drugged up."

Kelsey hesitated, and then moved to her friend's side and hugged her tightly. "Whatever I can do, I'll do it," she said softly.

"I know," said Alisha, returning the hug. "Girlfriend, I know."

Alisha placed her head back on the pillow, her long blond

hair fanning around her, and Kelsey and Quinn left the room after she assured them she would be fine.

Quinn took Kelsey's hand and led her to the couch. They dropped onto it together. They held each other for a minute, and then Quinn pulled away. He had something on his mind, Kelsey could tell. She waited for him to speak.

"Kels, some of the other dees were interviewing witnesses who were around the area of the crime scene, or who might have seen Jake Higgins and the murderer. Several people witnessed him pulling over to the side of the road. Two men called in after the news ran the story and they all say the same thing. A beautiful woman with long blond hair walked up to his truck and got in with him. They drove off together. Kelsey, all the descriptions match . . . Dammit, it sounds just like Alisha."

Chapter Seven

Anger gnawed at the inside of Calvin Reynolds' stomach, roiling and twisting, sharply, like a knife. Life just never worked out for him. Everything was so unfair.

Tonight it was Tessa that had him steaming. Damn slut thought she could say no to him. She'd never turned him down before.

Tonight, after they left the bar, was a first.

"I'm a w'mun an I'm sayin' no to you!" the drunken Tessa told him when he tried to go upstairs with her after giving her a ride home. "No means no, 'n' I have the right ta say no."

Hell, what did the bitch think? He was being nice? He gave her a ride home, bought her drinks all night, now he intended to get laid. She knew that was the way it worked. It was just understood.

He sat in his car, stewing, the radio blaring an old AC/DC tune. His eyes were fixed on the fifth-floor apartment where the lights were going on and off as if Tessa were a gerbil running from room to room. She finally settled on a room. The bedroom. Cal knew that. He'd been in there many times before.

His head bobbed forward with each pulsing beat of the fury-driven music.

She always loved it, the stupid bitch. Moaned and told him to "do it harder, Cal, fuck me harder."

Now she played hard to get. He made a snap decision, and turned the key off in the ignition, the music cutting off mid-beat, and the night suddenly silent and almost eerie. He stepped out and opened the car door, slamming it shut behind him, just to hear the noise.

He looked up at the window of Tessa's bedroom, and saw a shadow, the outline of a female head, peeking through the filmy, feminine drapes covering the window. A chill ran up the back of his spine and his scalp began to tingle, the hair on his arms standing up. Stopping for a moment, Cal nervously shuffled from foot to foot. What the hell was wrong with him? He stood in uncertainty until the sensation of extreme fear faded.

He was going to get laid tonight. All thoughts of his uneasiness fled his mind, and he strode forward, purposeful and intent.

The street was quiet, and he looked both ways before crossing to Tessa's apartment building. She was probably up there waiting for him right now. The thought made him move quickly up the five flights of stairs. The hospital maintenance worker was in good shape for a big man. He wasn't even breathing heavy when he reached her floor.

The apartment building had no security. Good for him, Cal thought as he walked to 5C. Preparing to knock sharply, so he would be sure the drunken woman inside would hear, he noticed the door was ajar. She was waiting for him. He knew it.

He pushed the door open and stepped inside, his eyes slowly adjusting to the dark. Cal could see only shapes. In the time he had taken to run up five flights, she'd turned off the bedroom light.

He walked quietly in the direction of the bedroom, bumping into furniture and tripping over the shoe a drunken Tessa had kicked off in the middle of the floor.

"Goddamn it," he cursed quietly.

"Whozzat?"

"It's me, Tess. I know you really wanted me to come up. You always do."

"Babee . . ."

He knew it. He could feel his dick hardening as he walked to the room. Good old Tessa.

Cal found the frame of the bedroom door with his groping left hand, and he put his right hand out to make sure there was nothing in his way. He touched a face and yelled out.

"You stupid bitch, you scared the bejezus out of me, you stupid cunt . . ."

The sudden glare of light blinded him, and he covered his eyes with his arms. He finally focused, squinting, at the face staring at him.

It wasn't Tessa.

Tessa lay on the floor by the side of her bed, looking up at them both in drunken amazement.

"Surprise," the face said.

He screamed, first in terror as he saw the glint of a surgeon's scalpel, then in pain as it ripped through his jeans and tore into his tender flesh.

"Damn, they go limp really fast," she said.

Chapter Eight

"You can't be serious. This has to be a joke."

Kelsey was shocked by Quinn's words.

Alisha and this man, this Jake Higgins, together today? Her mind was going in circles, cycling rapidly from belief, to disbelief, to shock, and then to anger. "Just a minute, Q, what are you saying? Huh? You saying you think Alisha had something to do with this creep's murder? You can't seriously believe that. You just can't."

She forced her mind to calm down, to think logically. This was California, land of the gorgeous beautiful blondes. It could have been anyone. She turned to Quinn, and he shook his head in disgust, pushing himself off of the sofa and away from her. Kelsey couldn't help but feel hurt, even though she knew his emotions were not targeted at her.

He paced the wood floor, hands behind his back.

"Of course, I don't believe she did it. I mean . . . Well, hell, Kelsey, you have to admit she had a motive. The man destroyed her. Shit, I would have wanted him dead. If Joe had known, well, damn . . . Joe. I can't believe he died. Just like that."

He moved even farther away from her, to the window looking out over the ocean. The sun had set hours ago, but the moon was full and rising, glowing luminously across the wavy water. Even from where she stood, it was a beautiful view.

Kelsey followed him to the window, standing behind him. She placed her small hand on his shoulder, and he turned quickly and pulled her to him. The tears came then, and Kelsey could feel the heat and pain of his grief.

Joe was not just Quinn's partner. He was his friend.

She knew, without an explanation, what he felt. She didn't speak, didn't try to stop his tears or say words that would mean nothing right now. She just let him hold her, felt his tears on her neck, letting them run down her back and not moving, not wiping them away. Kelsey stood perfectly still while he cried. His tears were silent and agonizing, and didn't last long. Finally, she could feel him sigh, could feel him tighten his chest and tense his arms. He was done with this part of his mourning, she knew. Done with this part of his grief. But there was still a long way to go. He held her for a long time, and then pulled back finally, and she reached up to his face and touched his cheek, stroking it gently.

Kelsey loved this man, as much as she was capable of loving anyone. She didn't believe any love could last; she knew all love was transitory and fickle. Someday, Quinn would not feel the same way about her anymore, and although she found it impossible to believe right then, the passion she felt for him might also be gone. But Kelsey would love him forever. He had been there for her, when no one else in her life had ever shown that kind of support. He would always be her friend.

Quinn touched Kelsey's face, slowly, running his finger from her chin down to her neck. She wore a short t-shirt she'd "borrowed" from Quinn, loving the feel of having him always close. The silly saying on the t-shirt was "Help, I've fallen and I can't reach my beer." He reached down and traced the imprint of her nipple through the flimsy cotton, watching as it became firm and hard beneath his caress.

He needed to be reaffirmed, she knew, needed to feel life flowing through him and into her, and she was silent as he reached to the bottom of the t-shirt and pulled it up over her head. She stood before him, naked except for her white bikini underpants.

Kelsey felt his desire as he pressed against her, and he moved her slowly toward the couch where he gently pushed her down onto her back, and knelt between her legs. He placed both palms on her stomach and ran them up and over her breasts, then abruptly moved them back down to her bottom, clad only in the flimsy cotton underwear. He pulled the panties down slowly over her legs, discarded them on the floor and moved his hands back to the spot previously hidden to his view. His fingers explored her gently and she moaned, quietly, aware they were not alone in the small house but unable to endure his caresses without making some noise.

"Come to me," she whispered, biting her lower lip as he stroked her most intimate parts, leaning in to kiss the insides of her thighs. "Oh, please, Quinn, please."

He explored her with his tongue and her moans became softer but more urgent, until she had to turn and bury her face in the side of the sofa as she climaxed.

Reaching down, she pulled him up to her and kissed him, tasting her own self on his lips. Quinn had been wearing a pair of shorts, a concession he had made upon moving in with Kelsey and Tia. The material was not thick, and Kelsey could feel the heat of his arousal through the thin material. She could also feel the animal strength of him as she reached inside his shorts, caressing him, loving him with her fingers. He groaned aloud, and moved his mouth down to cover her nipple, sucking greedily and hungrily. He stripped off his shorts as she pulled the blanket from the couch over the top of them. Tia was a heavy sleeper, but Kelsey took no chances of being discovered by the little girl and causing her any more shock than she had already suffered in her young life.

He moved himself inside her quickly, and as always, she was

overcome by the sense of completeness she felt when they moved together. He was almost ruthless, and it might have hurt, had she not been so wet from his previous ministrations. She let out small, muffled cries, like a baby kitten, holding herself back and yet unable to remain totally silent in the midst of their passion. It was agony not to yell, to shout, as the sensation grew, as they both neared orgasm and completion of this act of grief and desperation.

She moved with him until he shuddered, spent, and relaxed on top of her for just a second, before he moved to her side.

They stayed like that for a long time, not moving, not talking, just feeling. Kelsey loved this part as much as the incredible heat they shared while making love. She felt so close to him in the moments after they had sex. It was a feeling she wanted to last forever.

She finally forced herself to move, and they dressed silently, not talking. Quinn helped Kelsey put the t-shirt back on and he pulled her to him. She kissed him deeply on the lips, inserting her tongue between them and renewing their intimacy for one brief moment.

He whispered, "I love you," and she hugged him tightly. They were silent again for a moment.

"Alisha is not a murderer, Quinn. She was at the hospital all day."

"No, she wasn't." He stood up and crossed his arms, distancing himself from her, and the warmth left her body, leaving behind a trail of cold, frightening doubt.

"What do you mean she wasn't?"

Quinn's mouth formed a thin line of concentration and frustration. "She wasn't there all day. She was gone for two hours. The other nurses were pretty pissed off about it, since the ER was so busy. She was gone, Kelsey. Right at the time when Jake Higgins was murdered."

"It wasn't Alisha," Kelsey said stubbornly, standing up abruptly and preparing to return to her room. He grabbed her arm before she could flee and pulled her back to him. "You saw how distraught she is. She's never done anything to make you suspect her of something this . . . this . . . barbaric!"

"I'm not accusing her. I'm just giving you the facts. She wasn't there. She's going to have to account for her whereabouts. What does she drive?"

Kelsey shook her head in disbelief, and then said, "I know you're just doing your job, but you'll see. She'll have an excuse. She'll have a reason."

"What does she drive, Kelsey?"

"This is ridiculous, Quinn. She drives a small car. I don't know what kind."

"Four door? Two door? Coupe? Sedan? Color?"

"Well, officer, it's a four-door sedan, purple or burgundy or something."

"Kelsey, I want to believe in her as much as you do. Okay?"

She hesitated for a minute before answering. "Okay," she said, considering the time of night and high emotions they were both experiencing. She kissed his lips once more. They parted and she returned to her bed where her daughter slept, after gently pulling the cover over Quinn on the sofa bed.

The woman in the child's room stuffed her fist in her mouth to keep her sobs from being heard. Alisha was unsure she would ever sleep peacefully again. The agony of losing Joe too soon, combined with the shock of seeing Jake Higgins dead in *her* hospital, had jolted her into a realm of disbelief and dread.

This was not what they'd planned.

It didn't seem fair, didn't seem right that she'd been given no warning this was coming. Like so many other times in her life, it wasn't right that once again, she was unprepared for life's worst calamities and she had been knocked asunder. She'd spent the last fifteen years planning every single detail of every single day.

This wasn't right.

She got up from the bed abruptly and took off the t-shirt Kelsey had lent her. She pulled on her jeans and sweater, stepped into her shoes and quietly left the room, tiptoeing to the kitchen door and letting herself out.

She only knew she couldn't stay there any longer. Couldn't stay where two people still had each other. She wanted to be alone. To feel her grief alone.

As she got into her car, she looked out over the ocean. The moon was full and romantic, gliding across the water in a symphony of light. Alisha was alone. More alone than she had ever been in her life. She pulled the engagement ring out of her pocket and stared at it, moving it to see it sparkle in the moonlight. She believed most anything could be handled if you were just prepared. She was not ready for this.

At least she had the ring.

Chapter Nine

Kelsey stared into the eyes of a madman, subhuman, drooling and covered with mud and dirt.

She'd seen him somewhere before, but where?

He stepped closer to her, and she looked down to see her feet, once bare and covered with scratches and sores from running through rocky fields, were now encased in cement.

He neared, and her heart raced. She couldn't get away. It was happening again. He loomed closer and glared into her eyes, opening his mouth, and she waited for evil to pour forth, unstaunched and vile.

"Somebody get the phone," the monster man with the familiar face said.

The phone?

Kelsey jerked awake, her hand reaching over to the bedside table clumsily, knocking the alarm clock to the wood floor with a clatter.

"Damn!"

The phone followed the alarm clock closely, and she struggled to chase it. Somehow she had become entangled in the sheets—a restless sleep—and they were like the giant tentacles of an octopus, refusing to let her legs free as she swam through the deep waters of sleep. She landed on the floor butt first with a thud, her legs still wrapped tightly in the sheets that somehow stayed tucked into the bed.

Kelsey finally grabbed the phone and put it to her ear. "H'lo"

She heard a snort and looked up to see Quinn standing in the doorway, deeply amused and trying not to laugh out loud at her predicament. Tia slept soundly on the right side of the bed, minus her covers.

"H'lo?" she said again, her voice froggy with sleep.

"Kelshee? I neeed your 'elp," a familiar voice said.

"Huh?" She couldn't put a face to the voice in her groggy state. "Who is this?"

"Kelshee help meeeeee . . ."

The phone went dead.

"Who was it?" asked Quinn, as he moved forward to help her disentangle herself from the sheets. He quickly unwrapped the octopus tentacles from around her legs and pulled her to her feet. She still had the phone in her hand.

"I don't know. Whoever it was hung up."

She hit the star six-nine code on the phone's keypad.

"The number of your last incoming call was 555-9085."

Kelsey knew the number. "Tessa. And in the middle of the night. That woman has the worst sense of timing. She was drunk, too."

"Should you call her back?"

"No. She's probably passed out on the floor. Although she usually doesn't call in the middle of the night . . ." Kelsey paused thoughtfully, trying to decide if this distress call was real or another one of Tessa's "date rape" drunken experiences. Sometimes she regretted her decision to give out her phone number to the members of her group, but she knew the minute she stopped, someone would really need it.

"She is some piece of work, that Tessa," Quinn said with a small grin. He had answered the phone before when she called, and when he told her Kelsey wasn't available she used him as an unwilling substitute.

Kelsey pondered calling her back for a few more seconds,

and then decided it was a false alarm. It was always a false alarm with Tessa.

She climbed back into bed and Quinn straightened out the sheets and covered her gently with them. She felt comforted as he leaned over and kissed her gently on the lips.

"Night."

"Night. Quinn?"

"Yeah?"

"I do, you know. I just can't say it."

"I know. I love you, too."

Kelsey was just drifting back into slumber when the pealing of the phone jarred her awake.

"God dammit, Tessa!" She reached for the bedside table again, careful this time not to fall off the bed.

"Hello?"

"Kelsey, it's Franklin. Sorry to wake you. I need Quinn."

"Oh, okay. Hold on."

She looked at the clock on the bedside table. It had been two hours since the last phone call. *My, how time flies when you're sleeping.* Quinn stood in her bedroom doorway. His eyes looked dull and distant, and dark shadows below them told her about his lack of sleep and his grief. She doubted he had even dozed off.

"Franklin," Kelsey said, holding out the phone to him. He moved forward and took it.

"Anderson. Yeah? What? When? They found her when? A man? Shit! Okay, I'll be right there."

"What is it?" Kelsey asked, alarmed by the grim look on his face.

"Fuck. I don't even want to tell you. You're gonna blame yourself. I know you will."

"Quinn! What's going on? What?"

"Franklin and Munroe just responded to Tessa Morrow's

apartment. A neighbor called them about screaming. They found two bodies.

"Kelsey—she's dead."

Chapter Ten

She hadn't planned on killing Tessa, too. That certainly hadn't been part of the game plan. The woman was a slut, granted, but they were sisters, *compadres,* females.

It just happened when Tessa wouldn't quit screaming. The sight of blood gushing from the place on Calvin Reynolds where her favorite toy used to be just seemed to unnerve the woman, even in her drunken and drugged state.

Besides, the brown wig had fallen off and even though Tessa had been bombed out of her mind, there was still the chance she might be able to provide positive identification to the police.

Now there were three new mason jars lined up on the windowsill of the tiny shed. Honey, those breasts of Tessa's had been fake. No surprise, really. Tessa was a fake kind of girl. The silicone had gushed as she sliced them off.

She worked carefully on the bloodstains splotched all over her favorite pink blouse. It was stupid, she knew, to dress up for the sacrifices, but it just didn't seem right to not be decked out in her Sunday best.

Daddy, of course, had always liked the clothes she wore when she dressed up.

"Oh, baby, you look so pretty. Look at you all prettied up," he used to say. Of course, that was only when they were alone, their private time. When it wasn't just the two of them, he became belligerent and rude, pushing her around and yelling. She blamed the doctors. It was their fault this had happened.

She frowned as the memory of that time in her life came flooding back. Stupid doctors. Stupid.

She knew the doctors were wrong, of course. She'd always known. There was nothing wrong with her. She wasn't confused. It wasn't making her crazy. They were crazy.

"They're crazy. Not me."

She smiled at the growing collection. The little weenie belonging to Sadie Cabel's husband would make a great addition to her little windowsill garden.

It was time to plan.

Chapter Eleven

"Same killer, isn't it?" Franklin asked Quinn, his normally animated face bland, not changing expression as he surveyed the carnage in Tessa Morrow's bedroom.

"Looks like it."

"You sure you're up to this?"

"Yeah, I'm fine." Quinn, still reeling from the death of his close friend and partner Joe Malone, had no intention of letting it show. He would continue to do his job.

He carefully picked his way over the bodies being measured and photographed by the medical examiner's assistant. There was blood everywhere. He didn't think he would ever get used to the blood.

Todd McEnroe was the ME's assistant, and most of the time did a better job than Winston Sloane, the ME, who right now was on vacation in Aspen, Colorado.

The body of Calvin Reynolds had been identified easily. He still had his wallet, complete with an SBCH ID tag stating he was a maintenance worker with access to all areas of the hospital. His body was intact except for the missing penis. As was the case with Jake Higgins, the killer had left the testicles behind.

"He bleed to death?" Quinn asked McEnroe.

"Looks that way. Clean and precise. Severed the femoral artery, too. Very intentional. Man, what a way to go. This sucks."

All the male officers had winced as they stared at the victim.

The body of Tessa Morrow had been found on the other side of the bed, as if she'd died trying to escape out the window. The smell of cheap alcohol, mixed with blood and bile caused more than one seasoned detective to gag. They hadn't yet turned Tessa's body over, but a puddle of blood seeped from under her. McEnroe moved toward the woman's corpse at the urging of Quinn, and all the officers stood watching as he reluctantly turned her over, his neck muscles straining tightly.

"Ouch," commented Rita Jaramillo, who had just arrived on the scene. Tessa Morrow was missing both of her breasts.

Rita Jaramillo was one of four female detectives on the squad. Her partner, Terric Finch, was out on maternity leave. That made her Quinn's temporary partner, with the recent demise of Joe. Quinn didn't know how to feel about it. He didn't know how to feel about a lot of things right now.

His cell phone rang and he flipped it open. "Anderson."

"She's gone," said Kelsey's voice.

"Who's gone?"

"Alisha. I went in to check on her, and she was gone."

Chapter Twelve

Kelsey hadn't been able to go back to sleep after the second phone call. Quinn was right. She blamed herself. *If only she had called Tessa back . . .*

She'd fixed herself a cup of chamomile tea after he left, trying to be as quiet as possible so she wouldn't wake Tia and Alisha.

Tessa. Tessa was dead. This was tough.

Tessa Morrow saw herself as the perpetual victim. She liked being the victim, Tammy Rowe had assured Kelsey when she'd been sharing her concern with the therapist over one of Tessa's stories.

Tessa never failed to disrupt the Tuesday meetings and always had a story of exploitation to tell.

Kelsey, using her customary frankness, had told Tessa more than once her taste in men was atrocious, and she needed to change the places she hung out. Tessa would agree and cry, and then come back the next Tuesday with another story of her own stupidity.

Now she was dead. She'd called Kelsey for help, and now she was . . . Kelsey stood up abruptly and walked down the hallway, trying to escape from her thoughts. She listened at the door of Tia's room. There was no noise inside, and she hoped Alisha had managed to sleep through the racket of two phone calls. Tia could sleep through an earthquake, which was hard to believe considering what they had been through together.

The little girl had survived a kidnapping by her grandparents and a polygamous cult to return to California with her mother. There was so much ugliness in the world. So many people doing their best to destroy others.

She walked into the living room and sat on the sofa bed, picking up the pillow still wearing Quinn's scent, and holding it to her chest. She bent her head down and smelled his aroma, letting it permeate her senses. Usually, it would comfort her. Right now, she felt lost and alone.

She'd loved Joe Malone like a brother, and couldn't believe he was dead. So much death. Poor Alisha. Her chance to finally be happy had been taken from her with ruthless and callous speed, when she'd already been through so much.

Kelsey decided she would peek in the door of the bedroom and see if Alisha was asleep. She probably wasn't, and would need her friend. She walked down the hallway and quietly opened the door.

The twin bed was empty and made up neatly, the pink polka-dot bedspread pulled up over the small pillow. She scanned the room quickly, a futile gesture, for she could plainly see Alisha was gone.

Alisha was gone and there had been another murder. When had she left? Why had she left?

Kelsey walked back to the living room and took the cordless phone off its base, dialing the number of Quinn's cell phone.

"Anderson."

"She's gone."

"Who's gone?"

"Alisha. I went in to check on her and she was gone."

"Holy shit. Kelsey, that's bad."

"Come on, Quinn, it can't be Alisha. It can't be. All you have, anyway, is the fact she knew Jake Higgins and someone who looks like her was seen with him right before he died.

That's circumstantial evidence. I'm no cop, but I know that."

"Kels—"

"And there's no way she could be related to this murder. Okay, she knew Tessa, but only as well as I did. I could be just as much a suspect. I was so mad at Tessa on Tuesday I wanted to strangle her with my bare hands . . ."

"Kelsey," he said firmly.

"Sorry. What?"

"There are two bodies here. One is Tessa. The other one is a man named Calvin Reynolds. He worked maintenance at the hospital . . ."

He continued to speak but Kelsey could no longer hear him. She was in a tunnel and a train was headed straight toward her. She collapsed on the sofa.

"Kelsey? Kelsey? Are you there? Are you okay? Kelsey?"

"I'm still here," she said quietly.

"What's wrong?"

"Nothing. I'm just shocked . . ." She paused, her brain frantically grasping for reason and logic. "Alisha knew him."

"Calvin Reynolds?"

"Yeah, she knew him. She knew him well. Last month she filed a sexual harassment complaint against him. He was stalking her."

Chapter Thirteen

Satisfied the crime scene was under control, Quinn motioned to Rita and she followed him outside the door. He explained they needed to find Alisha Telford, and she nodded her head and followed him without asking questions.

Rita, a petite and curvaceous Latina with shoulder-length black hair, deep brown eyes, and an irrepressible laugh, had a knack for talking to murderers.

She had a reputation as the department "profiler," an unofficial title.

"So, you think this Alisha Telford did it?" she asked. They headed down the stairs of Tessa's apartment building, Quinn's long legs putting him two steps in front of her.

"No, I don't think she did it." He didn't turn to acknowledge her question, and he could hear her rapid footsteps behind him as she struggled to catch up.

"Just asking. Sheesh," Rita said when she reached his side. She pulled a stick of gum out of her jacket pocket and unwrapped it, crinkling up the foil wrapper in her left hand after she popped it in her mouth. "I just quit smoking for the umpteenth time. So far, I've gone twelve whole hours without a cigarette. Of course, this middle-of-the-night summons to a gruesome crime scene is *not* helping my resolve. Maybe I should get some nicotine gum."

Quinn gave her a look of impatience and immediately regretted it, knowing she hadn't asked to be paired with him, especially so soon after Joe's death. He knew she was a good cop, if he would just let her do her job. *If* he could let her.

"Gum?" she asked, holding out the package toward him. He kept walking across the street to his car, Rita almost running to keep up with his stride.

"No." Quinn walked briskly to the driver's side of the car and thrust the key into the lock, pulling the door open before his good manners finally caught up with him. He sighed deeply, and stopped before getting into the car, looking over the roof toward Rita, who eyed him with a look of compassion that irritated him.

The temperature in the early fall night hovered around fifty-five, and Quinn could smell the salty ocean in the slight breeze.

"Look, Alisha is a friend, okay? A close friend. She's like Kelsey's sister. So it makes it tough."

"I know. I met her with Joe just last week. She's a stunner. Speaking of Joe, I'm really sorry . . . I mean, I know you guys were close, and I'm sorry."

"Thanks," he said gruffly. He dropped his head and climbed into the driver's seat of the white Ford Taurus, standard issue for Santa Barbara detectives.

Quinn picked up the radio and clicked the mike button.

"Sierra eighteen to dispatch."

"Sierra eighteen."

"Need a ten-twenty-eight and ten-twenty-nine."

"Go ahead."

"Alisha Telford, date of birth unknown, early seventies. Address is on Cabrillo Avenue."

"Ten-four Sierra eighteen, ten-twelve."

They rode for a moment in silence, finally pulling up in front of Alisha's apartment building. She was on the eighth floor of a modern building, complete with security gates and cameras and underground parking. No one got in or out of the building without a pass card or checking with a twenty-four-hour attendant.

"Dispatch to Sierra eighteen," the radio crackled.

"Sierra eighteen," Quinn confirmed.

"Ten-ten on your ten-twenty-nine. No record of Alisha Telford with driver's license bureau, or car registration. Ten-ten on warrants."

"Ten-four, dispatch."

"Negative on the record search. Weird," Rita commented. As they exited the car, she eyed the iron bars, alarm signs, and closed entry. "She's a safety queen, huh?"

Quinn rounded the car and walked to her side.

"Joe always teases her she's the safest woman in California. 'Give her a chastity belt and *no one* will ever be able to touch her,' he always says . . . I mean he always said." He looked away from Rita's probing brown eyes.

"I guess considering her past experiences with men like Jake Higgins, it's understandable. I grew up in Santa Barbara. We never even locked our door. Of course, the motorized gates kept most of the riffraff out."

Rita came from money?

Funny, I wouldn't have known that.

Quinn gave Rita a puzzled look at her statement, but she didn't offer anything more, instead staring at the apartment building. "Come on, let's go," she finally said, moving briskly to the front doors, Quinn one step behind her.

Rita grew up the daughter of the in-house help for a wealthy film mogul whose second home was in Santa Barbara. Most of the time, her family had the house to themselves. When she was younger, she used to pretend she was wealthy and the mansion was *her* house. Her fantasies only lasted until the newest Mrs. Mogul showed up unexpectedly one weekend, went straight up to her bedroom, and shot herself in the head.

Not long after that, Rita decided money was not everything, especially as she helped her mother try to scrub blood from the walls and carpets.

The motivation of cash seemed to bring out murderous intent in ordinary people. It would never be a problem for her, Rita thought, since cops earned notoriously low pay.

They walked together to the east side of the building and Quinn rang the bell summoning the guard.

"Nice digs. How does she afford it? I didn't know nursing paid that well." Rita surveyed the immaculate gardens and elegant architecture as they waited.

"Yes?" a tinny voice pealed from the intercom.

"Here to see Alisha Telford."

"I'm sorry, but we don't ring tenants after ten p.m. unless we've been given special instructions."

Quinn hit the bell again, holding it down an extra second in irritation.

"He's just doing his job, Q," Rita reminded him.

He let up off the bell.

"Yes?"

"Police. Come open the door and I'll show you my ID. We need to speak to Alisha Telford."

After a moment, the young Hispanic guard appeared at the glass of the front doors. He looked a little leery. He'd probably heard this line before.

Quinn and Rita both flipped out their SBPD badges and he peered at them closely, comparing the pictures to the two individuals standing in front of the glass. He finally appeared to decide the identification was legitimate, and opened the door.

"Just doing your job, Mr. Garcia, huh?" Rita said with a friendly smile.

"Yeah, I have to be careful. Last month some drug dealers

tried to get in, said they were cops. Enrique let 'em in and they beat the shit out of some guy who owed them money. Rico got fired. I got a wife and kids. I can't afford to get fired."

"You know him?" Quinn questioned Rita, apparently confused by her use of the man's last name. She pointed to the man's nametag, that identified him as Julio Garcia, and gave Quinn a sharp look of irritation. She turned from him and back to the nervous young man who stood in front of them, moving his weight from one foot to the other.

"So, Mr. Garcia, you seen Alisha Telford tonight?" Rita didn't miss a beat, although she was inwardly seething at Quinn's remark.

"I don't know the names, man. I just know the apartments. Which one she in?"

Rita looked at Quinn.

"She's 8D. Tall, leggy blonde, blue eyes, nice body . . ."

"Oh, man, yeah. I know her. Nope, I ain't seen her at all. She's usually in and out of here all the time at night."

"Late at night?" Rita asked.

"All hours. She's a doctor or a nurse or something. Always wearing those hospital scrubs."

"But you haven't seen her tonight?" Quinn asked the question again.

"Nope. Not tonight."

"Ring her."

"Ahh, man, it's like after hours. These people don't like to be bothered, 'specially by the help. I could lose my job . . ."

"Mr. Garcia," Rita said in a conspiratorial voice. "We're the cops. You're just doing what you're told. The owners won't have any complaints."

"Sheeeet. Okay, man, but you gotta vouch for me if anyone questions it."

He walked over and picked up an intercom phone, punching

in the apartment number and waiting. After a minute, he put the phone back down.

"She's not home. Sorry."

"You have access to keys?"

"Quinn!" Rita reprimanded him.

"Right. Just curious. I think Kels has a key. If we can't track Alisha down, we'll use it later."

"Thanks, Mr. Garcia," Rita said as she followed Quinn out the door.

"Yeah, thanks, man," Quinn threw back over his shoulder as he hurried to his car.

Rita was silent as they drove back to the police station. Quinn, apparently caught up in the events of the past few days, did not notice her simmering anger, despite the fact she pictured herself with steam coming out of her ears. She finally decided she would take the initiative and tell him what was on her mind. If she had to work with him, he was going treat her right.

"So, you think all the Hispanic people know each other?" she asked.

"Huh?"

"You just asked me if I knew Julio Garcia without even thinking. Like I know every Mexican or Chicano in California?"

"Uh, Rita . . ."

"No, Quinn, just so you know, if you treat me right, I'll treat you right."

"I'm sorry."

"You're sorry?"

"Yeah, I'm sorry. I wasn't implying that you . . . I mean . . . I was just being stupid, okay? I didn't even notice his nametag. I've been so caught up in Joe's death and this murder case, and now two more murders that I didn't notice. I'm sorry. It wasn't a slur on you, I promise."

"Okay. Well, I was just making sure. Just so we have the rules straight."

"Rita, when it comes to women, I sincerely doubt any man will *ever* have the rules straight."

She laughed and he smiled, the tension between them temporarily dispelled.

They pulled into the station parking lot and both of them opened their doors and got out of the car. As they headed to the staff door, something occurred to Rita she hadn't thought of before.

"Hey, Quinn, remember those two bums they found? One on Las Positas Road and the other one on Cabrillo? Weren't they missing their, uh, male parts?"

"Yes."

"We checking that out?"

"Yes."

"Man, I'll be glad when Terrie gets back. No one to talk to around here."

Chapter Fourteen

The reports on the murdered transients were sitting on Quinn's desk. He'd printed them out before making a pot of coffee, and Rita sat down in his chair and started to go over them. He stood silently behind her, sipping at the scalding coffee, as she read. He didn't ask her to move. He needed her skills.

After a few minutes she seemed to become aware of his presence, and without speaking stood up with the reports in her hand and moved to another desk. Joe's desk.

Her own desk was located on the other side of the rather large office, separated by cubicle walls like a rat maze. His heart started beating faster as he watched her settle into Joe's chair.

"Damn! Sick SOB . . ." she stopped reading and put the reports on the desktop, pulling the chair toward him. Her look of disgust turned to concern as she stared into his eyes.

"Man, I'm sorry, Quinn, I'm not trying to . . . I mean . . . I'm not trying to take Joe's desk, it was just the closest and—"

"Don't. Okay? You aren't doing anything wrong. Just let it go."

Rita shook her head and bit her lower lip. She let out a deep sigh, and then turned back to the reports.

"Okay, well these are similar. Same MO, basically. Hacked off the penis with a very sharp knife or scalpel—"

"They weren't hacked, though," he interrupted, finally making the move to sit at his own desk next to Joe's. He breathed deeply and tried to force himself to relax. His desk was comforting. There were the familiar pencils in the holder, scarred with imprints of his teeth. The yellow number-two pencils were rarely used. He wrote with a pen. He only used the pencils when he pondered the perplexities of a case, like a talisman. His desk was neat and orderly, with a black-enamel "in" box filled with reports that needed to be attended to—reports that would have to wait.

The four senior detectives on the force shared space outside of Lieutenant Ron Bricker's office. Unlike the other detectives, they were not separated by cubicle walls. The lieutenant felt the walls hindered communication and slowed down investigations. Chief Eldon Hilliard did not agree. When the two quibbled, they compromised by separating the younger detectives with cubicles and placing four desks together in one room for the senior dees.

Quinn liked the open arrangement, as it allowed for communication among the detectives that were primary on most cases. It didn't sit well with the detectives who were separated, but he had no control over that.

Joe's desk was next to his. On the other side were the desks belonging to John Penny and Carlos Garcia. Now, one of those desks no longer had a full-time occupant. It would be a while before anyone could sit there without raising the ghost of Joe Malone.

Quinn tried to focus. "The ME said it was a surgeon's scalpel, or something very similar. A precision tool. And they weren't hacked. They were very carefully removed. And the killer made sure they both died, too. In both cases the femoral artery was severed. That probably wouldn't happen accidentally, especially considering the precision and delicacy involved."

"Souvenirs."

"Yep. The killer is a collector."

"There was no more info on these two transient murders

though. No sightings, no witness statements, *nada.* Who did the legwork?"

"Penny."

They were both silent. John Penny was a political statement. He was brought over from the civil division when Carson Fletcher was transferred out and reduced to serving subpoenas and warrants. It had been an exchange with a political motive. The chief, who wanted more of his "team" in the detective division, did not like Fletcher. They had butted heads on more than one occasion. He waited for the right time, and when the senior detective had been charged with police brutality by a young career criminal trying to avoid jail time, Chief Hilliard jumped on the opportunity and transferred Fletcher into civil. The charges proved unwarranted, but Fletch had not been reinstated. He walked around in his uniform with a bitter look on his face and a hand constantly holding his stomach. He chewed antacids like candy and spoke little.

Lieutenant Bricker still waited for the opportunity to have Fletcher reinstated. It hadn't happened yet, even though it was an election year, and rumor had it Chief Hilliard was not well-liked by the challenger to the mayoral seat, a young city councilman named John French. Polls were already showing in French's favor, and it looked like Mayor Fred Johnson would be ousted in November.

The likelihood of Lieutenant Bricker taking over Chief Hilliard's position had caused the chief to dig in his heels even harder, and one of his favorites, John Penny, had gone from serving warrants to investigating murders. He was young, brash, and cocky. He was also careless and thickheaded.

The only real attribute he seemed to possess, as far as Quinn could tell, was an innate ability to kiss ass.

"Well, we need to put in some more legwork then, don't we?" Rita rubbed her eyes and yawned.

"Rita, this is looking to me like a serial killer. When the press gets hold of it, they'll have a heyday. What do you think about it? I mean, do you think this is the work of a man? And why would a man do this?"

She popped her gum, chewing as she thought.

"Well, if you went with reason, you would say the killer's a woman. Last known person with Jake Higgins was a female. The killer is cutting off dicks. Somebody is mad. A woman would be the logical choice. But women don't usually commit serial murders. It's so rare, most of the time it's not even given a second thought. You have a serial killer, it's a guy."

"Do you think it's a guy?"

"My feel, you mean? My gist on it?" She grinned. Quinn knew her reputation amused her. Then she sobered up, and her face tightened as she considered the brutal murders they were investigating.

"It has a female touch to it, you know. While women rarely commit serial murder, it does happen. Look at Eileen Wuornos in Florida. She offed a bunch of johns, although some experts don't really think she fits the definition of a serial killer, since the motive appears to have been profit." Rita leaned back in the chair and stretched her arms above her head. "I need the reports from the Higgins murder and tonight's crime scene report. I need to spend more time surrounded by the details. But I'm thinking it's a woman, Quinn. It just feels 'feminine.' "

"Yeah, well if that's true, I wonder what the guy that pissed her off did. A little more than just stand her up."

"He probably did what all men do."

"What? Leave the toilet seat up?"

"Hey, that's a serious crime. You don't know shock until you've fallen into the cold toilet in the middle of the night. But nah, I meant the standard guy thing. You know. All men say 'I'll call you.' They never do. In this case, maybe it backfired."

"He doesn't call and gets his dick removed? I think I'll remember that one."

"You do that," Rita said with a weary smile. "I'll get on the horn first thing in the a.m. and find out if any other counties have reported similar killings. And I'll send a notice on the wire."

"I better call Kelsey," Quinn said.

Chapter Fifteen

Winston Cabel was a retired marine and a card-carrying member of the John Birch Society. He was a deacon in his church, the Carpinteria First Assembly of God, and a reserve officer for the Santa Barbara Sheriff's Office.

He was also married to an uppity bitch that needed to be reminded who was in charge—at least once a month.

Winston and Sadie had been married for forty-five years, and she had never reported him to the police. Until last week.

She's been getting mouthy lately. It's that stupid hen group of hers. Buncha women don't know their place in life. Had to keep her in line. Knock her around a bit, just to let her know who was boss. If she just didn't make me so mad . . . Hey, it was written in the Bible. Men were the ones in charge. Women needed to know their place.

His status as a reserve officer was now in question, and due to the current political climate, he would probably be asked to step down, even though Sadie had refused to press charges after she was treated at the hospital. Those stupid women, Alisha Telford and Kelsey Waite, had tried to change her mind, holding her hand and letting her cry to them about her miserable life.

He'd walked back into the hospital from taking a smoke break to hear them encouraging her to press charges. They even called in some tall, blond bitch with some fancy, shmancy title after her name. Psycho mumble jumble.

Winston had worked his ass off to provide well for Sadie, and this was the thanks he got. She turned to these two bitches—

probably lesbians—and called the police on him. Now, one of the things he truly loved was in jeopardy. He loved putting on the uniform twice a month and cruising the streets of Santa Barbara County. It made him feel powerful, alive and important.

Stupid bunch of hens. They needed to know who was in charge.

His stomach hurt, and he cursed as he tried to start the lawn mower. Sadie had gone to the grocery store to stock up their bare cupboards, something she should have done days ago. Always putting everything off until the last minute. It was no wonder he got so angry. His wrath built as he yanked at the pull cord on the lawn mower. It failed to turn over and he cursed and kicked it violently, hurting his foot, and causing a longer stream of angry words to flow from his mouth.

Damn bitch was taking forever, as usual. She's so fucking stupid. I'm hungry, that's why my stomach hurts, and none of the crap she has in the house is decent. Probably did it on purpose. She knows what I like to eat.

He'd sent her to the store for steak and eggs. She better come back with the right stuff, a good decent cut of meat, or there would be hell to pay.

One last pull of the lawnmower's cord convinced him it wasn't going to start without some tinkering, and muttering obscenities, he walked to the back of the yard and into the tool shed. After the bright sun of mid-day, the darkness of the shed was disconcerting, and he squinted as he tried to find the pull cord to the light, grasping around in the air like a cat batting at a string. He finally felt the string and pulled it.

He gasped as the light illuminated the beautiful blond woman with blue eyes. She watched him closely, a smile on her pink-tinted lips.

"What the . . . who the . . . What the fuck? Who are you? What are you doing in my shed? I'm a cop you know . . ." He tapered off as her loveliness hit him right between the legs. This girl was a looker.

"What are you doing in my shed?"

"Win?"

"Yeah . . . hey, how do you know my name? Answer my question? What are you doing in my shed?" His face hardened as recognition flashed through his brain. It was her!

"Winston Cabel? I'm a friend of Sadie's. You look happy to see me." She motioned to his crotch where the material of his jeans had suddenly become tight.

At the mention of Sadie's name his face tightened with anger and confusion, and he began to back away. This was weird. What was she doing in his tool shed? He needed to get out into the open. He needed to figure out what was going on. Why was his heart suddenly beating faster? He needed to get out of the shed.

It was too late.

Chapter Sixteen

Quinn slept for four hours after returning home. The combination of daylight and Joe's recent death made a peaceful sleep impossible, and he woke feeling just as tired as when he went to sleep.

Kelsey had taken Tia to a movie so the house would be quiet for him. It was too quiet.

He was in the queen-sized bed he shared with Kelsey, and he stared at the ceiling, his arms behind his head, as a tumult of thoughts ran through his brain. Joe. Alisha. Tessa. Reynolds. Where was Alisha?

The phone rang, causing him to start.

"Anderson," he barked.

"Quinn?" The female voice sounded tired, desperate and tinny, as though far away.

"Alisha?" He sat up abruptly. "Where the hell are you? Where did you go?"

"I had to think. I needed some time on my own. I'm here in Northern California, near my hometown. I'm calling from a pay phone. I just didn't want Kelsey . . . or you . . . to worry about me. I needed to come back here . . ."

"When did you leave?"

"When did I . . . Why? I mean, I left this morning. I left your house and went to my apartment, gathered some things, and just took off."

"Anybody see you? Anyone who can vouch for your whereabouts?"

"No, I've been on the road. Why are you asking me these questions, Quinn? I feel like you don't believe me."

"What time did you leave here?"

"I don't know. I didn't look. It was late and I was so upset. I don't know what time it was. Quinn, why are you talking to me like this? Am I a suspect? I was at the hospital when Jake Higgins was killed."

She couldn't have gone to her apartment. The night attendant hadn't seen her. Was there a back way in?

"Look, Alisha, you need to come back here, now, okay? We just need you here while we clear things up."

She sounded even more distant when she spoke again. "I understand. I just needed to do this. I'll drive back right away. I'll be there tonight. Tell Kelsey I'm sorry."

The click told him she had severed the connection, and he hit the disconnect button on his end and quickly dialed a number.

"Hi, this is Rita. You know the drill. Leave a message."

"Jaramillo, it's Anderson. We need to check back at Alisha's building and see if there's another way in, a way she could have used without the night guard seeing her. Get on that, please, and call me ASAP."

Since Alisha had disappeared from Kelsey's—and his—house, two more men and a woman had been murdered. The holes in Alisha's story seemed to be growing larger. Was it possible?

"Women aren't serial killers. It doesn't happen."

He knew it couldn't be a coincidence, the killer using the same MO on three male victims. The murder and maiming of Tessa Morrow didn't fit with the rest of the crimes, but her body was there right next to the male victim. Someone was killing people in Santa Barbara, and that someone shared a strong connection with Alisha Telford—who was officially MIA.

The medical precision used in every case was the same. The killer appeared to be escalating, and was not following the traditional patterns of serial murderers. Each of the murdered victims had a less than savory past, which added to motive, but why?

Before he'd left the office, he'd run the sheet on Calvin Reynolds. The man served time for assault and battery, and as recently as the past year had twice been charged with stalking and then released for lack of evidence.

The most telling charge, however, had been filed by Santa Barbara Community Hospital, just two weeks ago. The victim was Alisha Telford.

Quinn sat up and rubbed his temples, a lack-of-sleep headache disturbing his ability to think.

They needed help. The lieutenant had put in a call to the FBI that morning, requesting assistance from the Behavioral Science Unit. Quinn didn't look forward to working with the Feebs, but knew he had no choice.

The ringing phone interrupted Quinn's thoughts.

"Did I wake you up?"

"No, Kels, I wasn't sleeping."

"I didn't think you would be. I'm in my car and I just wanted . . . Well, I wondered . . ."

"She called."

A whispering sigh echoed across the phone lines, causing images of Kelsey's lips to flicker through his mind. He felt a stirring in his groin as he thought of her, and he wished she was there, lying beside him. He wanted to touch her.

He settled for the sound of her voice.

"Is she okay?"

"Yes."

"Did she say where she was, or why she left?"

"Not really. I'll tell you more later."

"We'll be home around five. Tia wants to go to the mall. You sleep. Please?"

"I'll try," he said, feeling lonely as they said goodbye.

They shared a connection, one formed almost from the day they met. He couldn't imagine his life without her. She couldn't see them together past tomorrow. It didn't mean she planned on leaving or wasn't committed to him and their relationship. It just meant she was only capable of living one day at a time. Past experience had scarred her.

Quinn didn't want it to hurt, but the fact she couldn't say "I love you" cut deep into his ego.

This line of thinking was getting him nowhere. He threw back the sheet and put his feet to the wood floor, staring down at his toes for a minute and wiggling them, before standing and crossing to the bathroom connected to the master suite.

He turned the water on in the shower and entered it, turning the temperature to hot and standing under the stinging spray, watching his skin redden under the heat and pressure.

Women are not serial killers.

As Quinn scrubbed his body with soap, he could hear the ringing of the phone. He considered jumping out to try and answer it, but decided it could wait. He heard the long beep of the answering machine and then a woman's voice—he couldn't tell who it was—leaving a message.

After he washed his hair and exited the shower stall, he dried off, wrapping the towel around his waist. He headed to kitchen phone, where the answering machine was located, and reached out to push the play button when he heard a distant ringing.

Work. Maybe it was Rita, getting back to him.

In the bedroom, he fished his cell phone out of the jacket he'd left hanging on a chair next to the nightstand.

"Anderson."

"It's Rita. We've got another one."

Chapter Seventeen

Kelsey pushed her way through the kitchen door, balancing two bags of groceries and three plastic bags from a kids' store at the mall. Tia pushed in behind her, causing the first of the bags to fall.

"Tia, look what you've done! Why couldn't you wait until I was through the door?"

Her daughter gave her an "I'm sorry" gap-toothed grin, and then danced around the kitchen holding the new boots they'd just purchased.

"But Mom, I wanted to show Quinn. Quinn, where are you? Quinn?"

Kelsey sighed as her impish daughter searched the house for Quinn, holding aloft the bright red shiny boots, one on each hand like gloves.

Kelsey set one of the grocery bags on the table, along with the other bags from the mall, and bent down to pick up the bag that had fallen to the floor, praying it didn't hold the eggs she'd just purchased.

As usual, her hopes didn't pay off.

"Damn! Tia, where are you?"

"Hallooo, dearie," said a trembling voice from the doorway. Kelsey jumped, dropping the sack she had just picked up, and giving new meaning to scrambled eggs.

She turned to see Mrs. Falconer, the neighbor from down the street, standing in her doorway and holding a cake pan.

"Hello, Mrs. Falconer."

"Call me Edie, please. I keep telling you that."

"Sorry, Edie," Kelsey said, a wry grin on her face. "Please come in."

"Thank you, dearie. I will. But just for a minute."

The odd seventy-something Mrs. Falconer had taken to popping over to Kelsey's ever since Quinn had moved in. Kelsey was convinced she harbored a secret crush on the handsome police detective, a suggestion Quinn refused to accept.

Nevertheless, Kelsey had never met the woman before the day Quinn had been working in the yard, and Edie just happened to walk up the street to "visit."

"Where's that handsome detective of yours, hmm, Kelsey?"

"He's around here somewhere, Mrs., er, Edie. Tia, did you find Quinn?"

The little girl came skipping back into the kitchen, her long brown hair flowing behind her. She never walked anywhere, and was almost always singing. Considering the things she had endured in her eight short years, Kelsey was amazed the child could be so happy. In the months since they had returned from Utah and Quinn came into their lives, Tia had blossomed from a sullen, difficult child to a bright, shiny sunflower, always raising her face to the rays of light. A light that seemed to come from Quinn, and not herself, Kelsey thought.

He has that effect on both of us. Make that all three of us.

Kelsey fought back an amused grin as she watched the tiny woman search the background for sight of Quinn.

"He's not in the house, Mom. Not anywhere."

"Oh, dear. I guess he got called back to work."

"Work?" inquired Edie, her plump elfin face lighting up at mention of Quinn's job, a career that seemed to hold endless fascination for her.

Kelsey emptied the grocery bags, tossing the scrambled eggs

into the garbage bin and opened the fridge, Tia pushing past her to grab a soft drink from the shelf.

"Tia, I just talked to you about pushing me. Honey, that's rude. Say 'excuse me.' And no soda for you. We had one at the mall."

"Moooom," was the little girl's reply, "Quinn would let me."

"Oh, no, you don't, little girl." She gave her daughter a stern gaze.

"Fine. I won't have one." Tia danced out of the room, scooping up the red boots she had dropped on the floor in her haste to grab the soda, and Kelsey heard the door of her room slam.

"Oh, my, she's full of spit and vinegar, isn't she?" Edie cooed.

Kelsey felt a stab of irritation at the elderly woman, who put the cake pan down on the kitchen table and pulled out a chair.

"Do you have some coffee?"

"I'll make some," Kelsey said, feeling peeved that Edie didn't take the hint and leave.

While the coffee brewed, she put away the rest of the groceries and picked up the bags from the mall. One contained some shirts she had picked up for Tia, on sale at Mervyns, and the other held a secret she was saving for Quinn, for a time when they were all alone and Tia wasn't around. She didn't know how she was going to finagle that one, but she intended to surprise him, and soon.

"So, what's that handsome man of yours working on?" Edie asked, her eyes twinkling and belying her age.

"Oh, a dreadful murder. Very gruesome."

Instead of scaring Edie off, the tidbits she offered served to whet the woman's strange appetite for information about crimes.

"Oh, do tell me. Please."

I sure hope I'm not living next to a serial killer.

"I don't really know much about it, Edie. Let me get you that coffee."

"Okay. And some of this cake I brought you would taste mighty fine with it."

Kelsey smiled, accepting that Edie was here to stay for a while, and she took the cake pan over to the counter, cutting a small slice for herself and a larger one for Edie. She put the cake on two small dishes she pulled out of the cupboard, and put one in front of Edie. Pouring the coffee into two mugs, she gave in and sat down at the table for a visit. The woman was a little odd, but very kind. Other than her curious interest in crime, she seemed harmless.

Yeah, well, I know very well that someone who seems harmless isn't always. I'm not leaving Tia alone with her.

"So, Edie, tell me about yourself. I don't know much about your past. Were you married? Do you have kids?"

"Oh, no, dearie, I don't have kids. I was married, once, to a son of a bitch. I hated him. He beat me for forty years. One day I got tired of it, finally found a backbone, and when he came home that night I was sitting up in the kitchen, waiting for him, holding his loaded hunting rifle. I threatened to shoot his unit off if he ever touched me again. He only lived five years after that. Luckily, he was a rich son of a bitch, pinched pennies all his life, so I get to live in luxury. Almost makes it worth it."

Kelsey's eyes grew wide at this revelation, offered like a casual comment on the weather.

"You look a little shocked, dearie. Sorry. I'm pretty shy, but once I get to know someone, I really open up. And I don't figure I'll be around much longer. Might as well get right to the point before I run out of time."

"Uh, well. I'm glad he's not around to hurt you anymore."

"Yes, you understand. I know you do."

"I'm not sure . . ."

"Well, I read about you in the paper, after you came back from Utah. They had a big write-up about the case in the *Salt*

Lake Tribune, you know. I found it online. But of course, the first place I found it was in the *World Speaks.*"

"You mean the tabloid paper?"

"Oh, yes, I buy all those newspapers every week. Don't miss a one. Did you know Hitler's nose has been cloned, and it's growing a mustache?"

Kelsey fought off the urge to put her face in her hands and giggle, as Edie had a very serious look on her face.

"My story was in there?"

"Oh, my, yes. I can't believe your father would sell you to that horrible madman for a hundred thousand dollars and a herd of cattle. Wanted you to be his twenty-sixth wife. Dreadful. Just dreadful."

"Um, Edie? That's not really what happened."

"Oh, I know. You're embarrassed. Don't worry. I don't tell anyone around here anything. I just know you've been through a lot. Like me. That's why I wanted to get to know you."

Tia ran back into the kitchen, apparently having forgotten her tantrum of a few moments before. "Mom, can I have some?"

Kelsey, who now had serious doubts about Edie Falconer's mental faculties, didn't want to touch her cake, and certainly didn't intend to let Tia eat any.

"Not until after dinner," she told her daughter firmly. "Why don't you go wash up and you can help me make a salad?"

"But Mom, you're eating some."

"You're right. I better save this for later. It's only fair." Kelsey stood up and scooped the cake back into the pan, pulling tinfoil out of a drawer to cover the rest of the cake. "Go ahead and finish yours, though, Edie."

"Okay," chirped the woman in her bird-like voice, as she happily scooped the cake into her mouth.

Kelsey fought back a smile as she pulled the ingredients out for a salad, every once in a while turning to watch the tiny woman eat her cake.

I sure hope she doesn't intend to stay for dinner.

Edie finished her cake and pushed the plate away. "Well, I better run. I guess Quinn isn't coming back any time soon. Would you ask him to come see me? I have a leak under my sink, and I'm just too old to get down there and fix it."

"Sure thing, Edie," Kelsey said, thinking to herself the old woman probably just wanted Quinn on his hands and knees under the sink so she could stare at his ass. Kelsey couldn't blame her. It was a mighty fine behind.

After Edie left, Kelsey put the cake dishes in the sink, and pulled out the cutting board. Thinking of Quinn, her eyes strayed to the phone, and she saw the flashing light of the answering machine, indicating someone had left a message. Moving toward it, she reached out just as the phone rang.

"Hello?" she answered.

"Hey Kels. Tried your cell phone, but you didn't answer."

"Hey hon, where are you? I just had a visit from Edie, again, and I'm telling you, she has got the hots for you something fierce. I mean—"

"Kelsey," Quinn said, interrupting her. "I'm at another murder scene."

Kelsey grew quiet, wondering where her friend Alisha was, and whether she would have an alibi. "Who?"

"Winston Cabel. Sadie Cabel's husband."

Kelsey moved quickly to a chair by the table and sat with a thump. Sadie Cabel was one of her group members, the victim of an abusive husband.

"Kelsey, I'm afraid this is definitely connected to you and Alisha. To your group. I need a list of the women who come to the meetings."

"I can't. Dammit, Quinn, I can't do that. You know we promise confidentiality. How can you ask me to break that?"

"Kelsey, we have a vicious killer on the loose here. We don't know when this person is going to strike next, but gauging from the closeness of these crimes, it will be soon. I need that list. Please don't make me get a subpoena."

Kelsey didn't speak. She couldn't do it. Couldn't betray the other women, even though one of them might be a killer.

"I can't."

"Kelsey," Quinn said, his voice tinged with exasperation.

"I can't," she repeated. "You're going to have to get the subpoena. Some of these women take their lives in their hands just coming to our meetings. You know that. I can't just turn it over to you. If I did that, who would ever trust me again?"

"Fine. We'll talk when I get home."

"Quinn, dammit," she started, but the dial tone told her he had already hung the phone up.

"Oh, God," she said, dropping her head into her hands. This was bad. And where the hell was Alisha? Things just kept getting worse.

Her eye caught the flashing light on the answering machine, and she stood up and almost ran to it, praying it was Alisha.

"This message is for Kelsey Waite. My name is Kendra Fowler, and I'm a doctor with LDS Hospital in Salt Lake City. I've been caring for your mother. I need you to call me as soon as a possible," a woman's voice intoned. She hurriedly scrambled for a pen and paper and wrote the number down.

My mother? What now? Oh, God, what now?

"Things are definitely going from bad to worse."

"You can say that again," said a voice from the kitchen door.

Chapter Eighteen

"Tammy!" Kelsey held her hand to her rapidly beating heart. "You scared the shit out of me."

The tall blond woman chuckled, and apologized.

"I'm sorry, Kelsey. I guess you're jumpy, with all the goings on right now. I just got your messages a little bit ago and I was in the neighborhood. Thought I'd stop by and see what you needed. How's Alisha?"

"Missing, right now."

The psychologist sat down in a chair by the table, and Kelsey dropped into one next to it, trying to calm her nerves.

"Oh, dear. That's horrible. I heard about the killings. It was on the radio. They're all related to our group, aren't they?"

"They seem to be. Quinn wants the membership records, and I can't do that to our women. I don't know what the hell to do."

"He'll just get a subpoena, you know, so you should probably turn them over. It will save you trouble with him, and it's inevitable anyway."

Kelsey studied Tammy's face, surprised at the woman's advice. Kelsey had believed that as a professional, Tammy would agree with her, and not want to divulge the women's names.

Tall and big-boned, Tammy was beautiful and strong, and made Kelsey, who stood only five feet two inches, feel like a pygmy. Kelsey knew Tammy worked hard to keep in shape, and she and Alisha jogged together three or four times a week. Her strength, however, had not stopped her from becoming a victim to her abusive boyfriend.

"I'm worried about Alisha, though, Kelsey. Do you know where she is?"

"No, but I think Quinn does. At least he said she called him, so she's okay."

"Well, that's good. She needs to come back here so we can help her."

Tammy looked around the kitchen at the vegetables and chopping board, and stood up. "You're fixing dinner, aren't you? I'm sorry I just dropped by. I was in the neighborhood, and just really concerned about Alisha, so I thought I'd stop."

"Don't apologize," Kelsey said, with a wave of her hand. "We're friends. You can stop by any time."

"Okay, well I have an appointment in forty-five minutes, so I have to run. Please call me if you need me, and let me know when Alisha gets back. I'm really worried about her."

"Tammy, you do realize she is tied to all the killings, don't you? I mean . . ."

"Alisha is not a killer, Kelsey. I think you know that as well as I do. Please don't worry about her. And it could just as easily be someone who is familiar with the group. I can't believe it's someone in our group, but maybe a husband or spouse. You know women aren't serial killers, right? It just doesn't happen."

"I know, but all the evidence is pointing toward Alisha, even though it's all circumstantial at this point. And the other women know they aren't supposed to share any of this information outside of our group," Kelsey protested, not wanting to believe someone was divulging dirty little secrets that were resulting in murders.

"I know. It's hard to believe. I might have pointed a finger at Tessa, except . . . well, she's dead. But how well do we really know these people, Kelsey? I mean, really?"

"Not well at all," Kelsey said with a sigh.

After Tammy left, she tried to sort her thoughts out, images of her catatonic mother, Tessa, and a grieving Alisha all tumbling through her mind.

She moved back to the phone and dialed the number she had written down on a pad by the phone, not wanting to hear what would be coming next. She wanted to leave her past behind, to forget about her father who betrayed her; to forget about her mother, whose betrayal hurt even more.

After the shock of escaping from the polygamist cult and David Stone's murderous wrath, her mother had fallen into a catatonic state that hadn't changed in months. Kelsey called the hospital every two weeks, inquiring about her mother's condition, wanting to be a good daughter. Not wanting to dwell on the injustices of the past. Things never changed. Until this phone call.

"LDS Hospital."

"I need to speak to a doctor. Kendra Fuller."

"Hold please."

Tinny music assaulted her ears, a schmaltzy remake of Boy George's "Do You Really Want to Hurt Me?"

Bad. Very bad omen.

Chapter Nineteen

The muted blue-and-green-toned wallpaper decorating the human resources office of Santa Barbara County Hospital was meant to soothe and calm. No bright reds or vibrant tones here. Quinn eyed the office with interest, wondering if the decorating scheme really had an impact on how an employee reacted to a situation.

He'd been a police officer long enough to know human nature was unpredictable. Years spent on the night shift had proven a definite link between a full moon and violent bizarre crime. When one considered that, it wasn't that far of a stretch to believe color could have an effect on the human psyche.

Human Resources Director Sandra Ball was behind her desk, on the phone, requesting permission from the hospital director to release information about Calvin Reynolds to the SBPD.

She drummed her fingers nervously on the desk, avoiding eye contact with Quinn, as she listened to something being said on the other end of the phone line, nodding her head occasionally, as though the person speaking could hear her.

"Well," she said after hanging up the phone. "I will do my best to help you."

The tall thin woman twirled her chair around and pulled the bottom drawer out of a tall filing cabinet. Leaning over, she ran her fingers over the different files, until she found the one she wanted, and pulled it out.

The brunette woman wore thick glasses, and had an oversized

nose incongruous with the rest of her petite features. Dressed in the same tones as the room, rather than exuding serenity and peace, she exuded tension and anxiety.

She twirled back to her desk and slapped the folder on the top, pulling her chair forward to get closer to the desk. She picked up the folder and opened it, then set it back on the desk, and looked at Quinn.

"Calvin Reynolds has been working here three years. In that time, we've had six different complaints about him harassing the nurses and female employees. He's attended sexual harassment training twice."

"Sounds like it worked."

"Detective, this is not humorous." Sandra Ball was offended, her mouth a thin line, her eyes wide and frog-like behind the thick glass frames. "The classes are intended to teach the employee how to treat fellow employees, and avoid problems of this nature. I designed the course myself, and we have had great success with it."

"Ms. Ball, I apologize if I've offended you. Can you tell me how a man with six complaints against him was allowed to continue working at the hospital?"

The question angered the woman even further, and she sniffed and rubbed at her nose furiously, before answering. "Two of the complaints were dismissed. They stemmed from Mr. Reynolds asking a person out, then becoming angry when she said no. However, it was determined both cases were blown out of proportion. Two of the complainants were satisfied with Mr. Reynolds attending the harassment course. The last two . . ."

"Yes?" Quinn urged her, as she trailed off.

"The last two were only reported in the past month, and we filed a police report on one, which appeared to be substantiated. The other claim was still under investigation."

"And one of those complainants was Alisha Telford."

"Yes, it appears you know that. The hospital director has advised me to cooperate, however I feel these files need to be kept confidential. I do not agree with this at all."

"Sorry to make you do this, but we have a pretty brutal murder on our hands, Ms. Ball. This is extremely important. What did Telford say happened?"

She looked back down at the file on her desk, and then at Quinn again. It was obvious she knew the circumstances, and did not need the file to repeat them. "She said Mr. Reynolds asked her out, and she said no. He became angry and berated her, calling her names, and using profane language. Then he began to call her at home and at work. One night she walked out to her car after a shift, and he was waiting there. She got scared and reported it. When we questioned him, he got angry and blew up at me. Called me a few horrid names. We called the police."

"And that was it?"

"Isn't that enough?"

"Yeah, that's enough. Who was the other claimant? The one still being investigated?"

"Detective, I don't think . . ."

"Ms. Ball, it's extremely important I have that name. I can certainly get a subpoena if you like, but that would result in you turning over your files. This way, you can just tell me and avoid a big mess. You've been given permission."

"Fine." She harrumphed angrily, and cleared her throat. "The other complainant was Dr. Rowe. Dr. Tamara Rowe."

Chapter Twenty

Rita sat on the bench outside the department, watching the orange-suited trustees from the jail work on the landscape surrounding the building. The bright jumpsuits with black letters signified to the world that the men and women wearing them had violated laws, and now had to pay.

"Wouldn't it be nice if all criminals automatically turned orange so we could spot them *before* they hurt people?" she mused. "Are you listening, God?"

"Don't know about God, but it sounds like a plan to me," Quinn said as he plopped on the bench beside her. "What are you doing out here?"

"I'm *not* smoking. What does it look like?"

She reached into her pocket and pulled out another stick of Juicy Fruit gum, nervously tapping her foot to the rhythm of some internal music.

"You picked a hell of a time to quit."

"You can say that again. What's up?"

"Oh, I needed a breath of fresh air. Just got off the phone with Kelsey. She won't turn over the records of her Women Against Violence group, or give us a roster. Says it would be a violation of the women's privacy."

"It would."

"Yeah, well people keep dying. You'd think she'd want to stop it."

"Come on, Quinn. Just get the subpoena. Then she doesn't

have to just hand them over, and you'll feel better about it."

"Yeah, I'm getting the subpoena. But, still, Kelsey should know better. She should just—"

"Just what?" Rita said, fixing him with a wide-eyed stare meant to send a message of rebuke. "Just do what you say? Just know how you're feeling? Abandon her ethics?"

"I don't know," Quinn said with a sigh. "I just want to catch this killer before anyone else dies."

"Understood," Rita said, tucking a flyaway strand of her shoulder-length hair behind her ear. She looked away from him, suddenly unable to hold the gaze. Quinn had the most startling blue eyes she'd ever seen in a man. Combined with his black hair, flecked with gray, he was incredibly handsome.

This man is taken. And, he's your partner, stupid. Knock it off.

"Damn, I need a cigarette."

"Those things will kill you," Quinn said.

"Yeah, if the job doesn't get me first."

"Just got off the phone with an agent from CASMIRC. Let her know we think we have a serial killer here. I hate having to turn to the FBI, but this killer's not leaving any clues."

The Child Abduction and Serial Murder Investigative Resources Center was set up to improve the investigation of major violent crimes, linking the FBI's vast resources with local law enforcement. Rita sighed, and wished once again for a cigarette. She wanted to find this killer, and didn't want the FBI taking credit.

"The ME come back with anything yet?"

"Nope. Killer's not leaving much behind. Crimes don't appear to be sexual, although they are definitely about sex—gender that is. No semen, no assault."

"Is the FBI agent going to come in?"

"She will if we want. She's okay. I worked with her last year in Utah. She recently transferred to CASMIRC. You'll like her."

"Wow, FBI's getting liberated, huh? A female profiler?"

"Name's Lexi Richards. She's sending me the profile questionnaire so we can fill it out and get some information back. Also need to put this through VICAP, see if any crimes come up anywhere else."

"And if they do?"

"If they do? God help us. We need to talk to Rowe. She was gone when I stopped by her office today."

Quinn took a moment and brought Rita up to date on what he had learned from the hospital human resources director.

"Shit. Sounds like our vic was a real creep. Both him and Higgins were lowlifes who preyed on women. Definite pattern there."

"Yeah, I know. You up for a beer?"

Rita looked surprised for a minute, then said, "Yeah, but whatever you do, no matter how I plead, *do not* let me smoke."

"You got it."

Rita and Quinn walked into the Rusty Pitcher, a local cop hangout not far from the office. Shouts of recognition and hellos went up across the bar, and both Rita and Quinn waved in acknowledgment.

Quinn spied a familiar face at the bar, and headed toward Carson Fletcher, who had two empty stools next to him.

"Stuff's bad for your gut," he said in way of greeting, pointing at the drink in front of Fletcher.

"Hey, Anderson. So what isn't? No worse than the job."

"Hey, Fletcher," Rita said across Quinn, and the man waved back, before turning to his drink.

"How's Sue?" Quinn asked, nodding to the bartender who held up a Guinness. Rita ordered a margarita, minus the umbrella, with extra salt.

"Gone," Fletcher replied morosely. "Said she can't put up

with my moods, so she packed it in and went to her mother's. Said she won't be back until I get it together."

"Well, this isn't helping you," Quinn said, pointing to the drink in front of him. Fletcher had become a regular at the Pitcher.

"Yeah, well, it's my only company."

"I need your help."

"Huh?"

"Penny was covering a bunch of attacks on homeless Joes, you know, the one's where the killer hacked off their units?"

"Penny," Fletcher snorted derisively. "He couldn't tell his asshole from his elbow."

"Yeah, well, I need some details on them, but I can't go snooping or he'll get suspicious. You still have that friend in records?"

"Suzy Q? Yeah, she's still there. We're still friends."

"Can you get those case files for me, check 'em out, see if they're missing anything? I need everything you've got. He's not going to help me or be happy I've been put on the case, but I think it's the same killer."

"Whoa, you mean the murders last night?"

"Yeah, same MO."

"Yeah, hey, yeah. I'll get on it in the morning. On the QT, right?"

"Yeah, keep it low."

"Done."

"One other thing."

"Yeah?"

"Looking for a car registration for Alisha Telford. Isn't anything under her name. But I know she has a car. Play with that, will you? See if you can't find her some other way. Birth date sometime in the seventies. I'll call you with the exact date, after we get her records from the hospital. Also do a search for bank records."

"Need a subpoena for that."

"Never stopped you before. I'll get you one first thing."

"Done."

After two drinks, Rita and Quinn excused themselves, and Fletcher said, "Yeah, I better get home, too."

Quinn took his keys away, and hailed him a cab, with little complaint, and he and Rita headed to the car.

"Uh, Quinn?"

"Yes, Rita."

"You have those case files."

"I know."

"You just trying to help the guy out?"

"Kind of, but he's a good cop. He might see something we're missing. Wouldn't be the first time."

"You're a soft touch, aren't ya?"

"No."

"Yeah, well, just don't get carried away. My mother always said those who tried to fix everyone around them usually ended up in the trash heap."

"Eloquent."

"It sounded better in Spanish."

They drove back to the station house in companionable silence, each quietly lost in their own thoughts. The loud voices as they entered the squad room shattered the serene atmosphere created by growing trust and partnership.

"This should be *my* case! I'm the primary on these murders!"

The strident yelling coming from the loo's office told Quinn and Rita that Penny had heard about the killings, and wasn't pleased he hadn't been called out.

The debate had apparently been stewing for quite a while, as it was now 7:30 p.m., and the lieutenant was usually long gone.

Quinn motioned with his head toward the office, then to the

door, and Rita grimaced, hurrying to her desk to grab her purse and jacket.

They were halfway to the exit when Lieutenant Bricker's voice halted them.

"Anderson, Jaramillo, my office."

"Shit," Rita swore under her breath and rolled her eyes before they turned and headed back to the office. The loo motioned them in and shut the door behind them. A simmering John Penny sat in one of the two chairs, glaring at both of them with the malice of a man who knows he's in over his head, but won't accept it.

"Sit down," Quinn directed Rita, "I'll stand."

"Yo," Rita said, giving him a dark look, her eyebrows knitted together. "You sit."

"This will just take a minute," the loo told them.

They glared at each other and both stayed standing, until Quinn sighed and sat in the chair. Rita leaned against the wall nonchalantly, a satisfied look on her face.

"Penny has pointed out he was the primary on the murders we believe are connected to these killings. Now, you two have done too much footwork on the most recent murders to take you off, so I've reached a compromise. Penny will work the murders with you."

"Whoa, Loo, hold on," Quinn interrupted, motioning with his hand. "We've got this thing going fine, me and Rita. You know three just mixes up the soup."

"Yeah, looks like you two are doing great," Penny muttered, glancing at Rita standing against the wall.

"Enough. Here's how it's working. Anderson is the primary. He's the senior detective. Rita's his partner, Penny you work the case with them, but if I hear there's trouble, you're off. Got it?"

"Got it." Penny was sullen, obviously not happy with being

relegated to second-team status.

"Fine," Quinn said, and stood. "That all?"

"That's all," the loo said, rubbing his temples.

"Fine," Rita echoed, and she opened the door and walked out, followed by Quinn and John Penny.

"You can't leave me out of the loop," Penny told them both as they walked toward the exit. "Where you going?"

"Just gonna grab a bite."

"Okay," Penny said. "You coming back tonight?"

"Maybe. Got some paperwork to do," Quinn answered. Rita stayed silent.

"Just paperwork?"

"Look, Penny, Loo told us to keep you in the loop. You're in the loop. You gonna shadow me now just to make sure we aren't playing without you?"

"No. But you better not leave me out."

"Christ, what is this, kindergarten?" Rita said in disgust.

Penny gave her a dirty look and walked away, muttering something about going home.

"Great. Just great," she said to Quinn, rolling her eyes again.

"You keep doing that, your eyes are going to stay that way," he said, fighting back a smile.

"Sorry, Mother."

Chapter Twenty-One

"I'm sorry, Dr. Fowler has left the hospital for the day. Would you like the number for her answering service?"

Kelsey sighed, the anxiety rising in the pit of her stomach. "Look, I'm in California. My mom is a patient there, and Dr. Fowler called me. Can't you tell me if something is wrong."

"Hold please," said the tinny voice, and the canned music came back on the line.

Kelsey shut her eyes and pinched the bridge of her nose, the tension in her neck making her head pound.

She watched the clock as the second hand moved slowly around the orb. Two minutes. Four minutes. Seven minutes. She was about ready to hang up when the hospital operator finally came back on the line.

"I'm sorry, but no one here knows anything about why she was calling you."

"Is my mother all right?" Kelsey asked, grimacing as she thought how stupid the question seemed. Last time she had seen her mother, the woman had been catatonic.

"I don't have that information. Do you want the number of Dr. Fowler's answering service?"

Accepting her lack of progress with the operator, Kelsey wrote down the number and disconnected from the hospital. Dialing quickly, she left a number and message with Dr. Fowler's answering service, and walked back over to her salad fixings, where the head of lettuce wilted and had turned a little brown around the edges.

"Damn!" In frustration, she scooped the lettuce and all the vegetables into the garbage and sat down heavily in the oak chair by the kitchen table. "Damn, damn, damn."

"Mom!"

Kelsey looked up to see her daughter standing in the doorway of the kitchen. The little girl had on her favorite blue skirt, which was getting too small, the bright red boots they'd just purchased, and a turquoise sweater. Her face was a mixture of cherubic child and aged woman, and Kelsey never knew which part of Tia she would see.

Some days the little girl would be so innocent, and at other times so mature Kelsey felt like the child.

"You said that word three times. That means you owe the jar seventy-five cents. You weren't going to swear, remember?"

"You're right. I'm going to single-handedly pay for your college education if I don't knock it off."

Tia ran over to the counter where the half-full jar sat, and pulled it toward her until it reached her chest. She wrapped both arms around the heavy container, and brought it to the table where Kelsey sat. A loud thump reverberated in Kelsey's rattled brain, and Tia ran to the other counter where her mother had left her purse when they first came back in the house.

"Here," she said, with a mischievous grin lighting up her brown eyes and dimpled cheeks. "Quinn said that's not for college. It's for Disneyland. Pay up."

"You, my dear, are a small extortionist."

"What's a "extor . . . extorshunest?"

"A blackmailer."

"What's a blackmailer?"

"Argh," Kelsey said, expelling a breath. "Someone who wants something, and will do anything to get it."

"Yep, that's me," the little girl cheerfully acknowledged, and then watched her mother carefully as Kelsey opened up her purse and pulled three quarters out of the worn wallet she'd carried for years.

"You know, I think you swore earlier when we were coming home from the mall," Tia said, her head cocked, the look on her face so adult Kelsey almost cried out in pain. Soon she would lose this little girl to adolescence, and sullen misbehavior.

"You're right. I did." Kelsey anted up with another quarter, dropping it into the jar, where it fell with a mechanical "plink."

"It was probably more than once—"

"Tia, enough! You little . . . rascal."

Giggling, the little girl returned the jar to the counter, pushed it back next to the answering machine, and skipped out of the room. Kelsey heard the TV go on in the living room.

"Read," she yelled.

"Aw, Mom . . ."

"Twenty minutes. Then you can watch TV."

The TV went silent, the grumbling stopped, and Kelsey groaned and stood up, walking to the freezer to see if they had some frozen pot pies.

She had a feeling Quinn wouldn't be home for dinner.

After haggling with Tia over the nutritional benefits of bologna sandwiches for dinner, Kelsey compromised and they shared a dinner of hot dogs and pork and beans. "At least there's protein in the beans," she said with a sigh.

After Kelsey watched a children's video with her daughter, she ushered a disappointed Tia to bed. "But Mom, I wanted to say goodnight to Quinn. Can't I just stay up until he gets home?"

"Goodnight, Tia."

As the door to her daughter's room shut with a loud bang, Kelsey shook her head and set about cleaning up the kitchen. When that chore was finished, she walked down the hallway and gently pushed the bedroom door open so she could peek inside at her sleeping daughter. Tia tossed restlessly, turning back and forth in her bed. "No. No. I won't. No."

Her cries were soft and low, but her mother, ever alert for danger since she'd come so close to losing her daughter, had heard them as though shouted through a bullhorn.

Kelsey walked into the room and sat on the edge of Tia's bed, gently stroking her arm and forehead. "Honey, it's Mommy. Wake up. You're having a bad dream. Wake up."

Tia tried to fight her way up from the bad dream, but her eyelids only fluttered, and the mumbling and thrashing continued. "Honey. It's okay. Mommy's here."

Tia suddenly quieted, her fighting limbs stilled. A deep sigh came from her small, slightly parted lips. Her eyes never completely opened, and Kelsey knew she'd manage to conquer the dream. She'd won this round.

She waited a moment more, and then stood and left her daughter, who now slept quietly, and, Kelsey hoped, dreamlessly. Her own dreams had long been vivid and colored with abuse and betrayal. She wanted those feelings erased from her daughter's subconscious. She wanted the little girl never to know that fear again.

They were seeing a counselor together, and separately, for that reason.

Kelsey's stomach began to ache, that familiar sharp twinge of pain she felt every time she thought of her daughter experiencing the ugliness life often handed out.

A crash from the kitchen interrupted her reverie, and set her pulse racing. She came to a complete stop in the hallway, not wanting the creaking floorboards to betray her position.

Wild thoughts raced through her mind. Was it Quinn? He had called several hours before to tell her he wouldn't be home until late, if at all. And she hadn't heard him open the door. He made enough noise coming home to raise the dead, and the ominous silence told her it couldn't be him.

Frozen, fear pounding through her, she tried to think of her options. The phone. It was in the kitchen. There was another one in her bedroom. Another quiet thump from the kitchen spurred her into action.

She stepped slowly backwards, headed to her bedroom, grimacing at the creaking of the floorboards. It took what seemed like hours to reach her open bedroom door, and she didn't dare close it for fear the intruder would hear.

In her bedroom, she grabbed the phone and pulled it into the closet with her, dropping to the floor. The cord of the telephone was stretched as far is it could go, and she prayed silently it wouldn't disconnect.

"Nine-one-one, what's your emergency?"

"Someone is in my house," she whispered, cupping her left hand around the phone so her voice wouldn't carry.

"What's your address, ma'am?"

She rattled off her address, and was prepared to continue when another noise from the other room caused her to freeze.

"Ma'am? Are you there? Ma'am?"

Kelsey heard the soft thump of footfalls, heading down the hallway. The swoosh-swoosh of cloth against cloth grew closer, and she heard the operator's voice, as though it came from miles away.

"Ma'am, an officer is on the way, he's almost there. Can you hear me? Are you okay?"

Kelsey could hear the roar of sirens in the distance, just above the roar of blood in her ears. Lightheaded, she realized her breaths were coming too quickly, and she tried to slow them down, not wanting to hyperventilate and pass out on the floor of the closet.

The intruder's footsteps stopped, as though the person also listened to the approaching sirens, which grew louder with each passing second.

"Ma'am? Are you okay, ma'am? Can you tell me if you are okay?"

Kelsey started, realizing she still held the phone in her frozen hand.

A louder creaking followed, as the footsteps grew heavier and headed in the direction of the living room.

"I'm . . . here . . ." she whispered into the phone.

"Okay, ma'am, the officers are in front of your house. As soon as I tell you, I want you to go straight to the front door and open it. Wait until I tell you, because the officer will be there."

"Okay," Kelsey whispered.

After a brief pause, the dispatcher's voice said, "Okay, go to the front door now. As fast as you can. Don't stop. He's right outside your front door."

Kelsey dropped the phone and pushed her way out of the closet, running to the front door and scrambling with the deadbolt.

"Kelsey?"

She screamed in terror and looked into the living room, where a shadowy figure stood by the window.

"Kelsey, it's me. It's Quinn." He reached over and flipped on the light and she saw it was indeed Quinn standing there, apparently drawn to the window by the sounds of the approaching sirens.

"Mom, what's going on?"

Tia stood in the doorway of the living room, sleepily rubbing her eyes and looking from Kelsey to Quinn.

"Oh my God, Quinn. Oh my God," was all Kelsey managed to say.

A pounding on the front door reminded her of the officer standing outside her door, and she finished opening the lock and threw the door open.

"It's okay," she told the worried-looking officer. "It was my . . . It was my roommate, Quinn."

Quinn walked over to the door and the young patrolman nodded in recognition, "Yo, Anderson."

"Hey Wilkes, guess I scared Kelsey. Told her I probably wouldn't be coming home. We were following some leads on the M&M murders, but those stalled, so I ended up coming home. Didn't want to wake Kelsey and Tia up. Guess that backfired."

The officer chuckled and spoke quickly into the radio tethered to his shoulder. "Guess my work here is done," he said, as his partner walked around from the house and nodded at Quinn and Kelsey.

"Yeah, I think we'll be okay. Of course when we shut this door, she's probably going to kill me."

After Kelsey tucked Tia back into bed, she found Quinn in the living room, idly flicking through channels on the television set.

"I guess I'm a little jumpy, but you are normally so loud when you come home, I thought there was no way it could be you."

"I'm not that loud."

"Yeah, you are," she said. A giggle burst from her throat, and she quickly dissolved into laughter. A hint of hysteria and relief mingled in with the tears that followed.

Quinn pulled her down to him on the couch, and held her close while she cried. "I'm sorry, Kelsey, I didn't mean to scare you."

"It's just everything. These murders. Alisha. Joe." She rubbed the tears from her eyes and pulled away from Quinn's embrace. They sat shoulder to shoulder staring at an infomercial featuring a large African-American woman wearing a head wrap and sporting a fake Jamaican accent exhorting them to call now—

she had important news for them.

"Maybe I should call her. At this point, she has more idea than we do about what is going on with these murders," Quinn said dispiritedly. "I'm sorry, Kels. I'm not trying to fight with you, but I really need to find the connection here before anyone else dies. The key has to be Alicia and that group. It's the common thread."

"Look, I know you're just trying to do your job, but Quinn, consider what I'm facing, here. I'm involved, too, and I know these people."

"Yeah, and you think that doesn't make this harder for me? Knowing you are so close to all of this?"

"Yes, but I'm missing something the killer seems to want . . ." Kelsey said, trying to make a joke of it, but it came out brittle and cold sounding.

"Remember Tessa?" Quinn said, no hint of a smile on his face or in his eyes.

"Look, I can't just turn the records over. I just can't."

"Guess all we can do is wait for the court order, then."

"Guess so," Kelsey said, sighing deeply and leaning back into the couch. Her body suddenly felt heavy and weak, and a hint of despair she hadn't experienced in a long time crept in.

They both sat in silence, watching the telephone psychic guess the deep dark secrets of her callers. "You have a boyfriend in prison, I see," intoned the dark-skinned woman with deep reverence.

Quinn chortled and hit the off button on the television remote.

"Is this going wrong? Are we headed in two different directions?" Kelsey asked, breaking the tense silence.

"I don't know, Kels. My guess is it's just one of the rough spots."

"Where were you tonight?"

"Working."

"I smell beer, and garlic."

"I caught a beer after work with Rita and Fletcher, and then we got a bite and discussed the case."

"Rita."

"Yes, Rita. She's temporarily my partner, Kelsey, and she's an excellent detective. You know that."

"Yeah, she's cute, too."

"If you like the type. It's just a rough spot, Kels. We'll make it through."

"Rough. Yeah, I guess that sums it up."

"Let's go to bed, okay? I'm too tired to think anymore about anything."

"Hey, what did you mean when you said M&M murders?" Kelsey asked, something he'd said to the patrolman suddenly jumping to the foreground of her jumbled mind.

"Oh, that's what we've tagged them. The Murdered Men."

"Plus one," Kelsey said quietly, thinking of Tessa. "Plus one."

Chapter Twenty-Two

Mel Gibson ran ahead of her on the stark white strand, wearing only the briefest of swimsuits and carrying a large knife. The turquoise water to their right dazzled, the sun's rays shining off it and temporarily blinding her.

She put a long, well manicured arm up to cover her eyes, the light blond hairs suddenly standing on end. A chill ran down her back. Mel wasn't running anymore. He waited for her, and she tried to stop, but her feet had taken over and seemed to have brains of their own. Closer and closer she came to him, and his smile turned to a leer, the knife suddenly dripping blood.

As she moved ever closer the man's handsome face dissolved and turned into liquid, and he reached up a hairy arm to wipe away the moisture.

The chill suddenly turned hot, electric hot, sparking up and down her back and legs, and her mouth became dry. Her heart thumped as she tried to dig down in the sand, to stop her feet from betraying her and taking her to the man.

When *he* moved his arm away from his face the familiar look was there. It was the look *he* always got when someone angered him. It wasn't Mel; it was a trick. It was the gaze loaded with forty thousand poisonous spiders prepared to launch an attack on a naked body left alone in a cellar.

She tried to scream, but no sound came, and he reached for her, the man with the face she'd never forget, the face she dreamed about every night, and she prepared herself for the shock of his touch, his icy hands running down her back and over her body.

"No," she groaned, the sweat pouring off her in rivers. "No."

Somewhere, a phone rang, and she watched his brow furrow in puzzlement, the anger on his face at being interrupted, his hand still reaching out for her, the knife raised high in the air.

The phone.

The beach faded, and more slowly, so did the pounding fear, the roar of the surf nothing more than blood rushing through her veins at top speed.

The phone rang and rang, and she reached over to the bedside table with a weak hand, surprised and grateful her limbs were working.

"Hello. It's late."

"You have to stop."

She paused for a moment, and the familiar voice made her pulse slow even further, an uneven calm beginning to take hold. Control flooded back into her icy body, slowly bringing the warmth of familiarity with it; the determination of her purpose became tangible.

"You have to stop," the low, whispery female voice repeated. Mother.

"I can't."

"Please. She wants to hurt you. If you keep going, she will."

"She loves me. I can't stop. If I do, they'll get me. They'll get you, too.

"I can't."

Chapter Twenty-Three

On Thursday morning, Quinn sat at his desk in the bustling office, poring over the membership roster of the Women Against Violence group. Nothing jumped out at him, no red flags, and he sat back and sighed.

"Anderson," yelled one of the detectives from across the room. "Line two."

He punched the button on his phone and answered, "Anderson."

"Hello, Quinn," a silky voice purred into his ear. "Long time no talk. Or see."

Memories of a leggy, blond anchorwoman flashed through his mind. Last time he'd seen her she'd thrown a glass of wine in his face before stomping out of his apartment.

Something about commitment and loyalty, words he found interesting issued from her deceptive mouth.

"Christy. Been a while. Is this just a friendly call? You just starting thinking of me, and decided you had to get in touch?"

"No, you're not that unforgettable, lover. You owe me, and I need some information."

"I owe you for what?"

"For a broken heart," Christy said.

"You don't have a heart, Christy. Remember, it's all business with you."

"Oh, you are still sore about that little news piece, aren't you?"

"That little news piece cost me six months of investigation, and allowed a killer to almost disappear."

"Well, you got him in the end. And I got promoted. So we're even."

"You're reasoning is a little twisted, Chris. What is it you want?"

"I'm a little twisted, remember?" She chuckled, and her rich, throaty laughter made his throat tighten a little as he remembered the sexual games she had enjoyed playing. His collar and necktie suddenly felt a little tighter, and he reached up and tugged at them sheepishly, angry she could still bring those feelings out in him.

"Yeah, I remember," Quinn said, pushing back in his chair. "What do you want?"

"Tell me about the M&M murders. I hear that's what you're calling them. Is it true we have a serial killer on our hands here in SB?"

"No comment."

"Come on, Quinn. Just a few details, for old time's sake."

"Sorry, Christy. No can do. Call someone you haven't already burned."

"You're such a baby, Quinn."

"Waah," he said into the phone, and hung up. He glared at the phone for a minute, muttering under his breath, and then looked up to find Rita watching him with curiosity etched on her face.

He glared at her, too, and she fought back a grin, as though she knew exactly what had happened.

"So, anything standing out in that roster, Quinn?" Rita said.

"No, not a damn thing. Time to pay some visits." Quinn stood and put his jacket on, nodding his head at Rita, who also stood and gathered her purse.

"Anderson. Franklin's on line two," one of the other detectives yelled across the room. Quinn grabbed the phone up and barked his name.

"Yo, Anderson, your girl's back."

"Kelsey?"

"No, Alisha Telford, dumbass," Franklin chortled, enjoying the chance to give Quinn some grief. "She just sashayed into her apartment building, as if she didn't have a care in the world—or a clue we were sitting here. You want us to pick her up?"

"I'm on my way."

"She still in there?" Quinn asked Franklin. He'd pulled the car up directly behind the other unmarked vehicle, and Rita got out more slowly than he did, eyeing the apartment building, a frown on her face as they watched people come and go.

Franklin was African-American, small and compact, with a face as dark as night. He was a notorious prankster, and also one of the best junior detectives on the force.

"Yup, hasn't come out. Hey, did you hear the one about the two leprechauns in the bar?" He leaned aback against the car expectantly, and Quinn groaned.

Rita surveyed the scene with a frown on her face, an eerie feeling running up the back of her spine.

An old lady walking her shih tzu carried a small plastic bag and wore rubber gloves. A young couple ran to a convertible, laughing as they jumped in and pealed out. From around the side of the building, a tall blond woman came. One hand held her keys, and a crumpled handkerchief, and with the other she wiped at her face. When she reached her car, she pulled out a compact, checking her lipstick before unlocking her car door.

There was something oddly familiar about the woman, and Rita searched her memory, an uneasy tingle starting in her toes and moving up. "Yo, Quinn, you see that lady?" Rita said, interrupting his conversation with Franklin. "Something's up here. Something isn't right."

"That's her," Franklin yelled, as he caught sight of the woman Rita referred to. The car pulled out into the street, and the driver made a U-turn, heading left on Cabrillo Street.

"Follow her," Quinn ordered Franklin, who jumped into the police sedan and took pursuit, hollering into his police radio as he drove away. Quinn followed Rita as she broke into a run, heading to the apartment building.

A young woman exited as they reached the entrance, and they pushed her aside and ran into the building, pounding up the stairs to Alisha's apartment. Breathing heavy, Quinn took the lead, and Rita let him, knowing he'd been there before.

They stood before 8D, and Quinn pushed open the door. A sickly sweet smell hit Rita in the face as they pushed open the unlocked door and Quinn moaned.

On the floor, surrounded by pools of blood, they saw the body of Detective John Penny.

"I lost her," Franklin told Quinn with chagrin. "Man, the woman drove like Mario Andretti. Had to slow down to avoid hitting civilians."

"Damn, damn, damn," Quinn swore, knowing the police directives about high-speed chases dictated what Franklin had done.

"Do you have an APB out? Did you get the license number?"

"Yeah, I called it in. Didn't come back to Telford, though."

"Yeah?"

"Car's registered to a Tamara Rowe."

"Tammy Rowe?"

"Quinn," Rita interrupted. "You know, I've only seen Alisha once, but this woman . . . well, she looked like her, but something was off. Something was wrong."

"You don't think it was Alisha?"

"Well, I can't swear, but I know I've seen her before, somewhere. So I guess it could have been her."

"Damn, these two women are both tied up in this together, somehow," Quinn said. "Well, this isn't getting us anywhere. CSU here yet?"

"Yeah," Franklin said, wearing a sad puppy-dog face, still upset he'd lost the woman in traffic. "They're processing the crime scene."

"Time to pay Ms. Rowe a visit."

Chapter Twenty-Four

They found Tamara Rowe sitting at her desk in the behavioral science unit of the hospital. The receptionist ushered them into the doctor's office, where she sat with her hair piled high on her head, wire-rimmed glasses perched on her nose.

Rita watched her closely, trying to determine if this was the woman she'd seen leave the apartment building where they found John Penny murdered. Although the hair color was similar, she couldn't tell about the woman's height, and the person she'd seen had not been dressed like this, nor had she worn her hair up.

"Detective Anderson, good to see you again. And your partner is?"

"Detective Rita Jaramillo," she offered before Quinn could introduce her. She stuck her hand out to shake the doctor's hand, and was struck by how firmly the woman returned the handshake.

"What can I do for you?" Tammy Rowe asked, easing back in her chair and bouncing a pen off her desk as she watched them expectantly.

"Have you left your office today, Ms. Rowe?" Quinn inquired.

"What's this about?" she asked, frowning, and pushing the wire-rimmed glasses up against her face with the tip of her right index finger.

"Can you please just tell us if you have left the office today?"

"Well, let's see, I went to the cafeteria for lunch. It's pot pie day, and I really enjoy a good . . ."

"Ms. Rowe," Rita interrupted, tapping her right foot nervously on the ground. They sat in two plush, high-backed chairs upholstered in a dark burgundy. The entire office was burgundy and dark green, with an elaborate mahogany desk sitting in the middle of the room. "Look, we need to know if you have left your office today, and we need to know where your car is."

"Oh, well, I loaned my car to a friend several days ago," she said, frowning. She stood up, and Rita was impressed with her height, tall for a woman, maybe five nine. Tammy Rowe walked around the desk and sat on the front, so she was closer to them. She was immaculately dressed in a smart beige pantsuit and designer shoes. Rita looked down at her own Payless black boots, off-the-rack suit bought at the local TJ Maxx, and she immediately felt frumpy and small.

"You loaned your car to whom?" Quinn countered.

"First things first. Tell me what this is about. Why are you wondering about my car?"

"Can anyone verify you loaned them the car?"

"Of course."

"Can you give me the name and number of the person you loaned the car to?"

"Look, detectives, this is starting to get tiresome, and I'm starting to feel like a suspect in something, so can you please explain yourself? I haven't left the hospital today. I'm backlogged on paperwork, and I spent yesterday with a suicidal patient, so if you'll quit playing games . . ."

"I'm not playing games here, Ms. Rowe. Who has your car?"

"It's Dr. Rowe, thank you very much. I loaned my car to Alisha Telford."

Tamara Rowe refused to give them any information about her

complaint against Calvin Reynolds, except to say he had verbally abused her when she said no, she did not want to go out with him.

"When are you men going to realize no means no?" she'd said with an angry glare in Quinn's direction.

"Lots of man hating going on there," he said to Rita as they left Rowe's office.

"Yeah, she didn't seem very fond of men, did she?"

"Definitely going to look deeper into her."

"I think she's scary. If I were you, I'd watch yourself."

Chapter Twenty-Five

Kelsey unloaded the groceries from the trunk of the car, and balanced two plastic bags with one hand, reaching in for a third. She frowned as she tried to figure out how to close the trunk with her hands full.

"Tia! Tia!" she hollered, trying to catch her daughter's attention, but the little girl had skipped on ahead, into the backyard, dancing to music on her Walkman.

Sighing, Kelsey decided she would have to come back and close the trunk, and she headed through the gate to the side door of her house, one eye on her daughter who danced around the backyard, singing into a make-believe microphone to the Backstreet Boys.

Kelsey set two of the bags on the ground and rummaged for her keys in the large bag she always carried.

"Gonna be gone for a while?" Quinn always teased her, whenever he spotted her with the purse he claimed to be the size of a large suitcase.

She listened for the jingle, and finally located the keys. She unlocked the door and pushed through, dropping the bags on the table. Walking back outside, she went first to the backyard where she'd last seen her daughter dancing like a maniac, but Tia wasn't there.

A quick catch in her throat made her feel vulnerable and exposed. Would she ever feel safe letting her daughter out of her sight, even for a minute?

Kelsey turned around and went back through the gate out onto the driveway, where she could see the dancing feet of her daughter, leaning over the trunk.

"Well, how unusual, she's actually helping without being asked," Kelsey mused, her hands on her hips. Tia's feet suddenly stilled, and the catch came back to her throat as she watched her daughter back away from the trunk, her eyes wide and round, shell-shocked. She backed away until she tripped over the curb and landed on her behind. She sat on the ground with a frozen look of terror on her face, still staring at the trunk of the car.

The hair rose up on Kelsey's arms and her scalp began to tingle as she crossed the short distance to her daughter and scooped her up.

Kelsey pulled the headphones off the little girl's ears and said "Baby, baby. What's wrong? What's wrong?"

Tia couldn't speak for a minute, and she gulped, forcing herself to breathe and swallow.

"Honey, talk to me."

Tia lifted up her right arm rigidly, and pointed to the open trunk, where only minutes before she had been gathering up bags to carry into the house.

Kelsey turned and eyed the trunk with foreboding, a pit in her stomach, and chills running up and down her body. She stood slowly, and walked the short distance to the vehicle, peering inside where she saw nothing at first. Nothing but grocery bags, an old blanket, and the glint of metal, and the smell . . . Oh God, the smell.

She reached her hand in and tugged gently at the blanket, knowing this was not hers and she'd never seen it before. The folded blanket unfurled and out tumbled a long, jagged knife, encrusted with red blood, no doubt blood, and next to it was—

"Kelsey, what's wrong? What's wrong?"

Kelsey jumped and screamed, turning to see her curious, elfin neighbor Edie Falconer.

The old woman peered into the trunk, frowned, scrunched up her eyes, and stood at straight, looking at Kelsey with confused eyes.

"Why, I do believe there's a penis in your trunk."

Kelsey sat on her lawn, watching the techs from the crime scene unit go through her trunk, unsure she'd ever be able to drive the vehicle again. A visibly shaken Tia was in the house, talking to Quinn and Rita Jaramillo.

Edie Falconer glowed as she told her story to Detective Franklin, seated in the back seat of a patrol car. Kelsey watched her with astonishment, wondering how this innocent-faced woman could be so enthralled with gruesome murder.

"Murder. Maybe it's not murder, maybe it's just—"

"Just what, Kelsey?" Quinn asked, causing her to start. She hadn't heard him approach from behind.

"Who does it belong to? The . . . the . . ."

"Probably Penny. Won't know for sure until the lab gets the tests back, of course, but his penis was missing."

"Oh, God, Quinn. This is bad. Did someone just put it in there when I was in the house? Or was it in there before? How *did* it get in there, anyway?"

"Don't know, Kels. We're trying to find out. But this is getting bad. Dangerous. I think you and Tia need to leave."

"And go where, Quinn? To visit my mother in the loony bin? No thanks. No Utah for me."

"My mom."

"Huh?"

"I want you and Tia to go stay with my Mom in Colorado. You'll be safe there."

"No, I can't leave here. I'm Alisha's friend, and I have the group—"

"Goddammit, Kelsey, Alisha could very well be the one killing people. Wake up and smell the roses. She's gone. We can't find her, and people keep dying. Somehow, she's involved."

"You can't just assume—"

"Mom?"

Kelsey turned quickly to see her daughter approaching with Rita. The little girl held the detective's hand tightly, her face still pale and ashen, her eyes watery and red.

"What did she say?" Kelsey whispered to Quinn.

"She's scared," he replied in a low voice. "Let's take her to my mother's."

"Mommy?" Tia and Rita had stopped several feet from where Kelsey and Quinn were standing.

"Tia, honey, I think it's time for a vacation," Kelsey announced. "Let's go visit Grandma Honey in Colorado."

Grandma Honey was a small, matronly woman with big, flashing blue eyes, a testament to her son's genetics. She had visited Quinn and Kelsey in California twice since they'd been together, and Tia had taken to her immediately.

Honey Anderson had raised a big family on her own, when her husband had passed away prematurely. A devout Catholic, she was a big fan of bingo, and loved the casinos located on the Indian reservation not far from Los Angeles.

Despite the fact Kelsey really liked Quinn's mother, staying in Colorado without Quinn did not sound like something she would be comfortable with.

"Oh, please come," Honey had urged on the phone when they'd called her. "All the other kids live close. Tia would have so many friends to play with, and you and I would have a great chance to get to know each other. It won't hurt for her to miss a little school, will it?"

Kelsey compromised. She would fly out with Tia and then

return home after two days, leaving the little girl in the safe hands of Quinn's mother.

It was not a decision she reached easily.

She packed a small overnight case for herself, and a larger suitcase full of Tia's clothes, Mr. Peepers, a worn stuffed animal that slept with the little girl every night, and a few small toys.

"Mom," Tia said as she watched her mother fill the suitcase. She sat on her twin bed, her eyes round and solemn. "What if they don't like me?"

"What? Who?"

"Them. The . . . the cousins. Grandma Honey's real grandkids."

"Oh, hush, silly child," Kelsey said, stopping her activities to grab Tia's chin and bend down so their foreheads touched. "What's not to like? You have a killer sense of style, tons of good jokes, and you're really good at checkers."

"Mom, I'm serious. I don't want to go, but I'm scared. I'm scared to stay here, and I don't want you here, either. Or Quinn."

"Honey, Quinn is a policeman. It's his job, and I guarantee you, I've seen him in action. He is really good at what he does. He can protect both of us."

"He couldn't before," Tia said, her frowning face a reminder she hadn't forgotten the events of last year.

"Yes, he could have, if I hadn't acted on my own, sweetheart. I told you, he got us out. I went back. It was my fault. I went back for Grandma . . . for my mom."

Kelsey knew the events in Utah were a blur for Tia, who had spent most of the time sedated and hidden.

"You never told me that."

"I didn't want to, sweetie. It's the past. It's over."

"Are you sure?"

"Yes, I'm sure. Now you go find Quinn and tell him we're almost ready to go the airport."

The little girl left the room, walking instead of performing her usual bouncing, skipping sidestep, and Kelsey shook her head as she watched.

Are you sure? Are you sure?

"God, I hope so."

They spent a reserved evening together, the three of them eating Kentucky Fried Chicken at the kitchen table. Afterward, Quinn pulled out a movie he had hidden away in a sack on the counter, and surprised Tia with *Spy Kids.*

"Oh, thank you, Quinn." The little girl ran to him and hugged him tightly. "Can we watch it now? Can I take it with me?"

"Yes, and yes," he said, and they moved into the living room and put the movie in the VCR, while Kelsey quietly cleaned up in the kitchen.

She joined them on the couch and reveled in Tia's childish laughter for the next hour, and then she sent Tia to brush her teeth.

Quinn and Kelsey sat for a minute in awkward silence, and then she stood and said, "I'm just going to check on Tia."

That night in bed, they didn't speak or touch, though each was restless. Kelsey thought of the Tori Amos song, "China," because that's how far away Quinn felt to her.

It's just a rough spot, that's all.

CHAPTER TWENTY-SIX

Quinn drove directly to the station after taking Kelsey and Tia to the airport the next morning. Distracted, he parked and exited his car, the noonday sun glaring off the metallic fenders of the automobiles in the lot. His left arm in the air to fight off the intense light, he reached into his suit jacket pocket to pluck out his sunglasses.

"Gonna hide those baby blues, huh, Quinn?" a familiar, honey-glazed voice said from behind his car.

He looked up to see Christy Frazier, a blond, immaculate, and stunning sight that used to make him weak in the knees. Now, she just made him feel tired.

"Christy, what are you doing here?"

"I came to buy you lunch."

"Not hungry."

"Come on, I owe you. Are you ever going to forgive me for that little faux pas?"

"Is that what you're calling it these days? You sold me out for a story, Christy. I call that betrayal. Besides, you're forgiven. It's over. Time to move on."

"I don't believe you. Let me atone for my sins."

"I have work to do."

"I might have some information that would be of interest to you, if I can talk you into joining me for lunch."

"What information?"

"Uh, uh, uh, first things first. Lunch."

Quinn stared at her with a hard look, removing his glasses so he could make eye contact. "What do you really want?"

"I want several things. First, I want you to forgive me. Second, I want to tell you what I know, and I believe it will help you."

"And last?" Quinn asked, a tinge of disbelief in his voice.

"I want exclusive right to the story when it breaks. And it will break . . ."

"Well, at least this time you are being honest."

"I was always honest, Quinn, you just didn't want to see it."

He watched her with curiosity, wondering at the small hint of bitterness he heard behind her golden tones. "It's early. Only eleven. Hell of a time for lunch."

"Call it brunch, then."

"Fine. Brunch. But I'm not making any promises."

"Good, neither am I. You can drive."

They drove in semi-silence, Quinn rebuffing Christy's occasional attempts at polite chitchat. She directed him to a trendy eatery in the middle of town, and he gave her a stern glare and a shake of his head. The place was well known among anchor people and town celebrities, and it was the last place he intended to show up with one of Santa Barbara's famous faces. Instead, he drove to an Italian restaurant on the outskirts of town, known for its excellent food and quiet atmosphere, and a genuine lack of trend-appeal.

"So, what's this news you have for me?" he said to her, after the waiter brought them their food.

Christy scooped up a big forkful of linguini and shook her head at Quinn while she chewed.

"I'm famished. Have to refuel. Business can wait," she finally said when she could talk with an empty mouth.

"You always did have a hearty appetite," he said to her with a half-smile, and she impishly grinned, causing his heart to race just a bit. She'd been hard to forget.

"In more ways than one," she drawled, and took another mouthful of food.

Quinn picked at his lasagna, thinking about Kelsey and Tia on their way to Colorado. Guilt washed over him as he sat having lunch with the woman he still had intense, erotic dreams about. He always woke up from them feeling dirty and used.

Christy was driven and focused, always had been, and her goal was to make her way to the top of the local news scene. She now anchored the weekend evening news, and was fast becoming a favorite among the Santa Barbara media.

"So, what's the word? When you taking over on the eleven o'clock broadcast?"

Christy laughed, finishing up the pasta with relish, and she grabbed the glass of white wine she'd ordered and gulped it down.

"All in good time. Viewer ratings keep coming back positive for me, and negative for Williams. She'll be gone in no time. She's close to forty, anyway, time to retire."

"Television news and sports. Only place in the world forty is old."

"Hey, I don't make the rules, Quinn," she said, wiping her mouth with the cloth napkin and setting it next to her empty plate. "I just make them work to my advantage. I'm thirty-two now, so I don't have much time to secure my place."

"I'm sure you'll get there, Christy. You always get what you want."

"Not always," Christy said, her bright smile suddenly disappearing as her right hand shot out across the table and grabbed his left hand.

Quinn pulled back abruptly, and looked away from her, embarrassed at the flash of raw desire he saw in her eyes, and felt in his groin.

"I'm involved."

"I heard."

"What, do you keep tabs on me?"

"Quinn," she said, leaning in toward him as she lowered her voice, "I miss you. We were good together. Remember that time in San Diego? On the balcony of the hotel? The scarf and feather . . ." Her voice trailed off dreamily as she closed her eyes and sat back, a host of emotions like passion and sexuality emanating from her in almost tangible waves.

"Stop!" Quinn reached out and grabbed her wrist this time, shaking her as she opened her eyes abruptly and frowned at him.

"I'm involved, I told you. And as I remember it, our whole relationship went on way too long, mainly because I was listening to the wrong head."

Christy shook her golden blond tresses and gave him a disappointed look. "Just one night? Haven't you ever just wanted to go back and try just one . . . more . . . time?"

She licked her lips, and Quinn swallowed, disgusted with himself for allowing his thoughts to travel to Christy's nether regions.

"You are a shallow, self-centered woman, okay?"

"You're turned on, and you know it," she countered, a knowing smile on her face.

"That's just sex. It doesn't mean anything."

Christy pouted for a minute, and then shrugged. "So, you going to take me up on my deal, or what?"

Quinn shook his head, amazed as always at how fast she could change gears. "Depends on what you have."

"Well, I might as well tell you now. I had a source in your department. John Penny."

"Penny fed you information?"

"Yeah, and now he's dead."

"Penny was . . . never mind. What did he know?"

"I'm not sure exactly what he knew, but he was looking at an angle all right. It involved the WAV group. Didn't I hear you are, uh, involved with Kelsey Waite, who runs the group? I interviewed her once. She's a little short, isn't she? I thought your tastes ran to long, leggy blondes?"

"My relationship is none of your business, Christy. What's the tie? What was he looking into?"

"He wouldn't tell me until he confirmed it. But he gave me three names. Alisha Telford, Tammy Rowe, and cute little Kelsey, all round and cuddly . . . ."

"Shut the fuck up, Christy."

"Ooh, you're protective."

"He didn't have anything. You haven't helped at all." Quinn stood and dropped his napkin to the table, motioning for the check to the waiter who hovered nearby. "No exclusive. This didn't help at all. I'm buying my own dinner, too."

"He said it was revenge."

"What?"

"He said he talked to someone who knew what it was about. It was all about revenge. Every man who ever wronged a woman in that group is going to die. I heard they found Penny's penis in your honey's car. She's had a warped past, hasn't she? Lots of years of being abused by men. Maybe she finally got tired of it. Maybe you better start going to bed wearing protective gear over your genitals, huh, Quinn?"

CHAPTER TWENTY-SEVEN

"Where the hell are you?" Rita said into the phone. There was no reply, because she was talking to Quinn's voice mail. "Call me, now. Something's up."

She slammed the phone down and leaned back in her chair, the desire for a cigarette pushing to the forefront of her mind. "Argh," she muttered, standing up and stretching. Where was Quinn? He should be in the office by now. When he called her earlier, he told her about sending Kelsey and Tia away.

"Didn't say he was going to *drive* them to Colorado, though."

"Talking to yourself is a very bad habit, Jaramillo."

"Ah, can it, Franklin." She tempered her terse greeting with a quick smile. "Penny was on to something."

"On to what?"

"Loo had me go through his desk, looking for clues. I found this." Rita handed Franklin a piece of notepaper. In messy handwriting the names "Telford, A.," "Rowe, T.," and "Waite, K." were scrawled. Next to the names stood one word, scrawled in big letters and underlined to the point the pen had torn through the paper.

"REVENGE."

"Revenge? Revenge for . . . Hey, that's Alisha Telford, Kelsey Waite, and Tammy Rowe, right?"

"I'd say yes to that, genius."

"Jaramillo, you are breaking my heart. Why you so mean to me?"

Franklin gave her his best puppy-dog impression, complete with pouting lower lip and wide brown eyes.

"Ick. Get away," she said laughing, pushing him with her hand. She sobered up quickly. "What does this mean? Why revenge?"

"The WAV group? All the victims are tied to it. It's not something we haven't thought of before. You know Quinn was getting a subpoena for the membership roster and group records."

"Yeah, but I think it's more than just that. Why did Penny have it underlined so many times. Like it really bugged him, you know?"

Franklin sat down in the chair next to Rita, and thoughtfully rubbed his chin. "Did you find anything else in his desk?"

"Just routine case files, notes, nothing groundbreaking or earth shattering."

"Yeah, that was the kind of detective he was. Nothing groundbreaking or earth shattering."

"You're speaking poorly of the dead. My grandmother would say you're putting a pox on yourself."

Franklin put his hands together in the shape of a cross and slowly backed off, an amused smile crossing his face.

Rita giggled to herself and shrugged as he walked away.

Revenge. Surely Alisha had reason to want revenge, to destroy the man who had raped her so many years ago. But a killing spree? And how was Tammy Rowe, the doctor, connected to the whole mess? The last name seemed even more of a stretch.

Could Quinn's lover Kelsey possibly be involved?

Rita finally reached Quinn on his cell phone, berating him for his absence as she drove with Franklin back to the hospital and Tammy Rowe's office.

"What the hell, Quinn, we're in the middle of a fucking

nightmare case and you just disappear? Why wasn't your cell phone turned on?"

"Rita, it is *not* charming when you say 'fuck.' "

"Fuck you."

She heard a sigh, and then Quinn said, "I was with an informant. Someone who knew Penny, and thinks there's a tie between him and WAV."

"That's what I've been trying to get a hold of you for. We found a note in Penny's desk. It had three names on it. Telford's, Rowe's, and, uh . . ."

"Kelsey's, right?"

"Yeah. That and the word 'revenge,' underlined. So hard it went through the paper."

"Kelsey is not a killer, Jaramillo."

"I didn't say she was, Anderson. I've got Franklin with me, and we're headed over to question Rowe again."

"Okay, I'm going to get Penny's personal effects from the morgue, see if he had any notes, or anything else on him that might be more concrete as to what he was investigating. He was probably just guessing anyway, trying to cover sloppy police work on the first three incidents."

"Quinn?"

"Yeah?"

"Don't disappear again."

"Who's in charge here, Jaramillo?"

"Fuck you."

"Later. I'm too tired right now."

"Argh," she cried as she clicked the off button. "I want Terri back. You men are impossible to work with."

"Ah, you love us and you know it," Franklin countered, grinning at her with his contagious smile.

She finally fought back a grin and smiled, shaking her head as she watched the road. Franklin pulled the car into the parking lot of the hospital, and they found a spot near the front of the building, one reserved for clergy.

Franklin stepped out, and looked up at the sky. "Forgive us, Father, for we have sinned."

Rita laughed as she slammed the passenger door. "You a lapsed Catholic, too, Franklin?"

"Nope. Good old Southern Baptist roots here. We keep our women barefoot and pregnant, thank you very much. Just watched a lot of movies growing up."

"Well, say a Hail Mary we catch this creep, then," Rita said as they moved together toward the entrance.

They walked through the hospital entrance, turning away from the bustle toward the quieter business offices on the south corridor. Rita walked ahead of Franklin. There was no secretary sitting at the desk in front of Dr. Rowe's office, and she glanced at her watch to see it was just a few minutes past one p.m.

Rita rapped briskly on the doctor's door. There was no answer.

Rita looked around, and then turned the knob and pushed open the door. The blinds were pulled, and the room was dark. She groped along the side wall looking for a light switch. She finally found it and flipped it up.

The room lit up brightly, papers, chair stuffing, and dirt from plants thrown everywhere. The expensive furniture had been gouged and hacked with something sharp. The office was destroyed.

Sitting on the beautiful mahogany desk was a small scalpel, covered in dried blood.

Chapter Twenty-Eight

Quinn pulled up at the station with the bag containing Penny's effects. It was nearing five p.m., and his face felt dirty, a shadow of beard starting to appear. He rubbed his chin roughly and sat back for a minute, leaning against the headrest of the sedan. He'd spent quite a while at the morgue, not his favorite place to be. After the rough night, the disastrous lunch with Christy Frazier, and the events of the past few days, he felt like he'd been turned inside out.

He had briefly gone through Penny's effects, but needed to pull everything out and go over the items one by one. Another late night loomed, but at least he didn't have to worry about Kelsey and Tia, who were safely in Colorado.

Quinn rubbed his eyes and then stepped out of the car. A bright yellow taxi caught his eye as it pulled up to the curb. Out of the taxi stepped Christy, and she gave him a dirty look as she marched past him to her car.

He ignored her and went into the police station, which was fairly empty as the nine-to-five dees had already cleared out for the weekend.

Just where he wanted to be on a Friday night. In a near-deserted office with the personal effects of John Penny, who had obviously lived a pallid and wan existence.

He spread the assorted items out in front of him on the desk and surveyed them. A key ring holding four keys: an automobile key, a possible apartment or house key, a small padlock key, and a large, silver key that looked as if it belonged to a door in an office building.

Penny's wallet contained a Visa credit card, his California driver's license—an unhappy Penny staring up at him from a small photo—and a receipt from a gas station in Redville, California. The receipt was dated the week before, a Saturday.

Puzzled, Quinn pulled out his own wallet and flipped it open, spying on top a picture of Kelsey and Tia, taken on the beach near the house a month or so before. They had their arms around each other and were smiling, their heads almost touching, the surf vivid blue behind them. He flipped through various other pictures, most of them of his nieces and nephews, pictures he received every year in Christmas cards.

Inside the billfold he had one hundred dollars in twenties and a bunch of receipts for purchases he could no longer remember. Tucked back in one hidden slot, he discovered, was a well-worn condom package.

His driver's license and credit cards were in neat slots lined up one on top of the other, one Visa and one American Express card. Tucked back in another hidden pocket was a poem, one he'd written the night after he and Kelsey returned home from Utah.

He unfolded the worn paper and read the poem, smiling at the memories it evoked.

Shining, she sits
on the beach, not knowing
the consequences of her
spell

Shining, she reflects
The man you know you are

And the child you once
Remembered

Shining, she beams
And you wonder, do I,
The man/child deserve
All this?

Shining, she sings
Come to me, into me, come to me
Shining

He hadn't written anything for quite a while. Had his muse deserted him, driven out by violence, murder, and the struggles of daily life and commitment?

Was it possible?

He folded the poem back up and put it back into the back slot of his wallet, stopping a minute to stroke the picture of Kelsey and Tia, before returning the wallet to his pocket.

She still shines, idiot.

Quinn sat staring at the contents of John Penny's life, or at least his life on the job. Did he have a special someone? Couldn't be Christy. She was a barracuda in a bathing suit, all curves and smiles on the outside, and razor sharp teeth that tore you apart if you dared to enter her realm, beguiled by her outer loveliness.

Penny was stolid, steady, dull. His lifestyle would not have attracted someone like Christy. She craved beauty, flavor, excitement, and adrenaline. Penny would have been nothing more than a stepping stone for her, a way to get what she wanted: the next big story.

His cell phone rang, and he answered, "Anderson."

"We've got a mess," Rita said without prelude. "Rowe's missing, her office has been thrown, and there's a bloody scalpel here. Crime scene is on the way. You should probably get over here."

"Be right there."

"You okay?"

"I'm fine. Little tired."

"Okay," she said, lingering a minute more before saying, "See you in a few."

He hit the off button on his phone, and stuck it back in his pocket, staring down at Penny's meager belongings. Was there more to it than this? What was bothering him?

It would have to wait.

Chapter Twenty-Nine

There was no sign of the missing Tammy Rowe, and the hospital administrator, contacted at home, gave them the phone number of her secretary, who, it turned out, had gone home sick after half a day.

Quinn made an appointment to interview the woman in the morning. He drove with a silent Rita to the home of Tamara Rowe, in an upscale suburb on a hillside high atop Santa Barbara. In the darkening gloom of nightfall, one could just see the sun dropping into the water of the ocean, reflecting across a wide expanse of the water.

"Ritzy," Rita commented, looking around. "She must have been some doctor."

"Must have been?"

"Slip of the tongue. I meant must be. Just seems every time we find some blood, or follow another path in this murder case, somebody else dies."

They left the car and walked through a nicely maintained yard to the cottage of Tammy Rowe. There were no lights on in the house, and Quinn knocked sharply at the door, then rang the bell. Rita walked to a side windowpane next to the heavy oak door and peered inside.

"Too dark. Can't see squat."

Quinn rang the doorbell again, and then tried the doorknob. It was locked, and didn't give in to his gentle pushing. They walked around the side of the house, noting the small windowless garage attached to the side.

Rita pushed up against a side door to the building, and found it open. Inside, she flipped on a light switch to see it was immaculate—and empty.

She stepped back and Quinn looked inside, seeing nothing that set off his inner alarms.

"Let's canvas the neighborhood," he said.

"I'm starving. It's gonna be a long night, isn't it?"

"Yep. We'll get takeout on the way back to the station."

They learned nothing much from Tammy Rowe's neighbors, other than she was quiet and kept to herself. No one could remember seeing her come or go that day, but most admitted they simply didn't pay attention.

Her closest neighbors on each side were not home, and both homes showed signs they'd been away for a while, with lawns a little too long, and papers on the porch.

Frustrated, Quinn and Rita had returned to the station house, stopping on the way to grab takeout from the closest fast food joint.

They ate at their desks, not talking, and when Quinn was finished he picked up Penny's personnel report, which he'd requisitioned earlier in the day.

"You know much about Penny?" he asked Rita, who still nibbled on French fries.

"Nope. He was quiet. Didn't talk much. Didn't seem real smart. A little too glib sometimes. Sloppy in his police work."

"You see signs of that?"

"Yeah, Terri and I caught a couple of cases where he'd done legwork or started on. He liked to tie things up, fast and easy. Didn't like complications."

"So, it doesn't make sense then. Why would he push the envelope in this case? Scream to investigate, make a stink with the loo, you know? It's nothing *but* complications."

"Personal interest?" Rita guessed.

"Okay, well, I know a news anchor who got inside information from him. She said he knew something, had a reason to believe the motive was revenge. And that Alisha, Tammy Rowe, and Kelsey were all involved."

"Could that have been sour grapes at you? I mean, him bringing in Kelsey's name?"

"I barely knew the guy. I also rarely talked to him."

"Oh, yeah, I forgot, you're the star. They don't saddle you with the pain-in-the-ass dees."

"You're becoming a real sore spot in my ass, Jaramillo."

She stuck out her pink tongue at him and giggled, taking another swig of her soda.

"So what's the tie? Why did he extend himself on this one? So far out he ended up murdered and mutilated. Why?"

"Personal interest?"

"I see no signs he was a person. I mean, look at his effects. A couple of dollars, a tiny bit of change, no pictures. Nothing but a receipt for gas in Northern California. Last Saturday."

"Northern California?"

"Redville. Where exactly is that anyway."

Rita's face became somber and her eyes darkened. "Tiny town. Saw it on the map yesterday. Right next to Chapel Grace."

Chapter Thirty

Saturday dawned early for Quinn and Rita, as they found themselves on the road for a trip to Chapel Grace, California, a tiny backwoods town near the Oregon border. Anxious to discover what John Penny had been doing in the small Northern California town, Quinn had called Rita around ten p.m. the night before and asked her if she wanted to tag along.

They'd alerted the local law enforcement, but there'd been no sign of Tammy Rowe, and Quinn knew he wouldn't rest if he didn't visit the place himself.

Rita read a James Patterson novel in the passenger seat, smacking and cracking the gum she chewed constantly. She was dressed in comfortable jeans and a baggy t-shirt, nothing like the suits she wore to the office.

"You look different today," Quinn said to her, glancing her way before turning back to watch the road.

"I may be working on the weekend, but it's still the weekend. You look different, too."

Quinn was also dressed casually, in denim pants and a short-sleeved shirt. His shoulder holster, with the gun inside, was draped over the back seat.

"We official here? Or are we on the QT?"

"For now, we're just two friends, taking a drive on our day off," Quinn said. "I'll fix it if things get ugly."

"Better hope they don't get too ugly."

They didn't talk much on the way, and only stopped twice.

Tired and road weary, they pulled into the small town of Redville almost nine hours later.

They found a small service station and pulled in. Rita stepped out of the car, stretching with relief, and hurried inside to use the ladies room.

Quinn searched for the slot to insert his credit card and automatically pump gas, but there wasn't one, and the pump wouldn't turn on, so he sauntered inside to talk to the attendant.

The man, short and grizzled, with a gray beard, green eyes, and a wad of chew bulging out his lower lip, spat into a soda can sitting on the desk next to him, and eyed Quinn.

"Need some help?" he finally said, spitting again into the can and grinning with stained teeth.

"Need gas. Do I have to pay in advance?"

"Yup," the man said. "Johnson boys keep stealing gas every time they get drunk and want to chase, so I got me one of those automatic shut offs. Means if I'm busy, those boys can't take the gas and run. 'Course, keeps strangers like yourself from running off without paying, too."

"Not much chance of that," Quinn said, handing the man his credit card.

"Well, now, I don't know that, do I? You look nice enough, in a pretty-boy way, but you can't judge a book by its cover. Ain't you heard that?"

"Pretty boy?" Quinn asked, his eyebrows raising a bit.

"Pretty boy, yep, that's Quinn," Rita volunteered, walking over to the desk. She picked up a pack of gum from a rack by the cash register, and set it down. "Pretty boy, will you buy me this gum?"

Quinn gave her an evil look, and she smiled her dazzling smile, the attendant watching both of them closely.

"Well, I guess I can trust you, since you have good taste in ladies," he said with a smile, causing Rita to wince at the sight of his decayed and brown teeth.

Quinn handed the man his card, and turned away, rolling his eyes. Rita put her hand to her mouth, as though trying to keep in a giggle.

"This'll take a minute," the attendant said. "Might as well get yourself a soda or something. He pointed to an ancient case full of drinks, all outrageously priced.

"There a restaurant, or a hotel, around here?" Quinn asked, ignoring the man's pointed gesture.

"Hotel? No hotels. There's a motel about a mile up the road. You could probably get a room there. No one much comes here. Mary runs the place. Calls it an 'inn.' All hoity toity. She's a good cook, though, so you could do worse."

He handed Quinn a receipt to sign, and kept the credit card in his hand, watching closely as Quinn penned his name. Snatching the receipt up, the man compared the signature on the back of the card to the one on the receipt. Finally, satisfied, he handed Quinn a copy and the card back.

Rita had been entertaining herself by examining the contents of the old service station, something that had been replaced by market/gas station combinations in most parts of the country.

She walked back over to the man and said, "You lived here long?"

"Yes'um," he said, offering her another brown-stained smile.

"How long?"

"Born here. Guess I'll die here, too."

"Do you know a woman named Alisha Telford?"

The man's face hardened, and his mouth turned down at the edge, his eyes narrowing and giving him a dangerous look.

"Who are you?" he asked roughly, spitting out tobacco on the floor close to her foot.

"SBPD," Quinn said, stepping in, flipping out his shield. "What's the problem here? You got a reason to be angry with

Alisha Telford?"

"Damn straight I do. Good-for-nothing bitch killed my brother. I ever see her face here again, I'll blow her to kingdom come."

Chapter Thirty-One

Quinn sat in the office of the Redville County sheriff, tapping his fingers nervously on the sides of the plastic chair. Rita paced from one end of the room to the other, making him nervous. They'd left the gum on the counter of the gas station when the man ordered them out, telling them to "get a warrant" if they wanted to come back.

"A warrant? A warrant for what?" Rita murmured as they left the man's business.

Now they waited for Sheriff Dave Sparks to appear. The woman who took them to his office had assured them she'd placed a call to his car, and he would be in as soon as he dealt with those "rascally Johnson brothers."

"Sounds like the Johnson brothers keep busy," Quinn commented, looking around the office. It was sparsely decorated, with no pictures on the old walls, and cheap-looking pressboard furniture. The chairs reminded Quinn of the kind they used in school cafeterias, at least in his day, and were just about as comfortable.

The Redville County Sheriff's Department consisted of one building, with approximately six different offices. From one open door across the hall from the sheriff's they could hear the sound of an occasional phone call, and a dispatcher's voice answering. It was nothing like the busy hub of the dispatchers in Santa Barbara.

"God, I need a cigarette," Rita moaned, finally dropping into the chair next to his. "What's up with this, Quinn?"

"That's what we're here to find out."

"Hey, Sheriff," they heard the receptionist say. "They're in your office."

A tall, well-built man dressed in a beige uniform sauntered into the room, nodding his head at them as he pushed his chair back and sat. "Sheriff Dave Sparks," he said, sticking his hand out across the desk to shake first Quinn's hand and then Rita's. "You're SBPD, huh? Took my wife down there for our honeymoon, about ten years ago. Nice place. Kind of spendy, but nice."

"A little different than here," Rita said with a smile.

"Yep. I started out with the LAPD. Didn't much like the pace, and decided to come back home. Wanted to raise my kids in a small-town atmosphere."

The sheriff had a pleasant, sharply angled face, dark brown hair, and azure-green eyes.

"Well, I hope you can help us, Sheriff," Quinn said. "Thing is, we've got a serial killer down in SB, who seems to have ties to your little town."

"Serial killer? Redville? Doesn't seem too likely."

"Do you know Alisha Telford?"

The sheriff's face tightened a bit, and he stroked an invisible beard on his chin, as though contemplating what he would say next.

"We don't get very good reactions around here when we say her name," Quinn offered, and Rita nodded.

"Well, thing is, Alisha's been gone from Redville a long time now. She's not actually from Redville, but about three miles over, small place called Chapel Grace. Pretty name for a two-bit nothing town. Maybe a hundred people. On a good day."

"Okay, but you obviously know her, or about her."

"I went to school with Alisha. Pretty thing. Sad though.

Father was an inhuman beast. Word was he pimped her out to get his drinking money. Beat the mother, Alisha, and her brother pretty severely."

"And she left here, when?"

"Sixteen years ago. The day her father's house burned down with him inside it."

Chapter Thirty-Two

Kelsey couldn't stay in Colorado, even though she never thought she'd leave her daughter alone again. The little girl had taken to all the new "cousins" and disappeared immediately after they arrived, and before they unpacked.

Quinn's mother had installed them in a small bedroom once occupied by Quinn, and Kelsey walked through the room touching his old possessions, caressing them, and wondering about the boy he'd once been.

With the small bedroom window ajar, she could hear the children running and yelling, squealing with fits of giggles, and the occasional heart-wrenching scream.

Oh, little girls could scream, so loud you thought they were dying, when it was only play.

A picture of Quinn, very young and handsome, with a strong burnished jaw and startling eyes, sat on top of a chest of drawers. He wore a graduation cap atop his head, and a crooked smile, his arms draped around two other young men on both sides of him. Graduation day.

Kelsey gazed with wonder at the boy he'd been, and missed with a heart-stopping ache the man he was.

"It's just been rocky, because we're under pressure. It'll be fine," she said to reassure herself.

Nothing had ever worked out for her fine before, at least not as far as relationships went. What if she was wrong?

"Can I get you an iced tea?" Honey said from the door, causing Kelsey to jump and start. "Or I can help you unpack if you'd like."

"Oh, you scared me. Deep in thought I guess."

"You don't really want to be here, do you?"

"It's not that, Honey. Really, it's not. It's just that . . . well . . . I don't want to leave Quinn right now. But I also don't want to leave Tia. I guess I'm torn."

"He wanted you here, dear. Out of harm's way."

"Honey, I've been in harm's way my whole life. I don't know how to live any other way."

The older woman chuckled and reached out to stroke Kelsey's cheek.

"It's just two days. Please. I want some time to get to know you. Plus, if I let you leave, Quinn will never forgive me. I don't like to incur my son's wrath."

Kelsey smiled and turned back to her suitcase. "I'll take that iced tea. Sounds great."

She finished unpacking Tia's clothes, putting them into the empty drawer Honey had cleared for her newest "granddaughter." Kelsey's own clothes would stay in her bag, as it would be no use to unpack them for such a short stay.

Just two days. It's just two days.

Chapter Thirty-Three

"Are you saying you suspect Alisha was responsible for her father's death?"

"Never any proof of that," Sheriff Sparks said. "She disappeared, so that was suspicious, but Carl Telford was a drinker. Found what was left of him in a chair, a bottle of cheap malt whiskey melted into his hand."

Rita grimaced.

"His wife was away at the time, had a night job serving tables at the Inn. She even bought it later, after Carl died. Believe it or not, she had a small life insurance policy on him. All of them did. Backwoods as they come, the Telfords, but they had insurance."

"Did you know Alisha well?" Rita asked.

The sheriff looked away from her, toward the door, then up at the ceiling. "Oh, yeah, I knew her. We were close, I guess. I liked her a lot. Even asked her out, but she was, well, damaged, I guess. Frail. She didn't know how to have a relationship. She'd come to me when she wanted not to be found. Wouldn't ever talk about it, though."

"So, you were high school sweethearts?" Rita asked.

"No, not at all. We were maybe thirteen or fourteen. Like I said, she'd come to me when she was afraid. Used to knock on my window at night, after my parents were in bed. I let her stay, and she'd slip out in the morning."

"And nothing ever happened between the two of you?" Quinn

asked skeptically, knowing well the hormonal needs of a teenage boy.

"If it did, it's damned sure none of your business," the sheriff said, his voice surprisingly calm, despite a spark of anger in his eyes.

"She ran away from the dangers night brought," Rita surmised, a thoughtful expression on her face.

"She was abused, and I don't know the details, but I know it was bad. I left it at that, and I protected her. I damned sure didn't take advantage of her!"

"I didn't mean to imply that," Quinn said. "Please accept my apology." His words were slightly brittle, but sincere.

"So, you never knew just exactly what was happening?" Rita asked.

"No. Like I said, heard rumors, but she never confirmed or denied them. The last half year she was here, she stopped coming. I tried to talk to her, but she just avoided me. Then the house burned, Carl Telford inside it, and Alisha and Tommy disappeared.

"Before that, they kept to themselves. Carl had his drinking buddies, disgusting in their own right, but he kept his family pretty isolated. Not much information ever trickled out about them."

"So, you knew Jake Higgins?"

"Unfortunately, yes. Good-for-nothing son of a bitch. Hasn't been around for a while, good riddance."

"Well, he won't be back."

Sheriff Sparks raised his eyebrows a minimal amount, and waited for Quinn to continue.

"He was murdered in Santa Barbara."

The sheriff sat with a studied expression on his face for a moment, and then spoke, shaking his head. "Yeah, I knew that. Poor Alisha. Bad luck always did follow her around."

"You were aware Alisha lived in Santa Barbara and Jake Higgins had been murdered there?"

"Found out both things, last week, when that other cop came nosing around."

"John Penny?"

"Yup."

"What did he want?"

"He just asked general questions about the family, at first. Then started in on Alisha. Trying to find out everything he could about her. How long she'd lived here. Whether or not she had been married. Hell, she was sixteen when she left here. Guess that's not too young to be married, but I sure never heard of her hooking up with anyone."

"And that's it."

"Yup. He didn't like my answers. Wasn't much I could tell him."

"What about Jake Higgins? Do you think it's possible they stayed in touch?"

"Hell, no! She hated the sight of the man. Tried to report he raped her once, this was when we were back in high school. Didn't go anywhere, of course."

"Why not?"

"Because Lance Higgins, the sheriff, was Jake's brother. Crooked as they come."

Sheriff Sparks drove the old sedan like a stereotypical country sheriff, slow and laid back. He pointed out different places in the town's history as they drove out to the place where Alisha Telford's family history had exploded and burned to the ground.

Quinn sat in the front seat, and Rita was in the back. He'd offered her the front, but she shook her head no. Pulling a stick of gum out of her pocket, she popped it into her mouth and climbed into the back of the car.

"So, what about Alisha's brother?" Quinn questioned after Sheriff Sparks pointed out the beauty parlor where the town ladies went for gossip.

"Oh, Tommy? Weird kid. He didn't talk at all. He and Alisha were always together at school, except during classes. He was kind of like a ghost child, spooky."

"You never heard him talk?"

"Heard him scream once."

"Scream?"

"Yeah, couple of boys started grabbing Alisha in the bus line after school, calling her names, grabbing for her crotch. I ran up to help, but before I got there he lost it and screamed bloody murder. Had a look on his face like he could kill. Scared those kids bad. Never bothered Alisha again. Nobody did. At least at school."

Quinn looked back at Rita, and she made funny shapes with her mouth, as though trying to think through the puzzle pieces the sheriff handed them one by one, out of order and without matching edges.

"Where is he?" Rita asked.

"He?"

"Tommy. What happened to him?"

"Alisha said he was dead. She told me at the hospital she used to have a brother," Quinn said.

"Don't know," Sheriff Sparks said, glancing at Quinn in the front seat beside him. "Didn't know he was dead. He left at the same time as Alisha."

They stood in a heavily wooded grove, giant redwoods towering overhead and dwarfing the people below. There was an empty clearing, full of weeds and pieces of metal and wire. There was no sign of the house that once sat in this clearing, at least as far as Quinn and Rita could see.

Stepping forward, Quinn walked out farther into the meadow, staring back at the narrow two-lane road leading to the lonely, mournful place. The last house they'd seen had been two miles before.

Walking closer to some wood, he saw the charred remains of several two-by-fours, blackened by fire and dirty and rotted with age. Nudging one with his foot, he watched the crumbly pieces of wood fall off, showering the ground.

Closing his eyes, he tried to imagine the life Alisha led here in remote Northern California, far away from neighbors, with a demon father who tortured her—maybe did worse to her. A brother who didn't speak, and a mother who was nothing but a ghost herself, unable or unwilling to protect the children to whom she'd given life.

He pictured her running away from the horrors of nightfall, heavy footsteps walking to her door, and the protector in him rose up, strong and powerful. Did this so seriously traumatize Alisha that she turned into a brutal killer?

"Where's the mother?" Quinn heard Rita ask Sheriff Sparks, as if she read his mind.

Quinn turned and waited for the answer.

"She runs the hotel now. Bought the place after Carl died."

"We need to talk to her."

"Yup," Sheriff Sparks replied, and turned to walk back to his car.

Quinn caught up to Rita, as she gave the isolated landscape one more look.

"There's something we're missing here. What is it?"

"I don't know," she replied. "But I intend to find out."

Chapter Thirty-Four

Quinn tried to call Franklin on his cell phone as they drove back toward the town, but he couldn't get a signal to dial out.

"No cell sites around here, much," the sheriff said, and picked up his radio mike.

"Charlie one to dispatch."

"Charlie one," replied the static-filled voice from the radio.

"Need you to patch a call through to this number, please." He looked at Quinn, who supplied Franklin's cell phone number.

"Ten-four, Charlie one. Stand by."

Sheriff Sparks handed the radio mike to Quinn, and he waited until the voice confirmed his call was on the line.

"Franklin."

"Yo, Frankie, any sign of Alisha Telford or Tammy Rowe?"

"*Nada,* my man, *nada.* How's it up there?"

"Lots to find out. Looks like we won't be back until tomorrow."

Franklin whistled into the phone, and Rita groaned in irritation, leaning back in her seat and muttering, "Men!"

"Cool it, Frankie. We're on to something here, just not sure what yet."

"Cool. Hey, got a call from Kelsey. She wanted you to know they arrived safely. Also heard from your feeb. She's flying in from Quantico in the morning. Guess the loo requested it."

"Thanks, Frankie. I'll touch base with her tonight. When we

find a place to stay, I'll let you know. No cell sites around here, so I can't call much."

"No prob, Anderson. Oh, hey, prints came back on the scalpel in Rowe's office. Matched 'em up pretty quickly, too. Wasn't hard, considering."

"Considering what?"

"They belonged to her."

"Hmmm. What about the blood on the scalpel?"

"Nothing on that yet."

"Thanks, Franklin. Put a rush on that, would you?"

Quinn handed the mike back to the sheriff, who hooked it back in place, and started off pointing out sights again as though they were on a tour and not trying to find the key to unlock the mysteries of a serial killer.

"That was where we waited for the bus when I was kid," the sheriff said, pointing out a strand of trees fronted by a yellow school bus sign.

"Oh, really?" Rita said, trying to act interested, and he caught her gaze in the rearview mirror. She saw amusement in his eyes, and realized this man was having fun at their expense.

"And where did you and Opie go to school? Did you spend lots of time with Sheriff Andy and Aunt Bea?" she asked, an innocent tone curling around the words, making them sounds homespun and warm.

The sheriff chuckled, and Quinn gazed at them both with a strange look.

"This is going to be a long night," he muttered, watching as the sun lowered behind the towering trees, and small birds chased dark into the sky.

Chapter Thirty-Five

Kelsey lasted until eight p.m. before her feeling of restlessness and unease got the best of her and she started to pace, returning to her room and picking up the packet holding her airline tickets. She walked back to the kitchen and picked up the phone, dialing the number of the airline.

Disappointed, she discovered the next flight out wasn't until ten the following morning. She changed her reservation, not hesitating at the fifty-dollar fee, and set the phone back down.

Kelsey looked up to see Honey watching her, standing in the doorway of the small kitchen, a half smile on her face.

"Done reading to the kids already?"

"Yes, they're watching a movie now, and Tia's nearly asleep. She wore herself out today, playing." Several of the girl cousins were staying over, to keep Tia company. Honey walked into the kitchen and opened up the cupboard, pulling out a canister of coffee and filling up the pot with water from the sink.

"Coffee?" she asked, setting the pot back on its base and pushing the on button.

The gurgle of an automatic coffee maker filled the air, punctuated with a few whispers and giggles from the other room. The rich, deep smell wafted over to Kelsey, and reminded her again of Quinn, since he was the only one who drank coffee in their house.

"I don't drink coffee. Being raised Mormon, I never picked up the habit. But I love the smell. Tried it once and hated the taste, but the smell, now that I like."

Honey sat down at the kitchen table and motioned to Kelsey to pull up a chair next to her. "So, you're headed back in the morning."

"Yes, I'm sorry. I'm not trying to dump Tia on you."

"Nonsense, no one is dumping anyone. She's a lovely child and I'm looking forward to getting to know her. She's safe here, and that's what really matters."

"I just have this feeling . . . I don't know, this urgency, to get back."

"Well, promise me one thing. Let Quinn take care of you. I know you're independent, and you've been taking care of yourself for a long time, but he loves you, and sometimes a man needs to take care of the woman he loves."

Kelsey smiled at the old-fashioned sentiment, and assured Honey, "He's already saved me more than once."

"But you're strong, I can see that. You're a good match, if you both don't let your stubborn pride get in the way."

"Tell me about him. Tell me what he was like when he was little."

"Oh, land sakes, let's see. He was a loner, really, even though I had a passel of kids. He liked time alone. He hated the snow and the cold. Spent the winter months inside, reading and writing. He was good, too. Really good."

Kelsey smiled at the thought of a young Quinn, shivering at the cold and refusing to play outside.

"Oh, my, I have to show you some of his things," Honey said with excitement, standing up and leaving the room. She quickly returned with a scrapbook thick with small mementos of the man Kelsey loved.

Honey sat back down and threw open the book, the first page showing a black-and-white picture of a beautiful baby, with a shock of black hair, bearing a toothless grin.

"Wasn't he beautiful? Oh, and those eyes. From the day he was born," Honey said, clicking her tongue against the roof of her mouth. "I knew when I saw him right after he was born that he was going to be a heartbreaker. I just always hoped it wasn't my heart he would break. I thought I would die when he moved, but I've adjusted."

Honey stood up briefly, filled a cup with the fresh-brewed coffee, added a teaspoon of sugar, and returned to the table.

She flipped the page and a picture of a young boy with a tall, thin man stared up at them, both of them sharing the same intense grin and sparkling eyes.

"Well, you can't see it here, in a black and white, of course, but Quinn has his father's eyes. All that man had to do was look at me and bam—I was pregnant."

Kelsey choked back a giggle and covered her mouth.

Honey glanced at her and then slid the book over toward her. "Why don't you look through this for a while. I have some of his first writing in here, and you can see how talented he was. Always winning awards. I was hoping he would keep it up, but, he chose to be a policeman."

"He still writes," Kelsey said, catching Honey's eye as the woman stood up.

"He does?" Quinn's mother asked in surprise. "I never knew."

"He does. And one day, I'm going to make him publish it."

"You're a good woman for him, Kelsey," Honey said as she left the room. "I'm going to check on the little ones and then take a nice, warm bath. My bones are creaking."

Kelsey savored the smell of coffee and the silence, looking at the full cup Honey had left sitting at her place at the table. She smiled, realizing the older woman had purposely left her alone to spend some time with Quinn's memories.

She missed him terribly, and for the first time said the words aloud, only to a picture of a small boy staring up at her, knobby knees and threadbare shorts, all elbows and angles.

"I love you."

Chapter Thirty-Six

"Can I help you?" the small, redheaded woman asked them as they walked into the main office of the hotel. The room held a counter with office supplies and a credit card machine. A vending machine sat in one corner, looking dusty and neglected and holding few treats. There were several metal-backed chairs pushed up against the walls, and a newspaper stand that stood empty. Through a small glass door they could see a nearly empty dining area, holding only four tables and several booths. A tiny kitchen was tucked in the very back of the room, and no one presently stood at the grill, although an elderly man wearing a John Deere baseball cap sat eating country-fried chicken, mashed potatoes and gravy, and corn. He looked up and waved at them, as though they were neighbors, and then turned his attention back to the food.

Rita eyed the woman they knew was Alisha Telford's mother, looking for some sign that would help them solve the puzzle.

"I'm Rita Jaramillo, detective, Santa Barbara Police Department. This is Quinn Anderson, my partner." She flipped her badge out for the woman to see, but the redhead didn't even glance at it. Instead, she began to look fearfully from one face to the other, anxiety sharpening the angles of an already thin and hollow face.

"First, we need a room."

"All right," the woman said cautiously. "Did you want a room with a queen?"

"I mean, we need two rooms. One for each of us."

"How long will you be staying?"

"Just one night," Quinn said, pulling out his department credit card and handing it to the woman, who reached out for it and dropped it, fumbling for it on the floor.

Mary Telford tried to put the card in the slot, but her hands shook so badly she couldn't pass it all the way through, and it took her three tries to get it in enough to register.

She dropped the card again as she attempted to hand it back to Quinn, and finally covered her face and cried out in anguish.

"I just wanted to see her!"

"Her?" Quinn asked, mystified. Sheriff Sparks, who had stayed behind to smoke a cigarette, walked through the door as the small woman fell apart, and he walked swiftly to her and guided her to the chair behind the counter.

"Now, now, Mary, no need to have a fit. They are just here to ask some questions."

He gave Quinn a sharp look, and turned back to the woman, comforting her until her anguished sobs quieted.

"Sheriff, we didn't do anything but tell her who we were and ask for a room," Rita said quietly. "I don't know why she fell apart."

Mary Telford looked up, her face red and blotchy from crying. She looked haggard, and old, haunted by the ghosts of many years passed, full of nightmares and mistakes.

"You're not here to arrest me?"

"Arrest you for what?" Rita asked gently, a puzzled look on her face. "What did you do?"

"The order. You know. The court order thing. I didn't mean to violate it. I just wanted to see her, to make sure she was all right. I didn't mean for her to get hurt, but I was so scared. So scared."

Quinn gave a look to the sheriff, who simply shrugged his shoulders. "What court order, Mary?" he asked.

"The one telling me to stay away from Alisha."

Quinn looked at Rita and nodded, then stepped outside while she moved forward to ask the woman more questions.

His phone was able to call out now that they were closer to towns, and out of the dense redwoods, and he quickly dialed the SBPD dispatch number. He asked the operator to run a warrants check on Mary Telford, and guessed at an approximate age. She searched through the database, and came back on the line quickly.

"Nothing on her, Detective, sorry," the dispatcher said.

"Can you do some more searches, with approximate ages, and see what comes up? Specifically, I'm looking for a protective order."

"Hold on, I have her driver's license up now. Mary Telford, born October twenty-first, nineteen forty-three. Here's her social. Let me do a BCI check and I'll call you back."

The night had turned chilly, nothing like the mild Santa Barbara fall nights he was used to, sitting in the backyard sipping a beer and barbecuing. An image of Kelsey flashed through his mind, a moving picture from earlier that summer.

Tia in bed, they had pulled chairs close together and watched the darkening surf as the sun set over the ocean. The fresh salt-tinged breeze spoke of surfboards, suntan oil, and naked bodies.

Quinn moved in closer to Kelsey, their heads touching, and Quinn pulled her into his arms, her plastic lawn chair falling to the ground as he scooped her onto his lap.

She giggled like a little girl, and he kissed her, lightly at first, then deeper, reveling in the soft touch of her full mouth, the gentle curves of her breasts pushing against his chest. She turned into him and the flimsy plastic chair creaked as she reached down and stroked his rising erection, her hand moving inside his shorts to grab him firmly, stroking as he groaned.

Quinn turned her around so she faced him, and he pushed aside the cotton shorts she wore, sneaking a finger inside the underpants until he found her sex, inserting a finger firmly inside her.

She was wet, and she moaned, arching her back as he moved the finger deeper, faster, until she shuddered and pushed hard against his hand.

With abandon, she stripped off her shorts and pulled him to the grass, pushing him to the bottom. She pulled off his shorts, and inserted him inside her, wet and silky and tight, and he struggled to hold back, struggled to keep from coming too quickly, but she wouldn't let him stop.

Kelsey moved and he cried out and came.

"Damn you, vixen," he said as she collapsed on top of him, flesh against flesh. "You drive me wild. I came too fast."

"Oh, there's always later," she whispered into his ear. "I have an appetite that needs tending to, and you're going to take care of it."

The memory of that night was ripe, a succulent peach, and he could almost smell it, smell her. Quinn realized he was erect and standing outside a motel—where he could be discovered at any time.

He briskly walked away from the building, dialing his cell phone as he moved. "Hey, Mom. Can I talk to Kelsey?"

When she came on the line, she sounded tired and lonely. "Hi, hon. Don't be mad, but I'm not staying two days. I'm flying back in the morning. I need to be there. I need to be with you."

"I'm not mad. Scared maybe, but not mad. I was just thinking about you. Do you remember when we were out on the lawn and . . ."

"No, you don't," she interrupted with a throaty giggle. "This is not the time or the place." Her voice dropped to a whisper. "Your mother is in the next room."

"Well, I just wanted you to know I remember how much you like it when I taste you. I miss tasting you."

"Quinn!"

"I do, though. I want . . ."

"Stop it!"

"Okay, okay. No dirty talk when my mother is so close. One question though. Just answer one question."

"All right, what?"

"Are you wet?"

There was a pause, before she answered.

"Soaking."

"I love you."

"Quinn, I love you, too."

There was a moment's stunned silence, as Quinn absorbed the words she'd never been able to say.

"Thank you," he said. "What time tomorrow?"

"Don't worry about me. I'll take a cab home. Plane comes in at ten a.m."

"I won't be back until late. I'm out of town on this case. But I'll see you tomorrow night. Don't wear underwear."

Chapter Thirty-Seven

After giving his arousal time to abate, Quinn went back inside the motel office, where Rita and Sheriff Sparks talked with Mary Telford.

The woman had calmed down some, and spoke in a flat monotone, answering all their questions.

Rita walked over to him, and in a quiet voice explained. "She thought, or Alisha told her, she had a protective order against her. I guess Alisha blamed her mother for not protecting her from Jake Higgins or her own father. Mary just found out last month she has cancer. She wanted to try to make amends, but got scared the police would arrest her for trying to talk to Alisha. Says she showed up at a WAV meeting, and watched Alisha, but left when she was confronted."

"Oh, man, Kelsey told me about that, but I just checked. There isn't any protective order against her. Maybe Alisha used it as a scare tactic to keep her away. Bad memories and all. Kelsey said she couldn't figure out what the woman was so scared about. Looked like she wore the weight of the world on her shoulders."

"I guess, in a way, she does," Rita replied, watching as Sheriff Sparks talked to Mary Telford gently.

"What about your son, Mrs. Telford," Quinn asked, striding forward so he was closer to her. "Where is he?"

The woman's pasty, ashen face hardened, a glint of steel in her eyes. "I don't have a son. My son is dead."

"When did he die?"

Mary Telford glowered at him for a moment, looking like a recalcitrant teen being forced to tell of misbehavior, and knowing the honesty would result in punishment.

"Sixteen years ago," she finally answered.

"Is that why Alisha left?" Sheriff Sparks asked.

"He's dead. I don't want to talk anymore. Am I under arrest?"

Sheriff Sparks looked to Quinn, who raised his eyebrows and shrugged.

"Of course not," Rita said. "But we really need some answers here, Mrs. Telford. You see, there've been some murders down in Santa Barbara, and they seem to be tied somehow to your daughter."

The woman's face changed yet again, a metamorphosis into greed, anger, and dark green jealousy. "Well, that's no surprise. Bad things always happen around Alisha. Somebody's dying? Definitely look in her direction. After all, she did kill her father."

After throwing out the provocative statement, Mary Telford refused to say any more. She tersely checked them in, processed the credit card, handed them their room keys and left. The man sitting in the diner calmly ate his dinner, seemingly unaware the cook/waitress had just left or that anything untoward was going on.

"Well, she's a study in personality changes, isn't she?" Rita mused, thinking of all the mood swings they had witnessed in a short time. "Do you think Alisha did kill her father?"

"I doubt we'll ever know," Sheriff Sparks said. "There wasn't any proof at the time, and unless Alisha shows up and confesses, that case is closed. Besides, it's not like Carl Telford was well liked around here. He was pretty universally hated. Only one who gave a rat's ass was his brother Leo, and people hate him just as much. We open up an old case, spending taxpayer money,

I'm going to have some angry council members and constituents to answer to."

"Does she just leave this unlocked?" Quinn asked, looking around the office, and eyeing the man in the diner.

"Oh, Charlie there takes forever to eat. She gets tired of waiting. He just puts his dishes in the sink and locks up when he leaves. He helps around here as a handyman, in exchange for food."

"Ah, love these quirky small towns," Rita commented, a wry grin on her face.

The three of them walked out of the office together, all quiet, trying to think through the pieces of the case.

"I'm just going to call Kelsey, and tell her and Tia goodnight," Quinn said, walking away from the sheriff and Rita. Rita watched as Quinn talked on the phone, his lowered tones and posture sending a message of intimacy.

"I'm going to go say bye to Charlie," the sheriff said, and stepped back inside the office.

Rita heard the name Kelsey as Quinn walked farther away from the motel, and she felt a bite of chagrin, remembering her reaction to him the day before, outside the police station.

The problem here isn't Quinn, Rita. It's you. Long time no sex.

Sighing, she rubbed her bare forearms in the brisk night, and leaned back against the main building of the hotel, the air cold enough she could see her breath. It reminded her of cigarette smoke, and another longing, sharp and pungent, coursed through her veins.

"I need to get laid."

"Well, all right then, your place or mine?"

"Oh my God," she gasped, jumping as she realized the sheriff had silently pushed out the door and stood just a few feet away. Deep in thought and longing, she hadn't noticed him.

"Oh, I'm so . . . Oh, man, I am so embarrassed. I'm sorry."

Rita was glad of the darkening gloom, hiding the blush on her face she knew was there.

"I'm not. I'm always happy to oblige a beautiful woman."

"Your wife and kids would really like that, wouldn't they?"

"What wife and kids?"

"Oh please. You told me you moved back here to have a safe place to raise your kids, remember?"

"Yeah, but I didn't say I had them yet, now did I?"

Rita gave him a skeptical look, and he threw both arms out palms forward, his idea of innocence pasted on his face.

"Please," she muttered, turning away, wishing for the burning in her face to simmer down.

"I'm not married. I was, once. Back in LA. She didn't want kids, and she didn't intend to leave. I'd had enough smog, crime, riots, and violence. We agreed to disagree, and I moved back home. Now, around here, the pickings are slim. Women like you don't come around very often."

Instead of easing the blush, Rita knew her face turned an even darker shade of red, and she fought back a silly grin at his words.

"Oh, you say that to all the girls who just said they need to get laid."

"Nah, only the beautiful ones."

"Beautiful, I am not."

"Broken mirror?"

She laughed, helplessly, and touched her right hand to her lips, turning away again, feeling like she was twelve, then turning back to examine his roughly handsome face.

"No sex?" he asked, a golly-darn-shucks look on his face.

She laughed again.

"Okay, how about dinner?"

"Uh, here?"

Rita looked back toward the motel, remembering the greasy

diner food she'd seen the old man devouring, and the now absent cook/waitress.

"No, my place. I cook a mean fettuccine Alfredo, and I have a bottle of pinot grigio begging to be opened. And just in case you change your mind, we'll be really close to my bed."

"Sheriff!"

"Please, don't call me 'sheriff.' Unless you're lying in my bed naked, under me of course, wearing my, ah, handcuffs."

Rita's mouth fell open as she blushed, feeling a warmth rise in her chest. She felt a dampness between her legs and she shivered with a hint of warning, a fear she would open desires she couldn't contain or control.

"Call me Dave," he said softly, pointing to her motel room. "You want to change before we go?"

This is insane, Rita. You can't do this.

"No. Let's just go."

Chapter Thirty-Eight

Quinn came back to the car after walking several miles, trying to burn off the nervous energy and sexual tension brought on by his memories and his chat with Kelsey.

He stuck his hand in his pocket and realized he still had the keys to the sedan, and Rita was stuck at the motel.

"Oh-oh. She's probably going to be madder than hell."

He took a quick glance at his watch, the illuminated dial showing him he'd been gone for over an hour, and quickened his pace, arriving back at the motel to see no sign of life.

On the windshield of the sedan, tucked under the wiper blade, he saw a note, flapping in the light, cool breeze. He read it and chuckled, tucking it in his pocket.

"That dog," he said. He tried the doors of the office and found them unlocked. Inside, sitting in the dark against a wall, watching him with a flat look on her face, was Christy Frazier.

"About time you got back. I was getting tired of waiting."

Chapter Thirty-Nine

"What the fuck are you doing here?" Quinn said harshly, anger burning in his gut and chest.

"Geez, you always say the nicest things."

"How the hell did you find me here? What's going on, Christy? Tell me the truth."

She shrugged, and pulled her white faux fur jacket tighter around here. "The guy let me wait in here. He's going to be back soon to lock up. We should go to your room."

Christy stood up and walked toward him, and he roughly pushed her away as she crowded close to him.

"You aren't going anywhere near my room. You might as well get back into your car and drive. And answer my question. How the hell did you find me here?"

"What makes you think your whereabouts are some big mystery, huh?"

Quinn grabbed her arm and tightened his grasp. "Why are you here?"

"Ouch, that hurts, you damn brute!" She yanked her arm away and brushed a piece of her long, blond bangs out of her eyes, flipping the rest of her hair behind her shoulder. "I like it rough, you know, but only in the right circumstances."

"I can't believe I ever saw anything in you," Quinn answered, his voice taut and low.

Her face fell, finally, arrogance and flippancy dissipating into hurt and anger.

"Damn you, Quinn," she said, brushing back a tear from her eye. "Damn you. I was just trying to be good at my job, just like you were trying to be good at yours."

"You sold me out, Christy. Bottom line. Now what are you doing here?"

"I knew you'd be here. I called the office, and thcy said you were on assignment out of town. I came here with John Penny, so it only made sense."

"How did John find out about this place, anyway?"

"I don't know. He didn't tell me."

"So, why are you here, now?"

"Because . . . Because I wanted to talk to you and I thought it would be a good chance, and because this story is mine, too!"

Exasperated, Quinn turned and stepped away from her, fighting back angry words and harsh sentiments.

"Look, Christy, go home. I promise you, you'll get the heads-up when the story breaks, okay? I promise."

"Why should I trust you?"

"Because I never did anything untrustworthy to you. Other way around, remember?"

"Isn't there any chance for us?" she asked, her voice softening, her arm reaching out to touch him.

He moved farther away. "I'm in love with someone else. And even if I wasn't, you wouldn't be in the running."

Her pretty face hardened, the look of seduction turning to wrath, the dark shadows in the room making her age in front of him. She spun away, headed out the door.

"You were never good enough for me anyway. And you better keep me informed on this, or I will make your life miserable."

She ran out and he heard a car starting somewhere in the parking lot, the silence of the small town so deep he almost swore he could hear frogs croaking in a pond somewhere.

"You always did," he said to the silent room.

Chapter Forty

She was on to them. The fake-nailed, brazen-bitch, stupid-hussy reporter knew something was up. Christy Frazier called the number several times, leaving messages. It was all Mary's fault. It was all John Penny's fault, too, but he was dead now. There would be no more trouble from him.

"I need to talk to you, it's important," the stupid honey-voiced brittle blonde said in the recorder.

She seethed as she listened nearby, wanting to smash the recorder to bits, to sweep it off the table and onto the floor, stomping on it like it was a little blond newspaper reporter's face.

The game wasn't over yet. This fake-breasted, two-faced TV anchor was not going to ruin it.

The game wasn't over. The tracks weren't covered.

She had to do something. She picked up the phone and dialed.

Chapter Forty-One

"Nice place," Rita commented as she walked around the living room of Dave Sparks' house. She handed him her jacket, and he hung it up on an old-fashioned coat rack in the entry.

"Belonged to my mom and dad. After they died, it came to me. Sister lives in Oregon, on a farm. They come down once in a while to visit, but most of the time it's just me."

The old house was homey and small, with the nooks and crannies common to houses of the era. A brief tour showed it had two bedrooms, one an obvious bachelor's pad, with a brass bed that was clearly an antique, a plain brown bedspread, and no real decorations.

Rita looked to the empty walls and the sheriff watched her, smiling.

"Mom's style wasn't my style. So I took her stuff down, most of it. Problem is, I don't know what my style is. So, I'm still waiting to figure it out."

He showed her the bathroom, small and simple, and the other room held a gym, complete with a treadmill and a weight set.

The kitchen was old-fashioned, but updated with the newest in appliances. Copper pots gleamed from above an island, and the stove had a microwave on top, and gas burners. The entire room was done in dark greens and burgundies, and Rita whistled.

"Wow, it's like I just stepped out of Bachelor Haven into Modern Kitchen."

"Well, I guess my style has kind of found its way into at least this room," he admitted with a chuckle.

"Sheriff, I am impressed."

"Please. Call me Dave. Remember?"

"Oh, yeah." She blushed as his comment about being naked, in bed, and handcuffed flew through her mind, a rapid-fire volley of mental images that left her weak in the knees.

He smiled knowingly, as if he could read her mind, and then poured her a glass of wine, pulling a crystal glass out of an oak-fronted cupboard.

"You can sit in the living room if you want, while I prepare dinner. Or would you rather stay here?"

Rita took the glass of wine he handed her and walked over to the island bar, pulling out a stool and sitting in it. "I'll stay here. I wouldn't miss this for the world."

He was adept in the kitchen, chopping and slicing with confidence and flair, and before long they sat at the table and enjoyed a lavish meal.

"I cannot eat one more bite. I will explode," Rita exclaimed, dropping the fork on the plate with a clink, and putting her hands up in defeat. "I think I just gained fifteen pounds on this one meal."

"What? No dessert? I could whip up a cheesecake," he said, smiling as Rita's eyes rolled back in her head and she groaned.

"No more food. Read my lips. Now, hoist me up here, I have to get going. Can you roll me out to the car?"

"How are you getting back?"

"You're taking me."

"What if I don't want to?" He stood up from his chair and slowly walked around the table to where she sat. She eyed him nervously as he pulled her chair out from the table and turned it outward, to face him. Stroking her neck with one hand, he bent over her and kissed her softly, then harder, until she arched her back and tried to pull away.

"Oh, God, no. I can't, Dave. I just . . ."

He silenced her protests and pulled her out of the chair and up against his hard chest and body, where she could feel his desire press against her.

She tried to speak again, but he shook his head and covered her mouth with his lips, stroking her body hungrily, reaching up inside her shirt to cup a breast, pushing at her bra.

He cupped her face in his hands and pulled back, watching her, their eyes locked, until she pulled away and slowly unbuttoned her shirt. She didn't want to think about what she was doing, she just wanted to feel it. She could worry about the consequences tomorrow. The guilt would come. It always did.

But not tonight . . .

Chapter Forty-Two

Bored in the motel room, Quinn booted up his ever-present laptop and checked the phone for a place to hook up his modem. Finding no success, he knelt down and followed the phone cord to the outlet, hoping to plug in there, but it was covered by a plate and inaccessible.

Frustrated, he let out a sigh and returned to the laptop, watching as a picture of Kelsey and Tia filled the screen, his wallpaper. He clicked on the Word icon on the desktop, and pulled up a file, something he had been working on for a long time.

It was a crime novel, featuring a frustrated detective with a long line of paramours. Every other chapter held a new sexual assignation with a woman. The book only made it to chapter six, where it had died a squalid and vulgar death.

Quinn read through some of it, and began to see where his protagonist had made errors. Empty sex and long nights in bars. Moving from one relationship to the next, only stopping long enough for a taste, and then moving on to the next flavor. Surely there should be more?

"Is this me? Is this where I was headed?"

Different now, living with Kelsey and Tia, Quinn considered the clichéd, hackneyed life of his protagonist, a lady-killing, booze-swilling cop with one testosterone-filled adventure after another.

It wasn't reality; it wasn't a life, at least to him. Not anymore.

He went back to chapter one, and began to reform his detective. Suddenly, this man looked a lot like Sheriff Sparks, and he gained an instant partner, in the comely Jo Ann Hernandez, a Latina detective with impeccable crime-fighting savvy and a good sense of profiling.

He began to type and lost himself in the world he was creating.

The cell phone in his pocket jarred him, pulling him out of the world in which he was a god and creator, and back into the one he inhabited.

"Anderson," he answered, rubbing his eyes, feeling the grainy tiredness.

"Man, that was quick. Don't you sleep?" Franklin's voice crackled across the line. "Oh, man, you're not . . ."

"Franklin, I am *not* with Rita. She's . . . she's asleep in her room. I was working. What's up? Why you calling if you expected me to be asleep?"

Quinn took a quick glance at his watch and was shocked to see that it was two a.m. and he had been writing for four hours.

"We've got another death. It looks to be related, although it's a little different. It's pretty . . . Oh, man, it's bad."

"Another guy?"

"No, this one is a celebrity of sorts, a news anchor."

Quinn's heart picked up an extra beat, and began to race, his breathing heavy. "Christy."

"Oh, man, how'd you know?" Franklin asked. "Christy Frazier. They found her about a half hour ago."

"She was just here at seven tonight. She couldn't be down there."

"She was *there?* Quinn, what the fuck is going on?"

"She couldn't have made it back," he said, not answering Franklin.

"Quinn, they didn't find her here. They found her in San

Francisco. SFPD called us because she was carrying your card and phone number."

"Was she—?" Quinn stopped, not wanting to know what had been done to her body. "Was she mutilated?"

"Yes. Both breasts. And worse. This animal just ripped her to shreds, her crotch . . . well, she's a mess they said."

"I'm on my way. Who do I contact?"

"Sergeant. Lon Thompson. Quinn?"

"Yeah, Franklin, what?"

"What's going on here? Why was she there?"

"She followed me up here. Said she was working the case with Penny. I sent her packing. I don't *know* what's going on, Franklin."

"You were the last one to see her alive."

"No, I wasn't. The killer was."

He disconnected the phone and began to pack up. When he finished, he picked up his cell phone and dialed Rita's cell phone number.

It rang four times before she picked it up, sounding groggy and distant.

"Jaramillo."

"Have the sheriff bring you back, Rita. We're heading to San Francisco. Christy Frazier just turned up dead there."

"Same killer?" Rita asked, suddenly sounding wide awake.

"Looks it."

"Why San Francisco?"

"She was on her way back from here."

"From here?"

"What are you, a parrot?" Quinn said, irritation flashing through him.

"Quinn, what the fuck was she doing here?"

"She came for me, and I sent her packing, okay? Now she's

dead. Somehow, I'm responsible. Are you coming, or not?"

"Be there in ten."

Chapter Forty-Three

Rita disconnected her phone and began searching for her clothes, which seemed to be in a trail that started in Dave's kitchen. She followed it backward, picking up first her panties and then her bra.

"Oh, no, please don't go," Dave said, moving up behind her and cupping her firm breasts in his hands. He ran his fingers down her body, brushing at the wet place between her legs, and she moaned.

"I have to," she said, pulling away, and putting on first her panties, then her bra. "Help me, Hansel, please. Follow the bread crumbs and get me my clothes." She pointed to the discarded garments on the floor of his living room and kitchen, and he laughed.

Pulling on a pair of sweat pants and a t-shirt, he walked into the living room from his bedroom, and picked up her pants and shirt. Walking farther, he found two socks and, in the kitchen, her shoes.

Dave brought them all to her and she dressed hurriedly, explaining what Quinn had told her on the phone.

"Was this a one-night stand?" Sheriff Sparks asked, pulling him to her for another blinding kiss.

"God, I sure hope not," she whispered, and then pulled away and finished putting on her socks and shoes.

"Me, too, Gretel, me, too."

Chapter Forty-Four

Quinn found the cell phone number he had been given for Lexi Richards, and hesitantly dialed. It was late, but she had an early flight and was on the East Coast.

"Agent Richards," she answered on the first ring.

"Agent Richards, it's Detective Quinn Anderson."

"Who?"

"Uh, Detective Quinn Anderson? We talked the other day? We met in Utah . . ."

A chuckle on the other end of the line confirmed she was teasing, and he shook his head, feeling like an idiot.

"Funny. Two in the morning here, and you think I'm going to be quick-witted?"

"Sorry. I'm punchy when it's early. I'm on my way to the airport right now. What's up?"

"We've had another killing, a news anchor chasing the story. She followed me up here, and I sent her packing, but I've got a feeling she didn't leave. She wouldn't tell me why, but our detective that was killed—John Penny—he had something he was working on. She got information from him. I'm wondering if she went somewhere between Redville, Chapel Grace, and San Francisco. Frisco's where they found her."

There was silence for a moment, and then Lexi asked, "Same MO?"

"Basically, from what I'm told. I'm on my way now. It's about two hours from here."

"You don't know what it is she might have known?"

"No. You have a profile yet?"

"Just basic. Nothing you didn't already know. I fed your facts into the computer and came back with a male serial killer, twenty-nine to thirty-five, white, attractive. You're familiar with the different types of serial killers?"

"Yeah, there's visionary, hedonist, missionary, and, uh, can't remember the last one."

"Power seeking. I would say yours appears to be a missionary, seeking vengeance for the victims of the world. Although the crimes are about sex, they aren't sexual. Make sense?"

"Yes, because he isn't getting a sexual thrill."

"No, in fact, he's stopping the victims from ever getting a sexual thrill again. Very effectively."

Sergeant Lon Thompson was a tall thin man, with a mustache, hard eyes, and hollow cheeks. He was dressed in civvies, denim jeans, and a sweatshirt, and smelled slightly of sweat and alcohol. Quinn shook his hand briefly, and then Rita did the same before the man led them to the crime scene.

The body had long ago been removed and transported to the morgue, and all that was left behind was crime scene tape and an air of discomfort, the knowledge something terribly amiss had happened there. The body had been found behind a convenience store, the victim's car was missing, and no one could remember seeing her.

A group of teenagers skateboarding through an alley found the body, when one of them tripped over her.

"No sign of a struggle here, so we think she was done someplace else and dumped here. Car is missing. Minimal blood, so the crime took place at least an hour before, ME says."

"Nobody saw anything."

"No, but the station has surveillance tapes, and we've got those now. Some of our guys are going over them back at the office. Oh, and your office called. An FBI agent will be arriving here in the morning. They're sending her straight here instead of to Santa Barbara."

"Thanks. He's escalating."

"Or she's escalating," Rita said, speaking for the first time since eyeing the crime scene. Images of violence kept flashing through her head, and the anger, fear, and confusion she felt disturbed her.

The sergeant eyed both of them, his eyebrows raised in a question mark.

"It's too brutal, Rita. It can't be a woman," Quinn said.

"But it could be a woman and man together," she offered, something clicking. "First thing tomorrow we need to search for a death certificate for Thomas Telford."

Chapter Forty-Five

Kelsey eyed the Pacific Ocean as the plane prepared to land in Los Angeles, and she breathed a little easier, feeling closer to Quinn, her sense of impending doom lightening just a little.

The plane taxied to the ground, and she sighed, glad to be back on solid and familiar ground.

She took a taxi from the airport and arrived home sometime after noon. She knew Quinn was working, but she still felt closer to him than ever before.

Kelsey paid the taxi driver and walked to her front door, where a box sat on her porch. Wrapped in brown paper, what would have seemed innocent just days before now was an ominous threat, seeming to grow larger as she stared. She stopped several feet short of the box, and images of severed body parts danced through her mind.

Kelsey looked around but could see no one near, and she decided to avoid the box by walking around to the back door and calling Quinn. Her heart racing, she dropped her bag just inside the kitchen door and rushed to the phone, dialing Quinn's cell number.

After four rings she was redirected to his voice mail, and her tension went up several notches.

"Quinn, it's Kelsey. I need you to call me now. It's important." Thinking of the events of the past few days, she added, "I'm okay, everything's fine, but I need you to call me. I'm at home."

She disconnected from the call, and dialed another number—

the SBPD offices.

"Detective Anderson, please."

The secretary who answered the phone came back promptly. Detective Anderson was unavailable, and could she take a message, please?

"Tell him Kelsey called, and I'm home," she said, and hung up the phone.

He must still be up in Northern California. Of course he was. He wouldn't be back until tonight. Was this an emergency?

Not wanting to get too alarmed, she still didn't dare open the box. Pacing the kitchen, she wondered what to do. Should she just call the police and let them investigate, or should she just open it up?

It could be a gift, maybe from a neighbor.

Who are you trying to kid? Who would bring you gifts?

A sharp rapping at the front door caused her to jump, and she hurried into the living room, looking through the peephole to see the top of Edie Falconer's head.

She opened the door to see the tiny woman holding the brown package, a look of mischief in her eyes. "Hello dear, you've been gone. I brought you something."

Edie extended the package toward Kelsey, and she reluctantly took it, unable to shake the jitters brought about by experiences and an overactive imagination.

"Hi, Edie. You're right. I just got home from Colorado. Haven't even unpacked, or I'd invite you in."

"Business or pleasure?"

"Excuse me?"

"Did you go to Colorado on business or for pleasure? I imagine if you had that handsome man of yours with you, it would have to be for pleasure."

The elderly woman chuckled and pushed her way through the door. "I won't take up much of your time. I just had something I knew you would want to see. I left it on your porch, but I guess you didn't see it."

Sighing, Kelsey followed the woman into the living room. Edie plopped down on the sofa and patted the cushion next to her.

"Sit down and I'll show you what I brought."

Kelsey handed the box back to the woman, and sat next to her, wondering what manner of surprise awaited her in the box.

As Edie pulled the top off the box, Kelsey saw it was filled with newspaper clippings, brown and old, some of them brittle and cracked around the edges.

"Newspaper clippings?" Kelsey asked, surprise in her voice. "I'm not sure why you gave me these, Edie."

"Read them, dear," Edie said. She pulled one out and Kelsey read the banner at the top of the page.

"Man Loses Penis in Tractor Accident," proclaimed the headline, and Kelsey cringed as her eyes widened.

"Oh, here's a good one. Look." The brittle newspaper almost crumpled and disintegrated in Edie's hand, and she held it carefully, as though trying to preserve some treasured memory. " 'Woman Mails Husband's Penis to His Mistress.' I really like that one. Wish I'd thought of it."

Kelsey sat staring at her neighbor Edie, a mix of emotions running through her mind. She didn't know whether to be amused or scared. Was Edie seriously disturbed, or just a lonely old woman with too much time on her hands, and a taste for the macabre?

"I'm not sure—"

"I've been collecting these stories for years. It started right after my husband died. I was angry and it gave me something to do. Don't worry, it's a harmless pursuit for a wicked old woman."

"Well, it's definitely unusual."

Edie chuckled, her eyes seeming to twinkle as she watched Kelsey's face. "I thought these articles might help you as you try to figure out what that penis was doing in your trunk. It's amazing how many ways a man can lose a penis. I'm sure glad I don't have one of those things sticking out at awkward moments."

"Well, that's very, uh, thoughtful of you, Edie."

"No problem, dear. None at all. Happy to help. You know, the real news people, the TV people, they never report on these things. You have to turn to the *Star* and some of those other magazines, real journalists if you ask me."

"Uh, Edie? They make most of that stuff up."

"Oh, no, dear. They can't. Someone would sue them."

Edie sat on the couch like a small child, her legs not quite touching, and her bird-like arms on each side of her. She swung her feet once or twice as she talked.

"Well, the thing is, Edie, people do sue them. And win. But they sell so many magazines, they just keep right on shoveling out lies."

"I've learned more from one issue of the *Star* than I learned in a year of reading the *Santa Barbara Sentinel,*" Edie said, wagging a finger in Kelsey's face. "They're just trying to fool you, dear. This is a sad, wicked, perverted world we live in."

When her little speech was finished, she sat back on the couch a little further. Her legs continued to swing, and she caught Kelsey's glance at her feet that didn't touch the floor.

"I'm shrinking, you know," she said, her bright green eyes twinkling. "If I keep going, they're going to have to bury me in a shoebox. Of course, with the arthritis gnarling up my fingers like twisted tree branches, and curving my spine, I'll be even more compact."

Kelsey couldn't help it; she laughed out loud. "Edie, you are a funny lady."

"Half the time you don't know how to take me, though, do you?" Edie pushed off from the couch, and crossed to the door in a flash, leaving Kelsey with narrowed eyes as she considered Edie's agility.

"You certainly don't seem to have any trouble getting around. How long have you had arthritis?"

"Oh, it comes and goes. The last five years have been tough. But I don't let it slow me down. Ta-ta, dear."

Kelsey shook her head as the woman closed the door behind her, and she looked down at the newspaper clippings still in the box. She picked a few up, and thumbed through them, grimacing at the lurid headlines her bird-like neighbor had clipped from supermarket tabloids, almost all of them having to do with dismembered sexual organs or odd sexual conditions.

"This woman is *not* right in the head. Could she be—?"

Kelsey thought again about how small Edie Falconer was, and also thought of her innocent face, and cherubic smile. Edie resembled one of the shrunken apple-head dolls Kelsey had seen when she was a child, after her father had relented and allowed them to visit the state fair.

Did Edie, and her odd interest in dismembered male organs, have anything to do with this case?

"She couldn't be a killer. She's too little."

Still, Kelsey looked again at the newspaper clippings. A stack three inches thick filled a cardboard box about four inches high and six inches wide.

"Aliens Remove Man's Penis While He Sleeps!"

"Ack! Enough already," Kelsey said with distaste, wrinkling her nose and dropping the clippings back into the box.

She pushed the box aside and stood up, stretching for a minute, and walked into the kitchen, where the flashing light on the answering machine indicated there were three messages.

She walked across the room and hit the play button.

"Kelsey, this is Tammy. It's about Alisha. I need to talk to you soon, so call me on my cell phone, 555-234-9687."

She moved forward to pick up the phone when the next message proceeded.

"Ms. Waite, this is Doctor Fowler calling again, from LDS Hospital in Salt Lake City? It's about your mother. My service told me you called, and I'm sorry I missed you. It's extremely important that you call me. The number is—"

"Oh, shit. What's wrong?"

The last message began, and chills crept up Kelsey's spine as she heard the voice of her nightmares, the man who still haunted her dreams. It couldn't be. God, no!

Kelsey moved away from the recorder as the deep, seductive baritone of polygamist cult leader David Stone filled the air around her, nipping at her skin like biting mosquitoes and filling her with dread and his own special brand of psychological poison.

"Kelsey. You can run, but you can't hide. Don't you know that by now? God's word will not be flaunted, no matter how long it takes me to get you. No matter how long. We'll meet again."

Chapter Forty-Six

Quinn turned the cell phone off and dropped it into his jacket pocket, turning to Rita with a mischievous look in his eye. They had gone over the details of the crime and compared evidence with the San Francisco Police Department for hours. It was now nearly one in the afternoon.

Rita's eyes felt gritty and dirty, and she rubbed them harshly, grateful she hadn't had time to reapply mascara after her love-making with Dave Sparks had worn it all off.

She'd nodded off briefly, her head just dropping to the table in a conference room of the San Francisco Police Department.

"I just got off the phone with your friend Dave. Seems Chapel Grace is pretty backward, and only switched over to computers five years ago. Of course, one of us has to go back there and search through years of files for a death certificate. I guess I should go."

He leaned back against his chair and put his arms behind his head, the beginnings of a grin twitching at the corners of his mouth.

"Oh, you are *so* not funny. I don't know how Kelsey puts up with you."

He smirked for a minute before finally giving in to a teasing grin.

"Just think, you might get lucky twice in a weekend. You owe me."

"I owe you?" she retorted. "Look Mr. Smug, you are not

exactly my matchmaker. You never even met this guy before. I think I'll take the credit on my own, okay?"

Quinn sobered for a minute and watched her with a serious look on his face. Finally, he spoke. "Look, Rita, he seems like a decent guy. A little 'countrified' for my taste, but still nice. But be careful. You don't know him."

"Oh, cut the big brother act, Quinn. I'm a grown woman," Rita said, fighting away the blush spreading across her cheeks as he tried to give her awkward advice.

"I just—"

"I know," she said, interrupting him. "I know. And thanks for caring. Your concerns are noted. Now, how I am going to get back there? We only have one car?"

"Department's springing for a rental. Be careful. Remember we don't know where Alisha is."

"Quinn?"

"Yeah?"

"You just said we don't know where Alisha is. Have you somehow decided she is the prime suspect?"

"Well, she's involved, and she's missing, as is Tammy Rowe. I have to consider that, Rita. And if it is a pair of killers, like you said, Rowe could be already dead. Or in great danger.

"We need to know if Thomas Telford is still alive, and if so, where he is."

"Quinn, what about John Penny's belief that Kelsey was involved? I know you are really close to her, but is there any chance . . . ?"

"No." His voice was flat and strong, brooking no argument. "Penny may have thought she was involved, but she wasn't. Kelsey didn't know squat about this. She didn't even know much about Alisha, except the stories she was told."

"But she's sort of protecting her."

"And if she was your friend, wouldn't you try to protect her, too?"

"Yeah," she murmured, running a finger over lips that felt bruised and swollen. "I would."

"Just be careful," Quinn added, a shadow of weariness under his eyes and tingeing his voice. "The killer or killers are out there. I just lost one partner. I don't want to lose another one."

Chapter Forty-Seven

Rita's drive back to Redville County passed in a blur of senses and emotions, swirling around her like fog on a brisk Santa Barbara–morning. She ruminated on the sins of premarital sex and passion, as extolled by a bevy of nuns and her own mother, fighting against the onslaught of shame.

"I'm not going to feel guilty. I'm not."

But what if she got back up there and the sheriff acted like he didn't know her? It'd happened before.

"Why buy the cow, if you can get the milk for free, *mi hija?*" her mother had always said.

"Oh my God, what have I done?" she wailed to the empty car.

Rita pulled in front of the small courthouse and parked, stopping to look around the town, trying to quell the butterflies hatching in her stomach.

Angry with herself, she jumped out of the car and slammed the door. Thirty-three years old and she still acted like a twelve-year-old caught masturbating.

The easy smile on Dave Sparks' face as he watched her walk into his office calmed her stomach butterflies into a state of gentle hovering.

"Files are all in here," Dave Sparks told Rita, leading her through a hallway and into a back room of the small Redville County Courthouse.

The clerk, in her mid-fifties with a bouffant hairdo and

clothes from the seventies, had offered to show Rita the way, her eyes opening in surprise as the sheriff declined her offer, and escorted the officer himself.

The clerk watched them as they walked away. Rita felt the eyes boring into her back, and she wanted to scratch away at the itch of small-town curiosity.

"Old girlfriend?" she asked him, after they were in the small storage room and he shut the door behind him.

He pulled her to him and kissed her hard, running his hands down her back and around to her front, caressing her breasts over her wrinkled shirt.

"Yes," he finally said, speaking into her neck as she leaned her head back. "Marge and I had a torrid, passionate affair last spring. She was just too much woman for me."

He moved his lips to the neck of her shirt and nuzzled there, bringing his hands up inside her shirt from the bottom. He reached her breasts, and pulled at the fabric of her bra, trying to touch her skin.

"Oh, Lord. Not here. Not even," Rita said, breathless. She tried to pull away but he wouldn't let her.

"Here. Now. I need you. I need to be inside you."

"Dave, please. I'm working."

Sighing, he pushed back, one hand resting on her breast, the other on the wall supporting them. "All right. But please do not plan on leaving this town again without being thoroughly ravaged. I intend to make you come until your eyeballs fall out."

"That is not a pleasant image," she said, and she pulled him down to meet her lips, gently kissing him, before pushing him away and straightening her mussed clothing.

"I don't normally do this, you know," she said as she tucked her shirt back into her jeans. Dave was watching her, his eyes shining with the promise of future plans for erotic adventures. "It's been a long time since my last . . . since I . . ."

"Don't," Dave said, putting a finger to her lips to hush her. "You don't owe me any explanations. We're not doing anything wrong, Rita. We're adults. I'm single. You're single . . . You are single, aren't you?"

Rita giggled and pushed him away, running her fingers through her lush black hair in an attempt to straighten the disarray. "Yes, I'm single, you goofball."

"Whew. Well that's a relief. Now, back to business. I did some asking around. Nobody remembers ever hearing that Thomas Telford died. In fact, he simply disappeared at the same time Alisha did, fifteen years ago. I drove by the Inn to talk to Mary Telford, but it was closed up tight. No customers, apparently, after you two left, and she wasn't there."

"Did you go to her house?"

"She has a small unit at the edge of the motel, and I knocked on her door and tried the knob, but it was locked. No answer and no noise."

Rita frowned as she gazed at all the files in the room. They filled shelves from the bottom of the floor clear to the ceiling, and the only good thing she could see was they appeared to be in alphabetical order.

"Isn't that odd? That she'd leave the Inn unmanned in the middle of the week, I mean?"

Dave walked over to the cabinet labeled "T" and pulled out a drawer. "Not really. We aren't very busy around here, especially during the week."

"But where would she go?"

"I don't know for sure. I can ask around after we're done here."

He shuffled through the files, made his way to the back, and then pulled out the next drawer. About halfway through he pulled out a manila folder with "Telford, Thomas" on the tab.

"Wow, that didn't take long. You know your filing system.

Uh, thought you told Quinn it would take a while."

Dave chuckled, and motioned to her to follow him out of the room. "I had to get you back here somehow, now didn't I?"

As she passed by him in the doorway, he grabbed her arm with his right hand, and gave her a quick kiss, his left arm lowering to her backside and staying there for a minute, before he released her.

She blushed as she looked up and caught Marge, who was passing through the hallway, staring at them wide-eyed. Embarrassed, the woman darted into a room with a "Ladies" sign on it.

"Busted," she muttered under her breath, and looked back at Dave, who was smiling.

"Oh, boy. They'll have something to talk about at bingo this week," he said. He led her into a room with a small table and four chairs, a refrigerator, and a microwave. Sitting in one corner was a soda machine, and next to it a snack machine.

Dave pulled out one of the chairs and she realized he was holding it for her. She dropped into the chair, and he scooted it in and sat in the chair next to her.

Still red and embarrassed, she propped her elbows on the table and dropped her face into her hands.

He laughed again, stroked the back of her neck, and then opened the file and fanned the contents out on the table. "Let's see, birth certificate, Thomas Telford, born March fifth, nineteen sixty-eight, Redville County Hospital." He looked up to tell her. "It's really just a clinic, but don't tell the docs that. Looks like the doctor who delivered him was James Prepont. He was the only family doctor around here at that time. He died a few years ago. His son took over the practice."

He looked at the few other papers in the file. "Got his driver's license when he was sixteen. Here's a photocopy. Looks like he was immunized properly, because the health department tracks those records. And that's it. Nothing more."

Rita picked up the copy of Thomas Telford's driver's license, and looked at the picture of a young, waifish boy, with small features and thick lips. Although he had been sixteen at the time the picture had been taken, he looked much younger, with no hint of manhood gracing his features.

"So, everybody has one of these files?"

"Yep."

"Can we look at Alisha's?"

Dave responded by standing up and walking out of the room, and Rita picked up the birth certificate and stared at it.

"Here we are," Dave said as he came back into the room and sat back down at the table. "Alisha Telford, born August fourth, nineteen seventy. That's it in her file, except for an immunization sheet. No driver's license, but she was just sixteen when she left. Maybe she never got a chance to get it."

"That's it, huh?"

"Yep. So, if he died, it wasn't here. Of course, we pretty much guessed that, or somebody around here would have known. I stopped at Mel's Diner, over across the street, before I came here and asked some of the old men that hang out there. They had lots of stories to tell about Mary's husband and his old buddy Jake Higgins, but not much else to say."

"What about the guy that runs the service station? Carl's brother? Did he run with Carl and Jake Higgins?"

"Leo Telford's his name. He's of the same ilk, no doubt, but he's a bit older than them. He's been in a few scrapes, spent some time in the county lockup, but mostly assault and battery and drunk and disorderly. Nothing major."

"Assault and battery is nothing major?" Rita asked, raising her eyebrows at him.

"Small town assault and battery isn't really the same thing as big town A&B. He got in some fights, hit a guy once with a beer bottle."

"Could you make him answer some questions?"

"Yeah, probably."

"Then let's go pay him a visit. I have an odd feeling we need to hurry."

Chapter Forty-Eight

Quinn finished up his paperwork with the SFPD and hit the road, playing over his conversations with Christy as he drove. What had she known? Obviously, she had more information than she'd given him. If he had played along, been a little bit nicer, would she have told him?

It didn't matter. Nothing could change what happened.

But what did she know?

His cell phone rang and he pulled it off the passenger side front seat, where he had tossed it when he got in the car, and answered.

"Anderson."

"It's Rita. We're on our way to question Leo Telford, better known to you as the bad-ass gas man."

"Ah, yes, Mr. Charming Disposition."

"Find out anything new?"

"No," Quinn said, driving with his left hand and holding the phone with his right. "There haven't been any similar unsolved murders in San Francisco. Killer left few clues. Their crime techs are poring over the body now, trying to find something to use in DNA analysis. I heard from Franklin, and he says all the sites have been clean, save for one thing we found on Tessa Morrow's body."

"What did they find?"

"She fought back. It was a long, blond hair."

"Shit."

"Yeah."

"Testing done?"

"Back tomorrow. I don't know, Rita, I don't see anything tying this to two killers. And the blond hair, well . . ."

"This thing is giving me a headache. We're at Leo Telford's place now. I'll call you back."

"Later," Quinn said, and hung the phone up.

Kelsey wasn't going to take this well, but at the very least, it looked like Alisha was involved. They'd opened her locker at the hospital and found a brush inside, so they had hair and DNA to compare. If it came back a match, then Alisha Telford could very well be a murderer. But why? And wouldn't Joe have had some idea, being so close to her?

Revenge. Somehow, this is about revenge.

Abused by her father, raped by a family friend, unprotected by a neglectful and troubled mother—was that enough to set a woman off on a rampage of vicious murder?

Quinn picked up the cell phone and dialed Franklin's number. "Anything yet from the state database?"

"No, boss, but we're searching, just like you asked."

"Don't call me boss."

Franklin chuckled. He liked to needle. "No driver's license listed in the state, and no property found on search. Really no trace of her at all.

"She's like a phantom."

Chapter Forty-Nine

The black-and-white police cruiser pulled up to Leo Telford's service station, and Rita and Dave sat staring at the storefront.

A "closed" sign was in the window, and there was no hint of activity inside. Rita looked quickly at Dave, and then got out of the car, moving her hand up to her side to touch the gun holstered to her side.

"I don't feel good about this," she told Dave, who exited from the driver's side and surveyed the desolate gas station, which had an abandoned look even when open. Now, it almost seemed to be ominous, with no lights on inside and no cars around.

"Where does he live?" Rita asked, her voice a whisper, the hair standing up on her arms and a chill running up her spine. "Something is wrong here. It's noon on a Thursday. Why isn't it open?"

"He has a place around back, just a shack really." Dave softly shut the car door and drew his weapon, following Rita's lead. She quietly shut her car door, following Dave with her eyes as he approached the front door and tried the knob.

He shook his head and walked over to the big front windows, peering inside.

Dave walked back to her swiftly. "There's no sign of life inside. No lights on. Can't see anyone. Let's head back to his house."

They made their way along the east side of the gas station,

staying close to the wall. Rita's heart pounded, and a knowing came to her in an electric wave, almost a premonition. They would find something bad here; she just didn't know what.

All around the cinderblock building were weeds decorated with trash—old hubcaps and tires, rusted red gas cans, empty soda containers, and unidentifiable hunks of metal and plastic.

Dave stopped as they neared the back and turned to her. "Maybe you better stay here while I check this out."

"This is *not* the time to go all heroic on me," Rita snapped, trying to keep her voice down. "I'm a cop. A big-city cop, no less. A homicide detective, even!"

Dave stared at her for a minute, then allowed himself a small grin, before he turned and slowly made his way out into the open, Rita covering his back.

Leo Telford's humble abode was approximately a hundred yards behind the main building. The yard was littered with even more trash, abandoned and rusting cars, hunks of metal, and several old washing machines.

There were several large redwood trees on both sides of the house, and the front door stood ajar.

Dave reached the gate and Rita followed, looking from side to side, even while she didn't understand her concern. There had been no signs of a struggle, no calls for help. What was wrong?

Dave pushed through the fence gate, and it swung back and forth, creaking in the silent atmosphere of tension. Each creak ripped through Rita like a gunshot, and she winced as she closed the gap between herself and Dave.

When they reached the front door, Dave tried to look in, and turned and shook his head at Rita. She could tell he could not see inside. As he stepped forward a large brown and white shape rushed through the door at Dave and landed on top of him.

The snarling, barking pit bull latched its teeth onto Dave's left arm, which he'd lifted in self-defense, and chomped down, causing him to cry out.

Afraid to shoot for fear of hitting Dave, Rita stuck her gun in her waistband and grabbed a large piece of rusted metal, swinging it with all her might at the dog's head.

With a solid crunch the metal bar connected, and the dog cried out in pain and loosened his jaws, allowing Dave to shake him off. The animal backed off, snarling and barking, shaking his head in confusion, and then charged at Rita.

She pulled her gun out of her waistband, but the dog dropped just inches from her, the shot roaring through her ears, and she saw Dave had raised his gun.

Skirting the vicious dog, now quiet and prone on the ground, she ran to Dave and examined his bleeding arm.

"You need medical attention."

"I'll be okay. But you're bleeding."

He grabbed her hands and turned them over, and she saw the raw jagged slice across one of her palms. Apparently she'd cut herself with the metal when she hit the dog.

"Wow, I didn't even know that. I didn't feel it. That dog must have been bionic. I can't believe he charged again after I hit him so hard."

Dave spoke into the radio clipped to his shoulder, and asked for additional help and medical assistance. "Go back to the car. In the trunk there's a first aid kit."

"You're bleeding, too," Rita pointed out, motioning to his torn, bloodstained sleeve. "I'm staying right here with you."

"Stubborn," Dave said, and then moved forward to the house. "You're going to need a tetanus shot. Those hurt."

"Don't sound so pleased."

"I want you to go back to the car."

Rita shook her head and ignored the uneasy gnawing in her stomach. *It's not that he doesn't trust you,* she told herself. *It's that he is worried about you.*

Sighing, Dave spoke again. "I think if someone was in there, they would have come out by now."

They made their way into the house, and the smell caused Rita to flinch. "I sure as hell hope that's not a dead body," she whispered.

"Smells like garbage to me," Dave said, wrinkling his nose with distaste.

They quickly searched the four-room shack and found lots of junk and deplorable living conditions, but no human life.

In a small kitchen they found rotting garbage piled up on the floor, and what must have been weeks and weeks of dirty dishes in the sink.

Rita headed back outside and breathed deeply, thankful to be out of the odiferous building. Dave motioned her to follow him and they walked back to the main building, stepping around the body of the dead dog. A door leading into the mechanic's area was open, and Dave cautiously approached it, standing flat against the building, trying to sneak a glance inside, before moving to the door, gun held high in front of him. He pushed the door fully open and stared, squinting to adjust his eyes in the darkened room.

Rita stood directly behind him, gun drawn.

"Oh shit." He turned to look at Rita, and then spoke into his radio again, then motioned her to follow.

She walked cautiously behind him and stopped cold, as she saw Leo Telford and Mary Telford hanging from the hydraulic lift, which had been jacked into the air.

They were both naked, their bodies slashed and disfigured, with breasts and genitals mutilated and missing.

"This killer gets around," Rita said under her breath.

CHAPTER FIFTY

Quinn sped up the highway toward Chapel Grace, engine roaring, dashboard light flashing a warning to other motorists. FBI Agent Lexi Richards sat next to him, reading the files they'd copied from the SFPD. The killer was in Chapel Grace, or close. Rita said the medical examiner believed the two victims had been dead less than two hours.

Rita's intuition to visit Leo Telford had paid off with one of the first real breaks in the case. The killer couldn't be far.

Unless there are two killers, and they have split up.

The California Highway Patrol had been notified and an APB had been reissued on Tammy Rowe's car, with descriptions of both her and Alisha Telford, as well as a warning about a possible male companion.

Concentrating on the road, the phone jarred through his roiling mind, halting the pieces of the case he was trying to construct.

"Anderson," he said gruffly into the phone.

"Quinn, oh my God, Quinn, he called me. He called me!"

"Kelsey? What? Who called you? Where are you?"

He could hear her muffled sobs, and knew she was trying to hold the terror back, her hand compressed against her mouth, her spine rigid. He'd seen her do it a few times before.

"David called me. David Stone. He said he'll see me again."

The car weaved for a minute as he took in her words, and then he pulled over to the side of the road.

"Okay, Kelsey, calm down. David Stone is in jail in Utah. You know that."

"It was him." Her voice had quieted, but the despair was still there, haunting her, haunting him.

"Shit, Kelsey. I'll call Franklin and have him send a squad car over. I'm halfway between San Francisco and Chapel Grace. It'll take a while to get home. Lock the doors, now, and don't open them to anyone."

"Okay," she whispered, fear ragged in her tone. "Quinn?"

"Yeah, hon?"

"I'm scared. Tell them to hurry."

Quinn explained in brief to Franklin about Kelsey's trauma the year before, when a cult leader from her past had arranged for her daughter's kidnapping in order to force Kelsey to return to Utah to marry him.

Franklin, only with the SBPD for six months after transferring from San Diego, admitted to having heard rumors about it in the department.

"Well, that's neither here nor there. You need to get to her and fast, okay? Also, call Utah, find out if Stone is out, and if so, how the fuck that could happen."

"Got it. You headed up to the crime scene?"

"I have to. I have Agent Richards with me. Get over there now, okay? And find a unit in the area. Get somebody there quick."

"David Stone?" Lexi asked him, her voice filled with strain. "It couldn't be. I know he's locked up in Gunnison. He hasn't faced a trial yet, as I'm sure you are aware, or Kelsey would have been called back to testify. His lawyer has managed to keep the whole case tangled up for over a year now. The only good thing is the judge wouldn't grant him bail."

"He could have phone privileges, though, couldn't he?"

"Of course. It's his constitutional right."

"Great. One more thing to worry about."

Lexi pulled her cell phone out of her pocket and dialed a number. She quietly gave the information to someone, asked a few questions, gave some orders, and hung up.

A few minutes later the phone rang.

"I see. Okay. Thank you. Yes, please. Put an agent on it. Thanks."

After she hung up again, she turned to Quinn. "I have someone on it. They checked, and David Stone is, indeed, in jail. The call could have come from him, though. We'll put a trace on your phone records and see what we come up with. There are lots of other possibilities, though. Other than Stone and a few key men, the rest of his flock are not in jail. They were let go, because there wasn't enough to charge them with. And they are still faithful believers."

"Shit."

"Yeah, shit."

Chapter Fifty-One

Rita questioned a few members of the crowd hanging around the crime scene, but nobody had much to offer. She walked back into the building and toward Dave, who was talking to the medical examiner. His face was grim and haggard, and she remembered how shortly before he'd looked young and vibrant as they made love. Murder, especially grisly murder, could age you fast.

Paramedics had cleaned his wound and recommended he get it stitched up, but he refused to leave the crime scene. He chose, instead, to ask the medical examiner to close it up. Rita found herself light-headed and woozy, and had to walk away. When she returned to Dave, the stitching was done.

"Time of death, I'd say, about an hour and half, two hours max," the ME said.

"So, he could still be close."

"Boy, you men are hard-headed," Rita said, and both men turned to her. "We don't know the killer is a man."

"What do you mean?" the ME asked. He was a middle-aged man, balding, with round chubby cheeks and large tufts of hair growing out of his nose and ears.

"Don't think I introduced you two," Dave said politely, as though this were a southern cotillion. "Doctor Prepont, this is Detective Rita Jaramillo, of the Santa Barbara Police department. Doc here does our medical examiner duties part time, since there isn't much call for his services."

"Doctor Prepont?"

"Yes, that's me."

"You delivered Alisha Telford?"

"Oh, no, that was my dad. I was still in medical school back then."

"Oh, I guess that makes sense."

"He delivered both of them, her and her brother, Thomas. Of course, he told me all about it. He'd never seen a case like it before. Said he hoped to never see another case like it again."

Rita's brow furrowed, and she looked at Dave, who shrugged, a puzzled look on his face.

"What was wrong with her?"

The doctor took a step back, as if he had said too much, and closed his mouth. "Her? Oh, I better not say anything. Doctor/patient privilege and all that."

"She wasn't your patient, so I don't think that applies," Rita said. "She also wasn't a murder suspect back then. What exactly is it you know and aren't telling?"

"More importantly, does it have relevance to this case?" the sheriff asked him.

"Well, I don't know. But you're going to have to convince me I'm not violating some ethics before I'll tell you any more."

Chapter Fifty-Two

Kelsey locked all the doors, and checked the windows, her heart beating rapidly as she secured all the entrances to her house.

Logically, she knew David Stone was not here in California. He was in jail in Utah. But he had followers who might be free and might do anything for him, including come to get her again.

"At least Tia is safe," Kelsey said, pacing as she waited for the police to arrive.

She walked back into the living room where she sat down on the couch, lifting another stack of clippings from the box Edie Falconer had left with her, trying to pass the time.

After several more gruesome stories about detached male sexual organs, she picked up a faded article with a big, bold headline. "It's a Boy—Or Is It?" She adjusted her eyes to the smaller type of the lead paragraph. "A Northern California couple gave birth several years ago to a male child, or so they thought. Doctors at a specialty hospital in Los Angeles recently discovered that young Thomas Telford was born with the sex organs of both a man and a woman.

"At the time of his birth, he appeared to have male genitals, and his parents were unaware of any problems until the boy began to dress in his sister's clothing and play with her dolls."

Kelsey stopped reading as the name penetrated her brain. Northern California. Thomas Telford.

Alisha's brother?

"Holy shit," Kelsey whispered, pulling the faded type closer to her face to read. A black-and-white picture next to the story showed a small boy, with blond hair and large, hollow eyes, staring into the camera, his lips tight and his body taut. A large hand placed firmly on his shoulder could also be seen, and Kelsey could see the wrinkles around the shirt where the hand clenched tightly.

Being forced to pose? For money?

She scanned the story again, reading how the parents had been told their child was a boy, only to discover when he was three that he actually was a hermaphrodite, born with sexual organs of both a male and a female.

"Hermaphrodite?"

A sudden knock on the front door startled her, and she almost screamed. Thinking it was the police, she hurried to the front door and peered through the peephole to see Tammy Rowe standing in front of her door, impeccably dressed as always.

Kelsey quickly unlocked the door and opened it, urging Tammy inside and then shutting the door and locking it behind her.

"Tammy, have you heard from Alisha?"

"Yes, that's why I came. I called you and left a message, but you didn't answer."

"I just got home from Colorado," Kelsey explained. "I took Tia to stay with Quinn's mom until things cool down here a little."

"You look terrible. Are you okay?"

"Not really. I just got a phone call from . . . Well, I think it was from David Stone."

"Oh, Lord, Kelsey, that's horrible," Tammy exclaimed, reaching a hand out to her. She touched her on the shoulder. "Are you okay? Isn't he in jail?"

Tammy had been the one to counsel Kelsey when she

returned, and she also referred her and Tia to their current doctor.

"Yes, the police are on the way over."

"Really? Actually, I came to tell you I found Alisha, and she wants to see you. But she's scared, because the police think she's responsible for the killings. So I need to take you to where she's hiding."

"Oh, God. Is she okay? She needs to turn herself in, Tammy. That's the only answer."

"She wants to talk to you first. It's not far. She's in a little hotel down by the beach. We'll be right back."

"Well, I have to call the police and tell them something."

"You can't tell them you are going to see her, Kelsey. They'll find her. She'll think you betrayed her. You need to talk her into turning herself in. I tried, but she just wouldn't listen to me. She's closer to you. She'll listen."

"Well, I don't know."

"Please, Kelsey. She needs your help worse than any of the other victims in the WAV group ever did."

Kelsey thought for a minute, then decided it was too risky. She loved Alisha like a sister, but she had to think of Tia and Quinn first. She couldn't put herself in danger, and something seemed off about this.

"I don't think I can, Tammy. Will you go and try to bring her here?"

Tammy shook her head and turned away. "No, she won't come. I already tried."

They still stood in the doorway of the house, and Kelsey turned to walk into the living room. "Let's sit down and think this out," she said. When she turned back, Tammy Rowe was holding a gun, pointing it directly at her chest.

"It's already been thought out, Kelsey. Now it's time to go."

Chapter Fifty-Three

Tammy Rowe's Volvo was the exact opposite of the woman. Filled with candy wrappers and empty fast food containers, it smelled of stale grease and old French fries.

She'd forced Kelsey into the front seat next to her, and kept the gun trained on her as she walked around the front of the car and got into the passenger seat.

"Sorry," Tammy said, as she pulled out a rope and bound Kelsey's hands in front of her. "Can't have you trying to jump out."

Tammy also pulled a bandana out of the back seat and secured it around her head and in front of her eyes.

"There," she said. "All ready."

The bandana smelled of grease and sweat, and Kelsey couldn't help but crinkle her nose as the smell wafted down toward her.

"Why are you doing this?" she asked Tammy. "I don't understand it."

"I know you don't. Most people don't get it at all."

Sudden clarity filled Kelsey's head as she looked at the place where she knew Tammy was sitting. "You're Thomas Telford, aren't you? You're Alisha's brother."

"I'm *not* Alisha's brother!" Tammy screamed at her, the calm, cool voice changing drastically into that of a wailing banshee. "I've never been her brother. Stupid small town doctor, and stupid small town, white trash parents. Stupid. Stupid." She muttered to herself for a minute longer. When she spoke again, her calm, modulated psychologist's voice was back in place.

"Can I explain it to you? It's not what you think," Tammy said.

"Yes, please explain." Kelsey kept her voice quiet and low, afraid of setting off another earthquake of emotion from the volatile woman—or man—sitting next to her.

"I was raised as a boy. I was born with a condition now known as intersexuality. Back then, we were considered freaks, or hermaphrodites. My mother was given progestin when she was pregnant with me, because she had had several miscarriages before I was born. Now, with modern research, we know that drug can cause a condition called progestin induced virilization. And it doesn't do anything to keep women from miscarrying. But back then, and especially in backwards Chapel Grace, they handed it out like candy."

"You look like a woman."

"I am a woman! I was born with an enlarged clitoris. Doctors told my mother she had an abnormal boy child, but that I was definitely a male. Common mistake. Doctors try to decide what sex a baby is without the knowledge they need. I looked like a boy on the outside. But I have ovaries and a uterus. I am a woman!"

Kelsey was quiet, allowing Tammy to talk, while an inner dialogue was taking place in her head.

Please, help me, Quinn. Please.

"They abused me. Took me to doctors, and did tests, making me strip, and lie on a cold table. Teams of doctors would come in and lift the sheet, stare at me, prod me, poke me!" Tammy shivered at the memory, and the car swerved.

Kelsey felt woozy because of the blindfold, and she couldn't tell where they were or if they were close to going off the road. What if they were near a cliff?

She forced herself to breathe in and regain her composure. Panicking now would not help her situation.

"Can you imagine, Kelsey, what it feels like, to be eight years old and not know what's going on? I didn't know. My good-for-nothing parents certainly didn't tell me. They just took me to doctors, let them poke and prod me. Made me pose for pictures in tabloid rags. Then took the money and drank it away.

"I got tired of being a victim. I decided it would never happen again. I also decided I would protect the other victims of the world. I was doing a pretty good job, too, except Alisha got scared. I didn't warn her about Jake Higgins. Set that one up nicely, though. He tried to rape her once, you know? Couldn't finish the deed. Too drunk."

"Where is Alisha? You didn't hurt her, did you?"

"Hurt her?"

Kelsey could hear the hint of incredulity in her voice.

"I would never hurt Alisha," Tammy said. "Don't you see? I did it to protect her. Her, and you, and all the others like us. I did it for us."

Chapter Fifty-Four

Doctor Prepont finally conceded to tell them what he knew about Alisha and Thomas Telford. The stern gazes of FBI Agent Lexi Richards and Detective Quinn Anderson helped him make his decision.

They had arrived back in Chapel Grace and met the others at the sheriff's department.

They sat in the sheriff's office: Rita, Quinn, Lexi, Dr. Prepont, and Dave Sparks. Too many folding chairs were crammed into the small room, and the air was hot and stale, inert.

Rita really wanted a cigarette. With a shock, she realized she hadn't thought much about smoking for the past twenty-four hours.

Substituting sex for cigarettes, she thought.

"Tell us what you know, Doctor," Lexi urged. "It's important you realize the level of violence here. Someone else is going to die if we don't track the murderer down. So far, Alisha Telford is the link."

"The only thing I know about Alisha is that my father believed she was being sexually abused. It's in her chart, and we talked about it after she left Chapel Grace. She would never admit it, and the mother only brought her in once, because Alisha had a high fever and extreme pain. Turned out to be gonorrhea. He tried to talk to Mary about it, but she tightened up and wouldn't discuss it. Never brought her back."

"How old was she?" Rita asked.

"I guess she was about eleven or twelve then. Too young to be sexually active, I think, but obviously something was going on."

"Did your father notify the authorities?"

"Yes, they investigated, but the family was tight-lipped, including Alisha, probably because she was scared, so they just dropped it."

"So what was it you were talking about in the field?" Sheriff Sparks asked him. He sat behind his desk, pushing a pencil around with his finger, picking it up every once in a while to chew on it.

Rita tried not to stare at the fingers that had performed magic on and in her body the night before.

"It's not about Alisha. It's Thomas. He was born with a . . . a condition. You probably know it as hermaphroditism, but today it's known as intersexuality. His mother was given progestin when she was pregnant, because she had suffered several miscarriages. He was born with an enlarged clitoris that looked like a small penis."

The doctor sweated, unpleasant large stains appearing under his arms and his brow beaded with moisture. He tugged at the collar of his shirt, as if he was uncomfortable talking about these things in mixed company. He kept darting glances at Lexi and Rita, but they both kept their faces straight and bland, not reacting.

"Back then, the standard practice was to perform surgery, a clitorectomy, and raise the child as a girl. They did this maybe ninety percent of the time. But Carl Telford refused. He said it was obvious his child was a boy, and he wouldn't have anyone trying to turn him into a girl."

The room was silent and still as they absorbed the doctor's words, and Quinn's cell phone shattered the glassy silence.

"Anderson. Yeah. Thanks. Uh-huh. Good God. It's confirmed? Okay, step up the search. I'll get back to you."

He disconnected the phone and looked around at the expectant eyes.

"Well, we found a record in San Francisco for one Thomas Telford. Only bit of information we could find, besides the driver's license here. But it wasn't a death certificate. It was a petition for name change. Thomas Telford changed his name to Tammy Rowe."

Chapter Fifty-Five

Agent Lexi Richards was silent, mouth drawn tight, lips pursed together, small wrinkle lines exposing the difficulty of her job. She slowly looked through the crime scene photos picturing the brutal demise of Leo Telford and Mary Telford.

Quinn, Lexi, Rita, and Dave Sparks were in his office after sending the doctor back to his practice. Lexi had called in an FBI forensic specialist from Quantico, and he was due to arrive later that day.

Lexi shook her head and sat the pictures on the desk face up. "Something's off here." She pointed to the other crime scene photographs Quinn had been showing her, now safely hidden in a manila folder. "These aren't quite the same as the others."

"I know," Rita said. "Something has been bugging me since I saw the bodies. It's different . . . more mechanical. More . . ."

"Savage?" Dave said.

"No, I mean they are worse than the other ones, but it's almost like it was staged. These vics were mutilated, rather than just having their sexual organs removed, but still—"

"Yes," Lexi interrupted, "but there is still savagery there, and anger."

"So the killer is either escalating into a frenzy—" Rita said.

"Or it's a different killer," Quinn finished the sentence.

"It's the two of them together, isn't it?" Rita said after a moment's silence.

Lexi shook her head, a frown marring her pleasant features,

as she tried to concentrate. "I don't know. It's most likely two different killers, but I can't say that for sure. There's been so little evidence."

"If you were going to make a list of all the possible people these two might target, assuming that it is them, who would be on it?" Rita asked, pulling a legal pad toward her. She picked up a pen and poised it to write. "There would be, of course, the parents. They are already gone. Jake Higgins, gone. His brother, the sheriff, who didn't do anything to stop him. Where's he?"

"Retired. Lives down on Oakley Road, in a small house. Ornery old coot. Keeps to himself."

"You need to send out officers and we need to watch his house," Lexi said, making notes in her notebook. "Do you need me to call in some backup?"

"Wouldn't hurt. I only have two deputies, and one of them is nearly blind and the other has a thing for the ladies. Spends most of his time in the coffee shop showing off his gun and badge."

Lexi shook her head and made more notes. She picked up Sheriff Sparks' phone and made the call to ask for reinforcements, and he stood up and walked across the hall to his dispatchers to send his deputies out to Higgins' place.

"I called the next county over, and they're sending a couple of guys down, right now. I told them to be on high alert. I also warned my guys to take it slow, and let us know if anything at all looks amiss."

"She could already have been there," Rita said, a sour look on her face. "I should have done this before."

"We all should have thought of it before," Quinn said, frowning.

"Okay, who else?" Rita asked, rubbing her arm where she'd been given the tetanus shot. Dave Sparks had made sure Doctor Prepont had given her one, despite her protestations. "We need to get all these people covered, so no one else dies. Those are the ones most closely related."

"We need to do a canvas on both of them, check their pasts. Anyone who might have harmed or wronged them. The M&M murders were mostly people they didn't know. Stalkers, wife beaters, and the connection was the WAV group. But things are too hot now, and things have escalated to the point where I don't seem to see them out hitting random bad guys," Lexi said.

Rita suddenly sat upright, her eyes open wide, blinking rapidly. "Oh God, I can't believe I didn't see it before."

"What? See what?" Quinn asked.

"The difference. The killings. One of them is killing off bad guys, likes Cabel and Reynolds. But the other one has made it personal. The Telfords. Jake Higgins. They are operating separately, but are still together. You have two totally different motives. One is mentally ill. The other is killing for revenge."

They were all quiet as they considered the possibility, and then Quinn spoke.

"She's right. But which one is which?"

Chapter Fifty-Six

"We need a search warrant for Tammy Rowe's house," Quinn said, standing up and stretching. "I'll call—"

His cellular phone rang and he lifted it out of his jacket pocket. "Anderson. What? *What?* Fuck! I'm on my way back."

He clicked the phone off and looked at the others in the room, who were all watching him expectantly.

"That was Franklin. Kelsey's missing. The uniforms got to her house to find it abandoned. Our neighbor said she drove off with a tall blond woman, and told the police it looked like they were playing hide and seek."

"Shit. Both Rowe and Telford are tall and blond," Rita said, as Quinn headed for the car.

"Wait, that's a long drive," Sheriff Sparks said to Quinn. "I have a rancher friend with an airplane, and a small airfield. He owes me. I'll put in a call."

"Thanks," Quinn said, trying to hide his emotions and fear.

Lexi Richards picked up her notes and tucked them into her briefcase. "You'll have backup here soon. I'll call and ask for a helicopter and put them on emergency status. We need to find the killer who is loose up here. I'm going with Quinn. You two can handle this?"

"Yeah," Rita said, glancing quickly at Dave.

"As soon as I call my friend, we'll take you out there, then head to Higgins' place."

"I think I need to go out there now," Rita said, her stern face brooking no argument. "You drop them off and meet me out there. Just give me directions."

"Hey, my deputies are out there. You can wait for me," Sheriff Sparks said, and a flash of anger crossed Rita's face.

"Later," Quinn said, interrupting them. "Let Rita go out. You take us to the plane now."

Sheriff Sparks raised his eyebrows at Quinn, and then agreed to the plan.

"Got it," he said. "Let's go."

Rita and Dave were the last to leave the room, and she patted him on the ass a little roughly, and whispered to him sharply. "I'm a cop, too. Don't you ever try to play that chauvinist game with me, Sheriff. It's not your job to protect me."

He gave her a hard look and then backed off, nodding, a little cold. Her heart twanged a bit, but she was also angry. If he thought of her as less than a cop, they could never be together. She had to have his respect, and it hurt that she didn't.

"No problem, Detective," he said. "You're coming in loud and clear." He walked briskly out of the office and to the car, where Agent Richards and Quinn stood waiting.

They left the parking lot at a high speed, and Rita followed closely behind in Quinn's car. She didn't put the lights and sirens on because there was no traffic on the road. Following the directions Dave had scribbled out on a piece of paper, she went straight when they turned into a long ranch driveway.

She seethed as she drove, and then got angry with herself. "Concentrate on the case, Jaramillo. The case."

She pulled up to a four-way stop and saw the dirt road to the right that Dave had noted. Turning, she whipped down the road, dust flying, until she reached a small, tidy house, barely big enough for one person. Parked out front were the two police cruisers, but there was no sign of either deputy. There was an old abandoned Ford on the side of the house, but she could see no other vehicles.

Swearing, she turned the car off and cautiously exited, her hand on the gun she'd pulled from her purse before she got out of the vehicle.

She moved cautiously forward, headed toward the door, which was suspiciously ajar, and then she heard a noise that sounded like a scream.

She couldn't wait. Two deputies might be in trouble. She moved rapidly and quietly toward the door, pushing it in slowly and trying to adjust her eyes to the dim interior. She heard the noise again, and headed down a small hallway, hoping the backup Agent Richards had mentioned was on the way, and fast. She moved to a small doorway in the back of the hall, and put her ear to it. Inside she could hear muffled noises and a thumping. As she prepared to throw open the door, across the hallway another door opened. She heard a click and felt cold metal push sharply against the side of her head.

"Well, hello," Alisha Telford said, reaching out and grabbing the gun Rita held in her right hand. "Another cop, come to join our party."

Chapter Fifty-Seven

Tammy Rowe weaved the car skillfully along the winding back road. She'd removed Kelsey's blindfold just moments before, and instead of relief, Kelsey felt even more anxious.

She had no idea where they were.

The only scenery was an occasional house or vineyard, and lots of grapes.

"Where are we going?" Kelsey asked in a friendly tone, not wanting to set her off again.

"You'll see."

Tammy pursed her lips and whistled a tune, then looked down at the radio as if her noise reminded her there was no music playing. She reached down toward the floor of the passenger seat, and Kelsey tried not to flinch. Tammy picked up a portable CD carrier and set it on Kelsey's lap.

"Pick some music. Anything you like," she said, turning to smile at Kelsey, before facing the road again.

I am in so much trouble. At least I know Alisha's not involved.

Kelsey opened the container and thumbed through the plastic sleeves holding the disks. She pulled out Rachmaninoff and prayed it was soothing, so Tammy's fragile mental balance wouldn't be unsettled before she could think of a way to escape.

Kelsey put the CD into the player, and soon soothing music played out through the car's speakers. Tammy nodded approvingly.

"Good choice. Very good driving music, Rachmaninoff."

They were quiet for a minute as Kelsey worked up the courage to ask another question.

"Ah, here we are," Tammy said, before Kelsey could get the words out. She turned down a dirt road with no markings. Kelsey strained to see where they were. She knew they had traveled up the coast and then slightly inland. When the salty, briny scent had faded, she'd deduced they were no longer close to the ocean.

Looking around her, though, she realized they could be anywhere in the vast Santa Barbara County.

After bumping up and down the dirt road for a mile or so, they came upon a small white cottage. Immaculately painted, the house was obviously not abandoned, despite how desolate the road had been.

"Wow," Kelsey said, unable to help herself.

"Isn't it lovely?" Tammy asked, excitement tingeing her voice. "This is my little getaway. I had to take your blindfold off, because I knew you would appreciate this."

The little bungalow sat on dark brown, rich-looking earth, surrounded by tall trees. A small vineyard graced the back of the house. There was an immaculately groomed flower garden in front of the house, although there were only a few plants left blooming in the cool October nights.

The house had dark green shutters, and Kelsey could see window treatments on the insides of the large glass windows.

"Let's go in. I can hardly wait for you to see."

Tammy walked around the front of the car until she reached Kelsey's door and opened it, reaching in and pulling her out by the right arm.

"Can you untie these?" Kelsey asked, raising her bound hands. "I promise I won't try to get away."

"Oh, no. I'm not that dumb." Tammy chuckled. She led Kelsey toward the front door of the house, and pushed her roughly to the wall as she pulled out her key and unlocked the front door.

"You first," she said, shoving Kelsey inside.

The home was as immaculate inside as it was out, with light pine furniture, and lots of white accents. The floors were wood, also light pine, and there were expensive Persian rugs on the floors. "It's so different from how I was raised. I love it," Tammy exclaimed.

"Different from how I was raised, too," Kelsey said quietly, admiring Tammy's taste.

Tammy pushed Kelsey farther into the room, and pointed to a large, leather chair, upholstered in burgundy leather.

"Sit there."

Kelsey sat, and Tammy dropped her purse and walked to the window, opening the blinds, and letting the sun in.

"This is my escape. I don't share it with many people. No one else knows it's here but Alisha."

Alisha. Oh, please, let Alisha save her, or at least tell Quinn where this place is.

Tammy watched her closely, and shook her head, her radiant smile and frown dropping away to reveal the cold, hard mask of the killer. "Don't get any ideas. Alisha would never turn on me. I've taken care of her for too long. She owes me.

"Your boyfriend is next."

Chapter Fifty-Eight

The cold metal on her face caused Rita to instinctively step back. Alisha moved forward, pushing the gun into her temple harder. She tucked Rita's gun into her waistband with her left hand, and never took her eyes off Rita.

"Don't move," the woman told her in a harsh, strident voice. "I will not feel bad at all about getting rid of yet another dirty cop."

Rita stopped in her tracks, wondering what Alisha had against cops, besides her encounters with the now-retired Sheriff Higgins, who was hopefully still alive in this house.

"Where are the deputies and Sheriff Higgins?" Rita asked her.

Alisha waved the gun carelessly and Rita flinched at the way she handled it, worried it would go off. "In there," she finally said, pointing to the room where Rita had heard the noise. "Open it."

Rita hesitated, then seeing the firm set of Alisha's face, she pushed through the door. Inside, lying on the floor, were the bodies of an old man—presumably Higgins—and one of the deputies. Both had been shot in the head, and blood pooled around them. In a chair in the middle of the small room, which was empty save for a few boxes and old furniture pushed up against the wall, was the other deputy. He had a boyishly handsome face and fear in his eyes, and Rita supposed this was the detective who liked the ladies. He didn't look like much right now, as he was stripped naked, his clothes in a pile several feet from the chair.

"Don't mind them," Alisha said, motioning toward the dead bodies, as though they were at a cocktail party and some gatecrashers had just come in. "They won't bother us."

"Why are you doing this?" Rita asked her. "The FBI has been called in, there are police everywhere looking for you. You can't get out of this county."

Alisha's face hardened. "You don't know me. I guarantee you I can."

She motioned to the detective in the chair, and said "Go sit at his feet."

Rita hesitated, and Alisha screamed, *"Move!"*

As Rita slowly walked to the middle of the room, Alisha moved back toward the bodies, and a hand reached up and grabbed her ankle.

She screamed and dropped the gun, and Rita dove for it.

Realizing her mistake, Alisha dove, too, and they wrestled for the gun on the floor, until Rita pulled it away from her and grabbed at Alisha's waistband for her own gun.

Twisting away from Rita's probing hands, Alisha kicked the gun from Rita's grasp. It skittered across the floor, landing under the chair that held the naked, bound deputy.

Alisha scooted away quickly and scrambled to her feet, touching the gun in her waistband as she took off running through the house. Rita jumped up and raced to the chair, grabbing the gun and telling the sad-eyed deputy, "I'm coming back. I promise." She turned and raced down the hallway after Alisha, rushing out the front door in time to see the woman jump into one of the police cars and start it, speeding away.

"Damn country cops!" Rita cursed, knowing the keys had been inside the car. She raced to the other police car and jumped in, turning on the lights and sirens as she chased Alisha down the road.

Rita grabbed the radio mike and screamed into it, "Ten-thirty-three dispatch, this is Detective Rita Jaramillo, SBPD. I am in pursuit of a stolen police car, driven by murder suspect Alisha Telford. We have officers down at the Higgins place. Suspect has just turned onto Oakley Road."

"This is dispatch," crackled the voice on the radio before another one broke in and starting giving instructions. Relieved, Rita recognized Dave's voice, and she concentrated on turning left on Oakley to follow Alisha. She rounded a bend to find Alisha had stopped, parking the car in the middle of the road. Rita slammed on the brakes, the vehicle going into a skid before smashing into the side of the other police car. Rita's head and shoulders, unprotected by a seat belt harness in her hurry to follow Alisha, flew forward into the windshield and Rita heard a sharp crack before she felt the pain in her head and drifted off to nothingness.

Chapter Fifty-Nine

Detective Quinn Anderson and FBI Agent Lexi Richards didn't speak much on the flight back, a bumpy ride on board a small Cessna.

Lexi spent the time studying the pictures and notes from the first crimes, including Christy Frazier's murder in San Francisco. They had learned from the SFPD medical examiner that she had been dead approximately two hours when her body was discovered.

"This killer is making no attempt to hide the bodies, or avoid discovery. Is that a sign of inexperience, or is he or she trying to tell us something?" she wondered aloud.

"It's a message. Come on, the bodies hanging from the hydraulic lift at the service station? It was blatant. Admire me." Quinn looked out the window again, and rubbed at his stomach, which felt as though someone had ripped it out, tied it in knots, and put it back into his body.

"I don't know. It could have been because the North Cal M&M killer wanted us to think he and the South Cal killer are one and the same. Leaving the bodies out like that, same MO, only different. Could he have known they were different?"

"You still don't think it's possible this could be Alisha and Tammy?"

"Tammy could fit. Intersexed children often see their childhood as one of trauma and abuse, much like sexually abused or physically abused children. Medical procedures, involving things they aren't told about, doctors and nurses looking at their genitals, when they've been taught to be ashamed of them. It all adds up to abuse."

"But is Tammy Rowe a man or a woman?"

"I don't know. She believes she's female, that's obvious. And they're finding sometimes the only way to know is to the let the child determine what sex they are. Did you hear about the boy who had his penis damaged during a routine circumcision?"

"Ouch. No."

"Well, doctors decided it would be better to remove what was left, and raise him as a girl. They believed the psychological trauma of not having a functional penis would be worse, and they also believed they could give him hormones and he would do better as a girl."

"Did he?"

"No. It was a complete failure. He blamed his parents, considered it abuse, and is now living as a man. You can't pick and choose someone's sexuality and gender—at least that's what I believe."

Quinn raised his eyebrows. He knew Lexi was a believing Mormon, and her church frowned on homosexuality, viewing it as an offense to God's laws.

"What?" she said, giving him an irritated look.

"Nothing. Just surprised, that's all."

"Look, I have a brain, okay. I don't have to agree with everything church authorities say."

"I thought they didn't like it when members didn't toe the line."

"Quinn, here's the deal, okay? My mother and father were Mormon. My grandparents were Mormon. My great-grandparents were Mormon, and my great-grandfather even knew Brigham Young. I was born and raised in Utah. It's cultural. You can't wipe it off. It's part of who I am."

"You don't owe me an explanation, Lexi."

"No kidding. But you're getting one, anyway."

"I get it. I was raised Catholic. I still do the sign of the cross myself sometimes, out of habit."

"Anyway, back to this," Lexi said, and turned away from him and put on a pair of reading glasses, poring over the material once again. With her short dark hair and stylish suits, she looked like she could have been reading *Cosmopolitan* and drinking martinis, instead of studying grisly crime photos and details, and defending her fundamental faith.

"Fucking whacked-out world we live in," Quinn said, leaning back against the headrest and rubbing his eyes with his left hand. "God, I hope she's okay."

"Me, too," Lexi said. A small grimace crossed her face, although she didn't look up from her reading material. "I think she's been through enough."

Chapter Sixty

Tammy Rowe led Kelsey to a back bedroom and pushed her inside. "Sit there," she said, pointing to the bed, covered with a lacy eyelet bedspread and stacked with stuffed animals.

Kelsey sat on the side of the bed, surveying the room and its contents. An ornate cabinet of oak reached to the ceiling, and inside the glass panes she could see beautiful china dolls, of all shapes and sizes, all sitting on stands and gazing out sightlessly at the scene unfolding in front of them. A wallpaper border running around the top room was made up of ballet shoes, in various poses and directions.

On a small vanity with a big round mirror, there were bottles of bubble bath and perfume, nail polish and makeup. A silver brush and comb sat next to a round powder puff, and around the top of the mirror were feather boas and girlish hats, the types of bonnets one might wear at Easter.

Kelsey saw a door she supposed was the closet, shut tight, and then a nice stereo system, in pink, with forty-fives and LPs in their original cases, stacked neatly by the side.

Tammy watched her admire the room with a big smile, standing back with her arms crossed.

"Neat, huh?" she said, when Kelsey made eye contact with her again. "I scoured the secondhand stores to find those records. David Cassidy. Bobby Sherman. Donny Osmond. I found them all."

"This is incredible! It's like a childhood dream," Kelsey said, her mouth open wide as she scanned all the treasures.

"Come, come," Tammy said suddenly, pulling Kelsey to her feet and dragging her into a different room. She'd taken the gun and tucked it into the front waistband of her stylish suit. It was an odd sight, marring the woman's studied elegance and perfection.

Tammy threw open a door and they walked into a room full to the brim with toys. Kelsey saw an Easy-Bake Oven, something she'd coveted as a child but had never owned. There were dolls of all types, sizes, and colors. One doll with long red hair she remembered from the commercials. It was a Chrissy doll, and the hair grew shorter and longer, controlled by a knob on the head. Kelsey remembered holding her childhood friend's doll, rocking it, and wishing her parents would buy her one.

"All I ever got for Christmas were scriptures and homemade clothes," she said, mostly to herself, eyeing the Candyland game, the Chutes and Ladders, Monopoly, Life, checkers, and at least twenty more, all stacked neatly on top of each other.

There were jump ropes, and Hoppy Taw hopscotch markers, and a big open chest full of dress-up clothes, tiaras, costume jewelry, and shoes.

A canopy bed took up most of the room, covered with a fluffy pink quilted bedspread and five big pillows.

"Fun, huh?" Tammy said, jumping up and down a little, and clapping. "Everything here I never got as a girl. Stupid BB guns, and Ken dolls. I used to cut the hair off Alisha's dolls and make little wigs for my Ken, so he could be a girl, too." Her face hardened. "It wasn't the same, though. He didn't have the shape, like Barbie did. It was pretty obvious *he* was a man."

Her face lightened again and she grabbed Kelsey's arm. "I have a great idea. Come on." She pulled her back into the bedroom and threw open the cupboard. Inside were many pairs of pajamas, baby-doll style, all in different colors, materials, and patterns.

"Pick one. We're going to have a sleepover. It'll be so much fun."

Kelsey's eyes widened, as she took in the full breadth of Tammy's dementia.

Sleepover with a Psycho. Sounds like a B movie.

"You change in here," Tammy said. "Pick whichever one you want. Let me know when you're ready. I'm going into my room to change, and then we'll pop some popcorn, watch movies, and tell scary stories. Sound good? Good!"

With that, she hustled to the door and Kelsey stood in the middle of the room, shaking her head, wondering what the hell was going on. Sleepover? Popcorn? Movies?"

She heard a cll-iick as a metal key entered a lock on the outside of the door and reality hit her again. This was no party. Tammy was a murderer, and one who was in serious la la land. She was in deep trouble.

Kelsey walked over to the closet and pulled out a pink number with puffy sleeves and no pattern.

"I guess I better play along."

Chapter Sixty-One

Quinn wandered from room to room of the oceanside cottage, looking for clues, desperate to find some trace of evidence that would lead him to Kelsey's side.

Lexi talked quietly with an FBI agent while crime scene technicians dusted for fingerprints. Franklin was bringing Edie Falconer over to speak with them, but other than the box of old clippings, there was no clue—no sign of where Tammy Rowe was headed and where she was taking Kelsey.

Quinn walked over to the window and stared out at the ocean, taking in Kelsey's favorite view. She loved this place, loved the sound of the waves, and the salty smell of the water.

"Detective Anderson?"

Quinn turned to see a small, visibly shaken Edie Falconer standing before him. Franklin stood in the background, and watched.

"Come sit down, Edie. We need to talk."

"I didn't realize she was in trouble," the cherubic woman said, her large eyes pooling with tears that threatened to set off a landslide down the craggy, wrinkled face. "I thought it was a friend. She didn't look like she was upset. Of course, I was kind of far away, but still . . ."

Quinn led Edie to the sofa and sat her down. He sat next to her, and patted her hand.

"What else can you tell us about the woman, Edie? Was she tall? Short? Fat?"

"Oh, tall. Very pretty, very elegant. I told that other nice detective all about it," she said, her voice little more than a whisper.

"Detective Franklin?"

"Yes," she said with a slight nod, her voice still low and lacking its usual animation and inflection. Quinn nodded to a detective standing in the background, and he moved forward and handed him a manila envelope. Inside were black-and-white photos of Alisha Telford and Tammy Rowe, supplied by the hospital human resources department.

"Can you tell me if it was one of these women."

Edie brightened.

"Oh, yes, definitely it was her!" She pointed to the picture of Alisha Telford. Quinn started to turn to bark an order at the detective, while Lexi began to walk over toward them.

Edie's gaze shifted to the second picture, and the bright look on her face faded to a puzzled frown. "Oh wait, I think it was her. Oh my goodness, they look a lot alike don't they?"

Quinn caught Lexi's gaze, her head tipped, asking him a silent question. He looked at the pictures again. Although the two were decidedly similar—long blond hair, blue eyes, full lips, closed-mouth smile—Tammy Rowe's face was broader, her nose a hair shorter, her eyebrows closer together.

While Alisha was a stunning beauty, Quinn realized, Tammy's beauty was more forced, less natural—almost artificial.

"They do look a bit similar, don't they," he said to Edie, knowing from her front yard, she wouldn't have had a close view of Kelsey or her abductor. "Thanks for your help, Edie. Detective Franklin will see you home."

"I hope you find her, Quinn," said the elderly woman, her lips thin and trembling. She transformed as Franklin walked forward and offered her his arm.

"My, aren't you a handsome black stallion," she cooed to

Franklin, and he turned away from her and rolled his eyes. Quinn fought back a quick grin, before the heaviness of the situation settled back upon him.

In other circumstances, he would have been highly amused by Edie's shameless come-on to Franklin, but with Kelsey missing, he was hard pressed to feel anything but tension and desperation.

"They are similar," Lexi said, as they watched the only witness disappear out the front door. "Height is around the same, as is weight. Looking at the two of them, I would think sisters."

"They were never together. Once in a while. No closer than Kelsey was with Tammy, or the Tammy she thought she knew. Kelsey never said anything about them having a close bond."

Quinn thought for a minute, and then considered what he knew of the two women. "I saw Alisha more, of course. She was tall, thin, but curvy, hips and indented waist. When she wasn't on duty she was always wearing tight jeans, or shorts and miniskirts. Not obscene, mind you, but always sexy. Tammy, she was more professional. Same height, or close, but less curvy, more straight up and down. She wore a lot of tailored suits and professional clothing.

"Two girls. Just two girls, with fucked-up parents, no way to escape, and one with a medical condition that caused the parents to become abusive in order to hide it."

"Yeah, two girls." Lexi sighed and rubbed her eyes. "Where the hell are they?"

Franklin, who had made his way across the room to one of the uniforms and had obviously been retelling the story of Edie, walked back toward them, his phone to his ear, a grim expression on his face.

He hung up and faced both Lexi and Quinn, shaking his head. "DNA's back on the scalpel from Rowe's office. They dusted the entire office for prints, too, including those of Alisha

Telford, and there were lots of unidentifiable partials and prints, but the bottom line was that the prints belong to Rowe. Even on the chairs and furniture that was overturned, and the files that were on the floor. It looks like she tossed the place herself."

"Rage, maybe?" Lexi wondered.

"The blood?" Quinn asked.

"The blood was John Penny's."

Chapter Sixty-Two

"Rita? Oh my God, Rita? Are you okay?"

Dave Sparks tore at the door of the crumpled police cruiser, which had hit the abandoned cruiser at about forty-five miles an hour as Rita rounded the curve.

He got the door open and pushed at the deflated material of the car's air bag, trying to get it out of the way so he could pull her out of the burning vehicle. Behind him, he could hear sirens, more than just the usual emergency vehicles and police cruisers from another county.

Reinforcements had arrived. Hopefully, he thought, not too late for Rita.

She moaned and he grasped harder, pushing the bag away and getting his arms around her torso.

He pulled her out of the car and carried her awkwardly, legs dragging, to the side of the road, away from the burning vehicles and any danger of explosion. He could see no one was inside the second cruiser, but he knew whoever had been driving couldn't be far away. He spoke into the radio clipped to the shoulder of his uniform and told the dispatcher to alert the other authorities: the suspect was loose.

That done, he knelt by Rita, lying in the soft grass off the side of the road, a cut on her head bleeding slightly. She appeared to have no other injuries.

Rita opened her eyes and looked up at him, blinking to focus. "Ouch. That hurt."

"I bet it did."

"Are you going to say I told you so?"

"Only if you want me to."

"I don't."

"Then I won't."

"It could have happened to anyone, male or female. It doesn't matter who went out there, it would have happened. Dave?"

"Yeah?"

"One of your deputies is dead. I'm sorry. The other one is tied up back there. At the sheriff's house."

"Higgins?"

"He's dead, too."

"Ah, shit. Who was it?"

"Alisha Telford."

Dave shook his head slowly, not looking forward to visiting Millie, Deputy Larsen's widow. Forty years on the job, and now he was dead. Never wanted to move up. Just liked to cruise around the county giving tickets to teenaged speeders and juvenile delinquents. Once in a while a crime, a robbery, but never anything too complicated. Evil had swept into town with Detective Rita Jaramillo and her partner. Dave couldn't regret her coming here, though. He wouldn't, even though now they were seeing a crime wave unlike any they'd ever experienced before. Now one of his deputies was dead.

That evil started right here. It just made its way back.

The paramedics arrived and examined Rita, who shooed them away saying she was fine, just a little dazed. They cleaned up and bandaged the small cut on her head, while the FBI and their crime scene techs pored over the two vehicles. A small fire truck had effectively put out the flames, and now both cars were just smoldering.

In the woods, several officers were searching with dogs, an occasional shout coming up as they worked.

When the paramedics were done, Rita walked over to Dave, who stood against his car talking to one of the FBI agents. She moved to the passenger side and opened the door, standing just inside it, leaning against the roof for support. Once there, she pulled out her phone and dialed.

"Quinn? Yeah, it's me Rita. Bad scene up here. What? No, it's not Kelsey. But Alisha doesn't have her, Quinn. I just met her face to face here. She killed the old sheriff, Jake Higgins' brother, and a deputy. Almost got me, too . . . No, I'm okay. She got away. Not sure how. I don't think on foot. She stole a cruiser, but left it in the middle of the road and I plowed into it in another cruiser. I'm okay . . . No, I'm okay. We're going to go shake down Mary Telford's place. See if we can find a clue . . . Really? . . . Really? Okay . . . Yeah. Sounds good."

Rita hung up and saw Dave had ended his conversation with the agent. Now he was watching her carefully.

"So, we're headed to Mary's motel, huh?"

"It's an *inn*, Sparks. Get it right."

"You still mad?"

"Maybe a little."

He shrugged, and said, "So Tammy Rowe has Kelsey. At least as far as we know."

"As far as we know," she parroted him, and then moved into the seat and slammed the door. He entered the car and sat next to her. She avoided his eyes, watching instead the scene in front of them, as crews worked to get fingerprints and evidence, and clear the accident from the road.

"Rita, look at me, please?"

She focused on his face, a sardonic expression crossing her brow and eyes.

"I'm starting to care, okay? I'm starting to care a lot. I didn't want you hurt. I didn't mean to imply you couldn't take care of yourself."

"But you did."

"Now you're being stubborn. Won't even accept my apology."

"If I were a man, you wouldn't have said one damn word to me about it. Not one."

"If you were a man, I wouldn't be sleeping with you."

"Well, just consider me a man, then."

Dave knew he'd hit it where it hurt the most—her job. But now she was being stubborn.

He gave up, threw his hands in the air, and started the car. He knew the fact that she'd almost gotten killed, and that the murderer had escaped, made his attempts to protect her all the harder for her to swallow. It was important to her to do her job right and prove she was just as capable as any man.

"You were right, you know. Out here, we go out, often there is no backup. If someone is at lunch, or out on another call, you're most likely on your own. One of my deputies even got killed, and you didn't. You got away."

"So did she," Rita said tersely, looking out at the passing scenery.

Chapter Sixty-Three

A sympathetic judge had rushed through an emergency search warrant for Tammy Rowe's bungalow in the hills of Santa Barbara, and Quinn and Franklin were standing in front of the door, waiting for the SWAT team to gain entry and secure the premises.

Neighbors all along the swanky winding road came out and stood in front of their homes, watching the police in action.

"Media will be here soon," Franklin commented.

"Yeah, let's just get in and out as quickly as we can," Quinn said, grimacing, knowing the media would be twice as bad once word got out that one of their own—television anchor Christy Frazier—had been killed.

They searched the immaculate French country-style house for any clues, and found nothing. No signs of a weapon or clothes used in the attacks. Quinn hadn't expected any.

Tammy Rowe lived a very closed life. She had no television, not in any of the four bedrooms or the living room. There was an old radio on the mantle of the fireplace, and an ancient stereo system that had a turntable for playing records. They searched through the albums and forty-fives, finding old songs from the sixties and seventies.

She had only business wear and casual suits in her closet. There were no shorts, no sweats, and no lounging wear. In one drawer they found several pairs of silk pajamas in bright colors. Underwear was expensive looking, silky, no tears or rips. Shoes were all perfectly shined and looked new.

"Weird," Franklin commented, coming out of the master bath attached to the main bedroom.

"What?"

"Toothbrush in there, toothpaste, Tylenol, petroleum jelly, toilet paper—all the standards. But nothing personal."

"A toothbrush is personal."

"Yeah," Franklin said, smiling, holding up the baggie holding Tammy Rowe's clean, pink-and-white-striped toothbrush. "But nothing, like, that says who she is. You know, people lay claim to their bathrooms. My old lady used to use so much hairspray, the room smelled of it for weeks after she was gone. I had to scrape the gunk off the mirror. That bathroom doesn't even look used. Toilet paper folded in a nice triangle, like they do in motels and hotels. Nothing in the medicine cabinets. It's like the light's on but nobody's home, you know?"

The entire house had that feeling. Quinn rummaged through the drawers of Tammy Rowe's home office. He found her recent bills neatly stacked in one drawer. The rest were filed neatly away.

"We could be here all night," he muttered. She didn't have a computer. There was nothing about the house that screamed "Lunatic!"

Lexi Richards walked into the room and he turned to her.

"Find anything?"

"Nothing. But the guys are about to open her garden shed out back. Maybe you should come out."

He jumped to his feet, still carrying the bills, and sat them back on the desk. They walked through the house, and opened French doors that went out onto a patio. There was no furniture or signs of life out here, other than an immaculate yard and trimmed bushes. The six agents at the woodshed were waiting for Lexi's okay, and she nodded her head as they broke down the locked door and checked the inside. Quinn was right behind the first man, who entered gun drawn and in crouch position, moving back and forth checking for intruders.

A spider scuttled away at the sudden influx of light, but other than a lawnmower, some hoes and rakes, and a coiled up hose, the shed was empty.

Chapter Sixty-Four

"Popcorn," Tammy Rowe called out gaily, as she unlocked the door to Kelsey's pink prison and came in. "Sit," she said, indicating the floor by the side of the bed. "We'll chat, just like friends do. What fun."

Kelsey sat, uncomfortable in the fluffy pink baby-doll gown she wore. Tammy sat next to her, placing the popcorn between them. She wore another baby-doll gown, purple with pink lining, and huge puffy sleeves. The gun was tucked into a pink sash she had tied tightly at her waist. *Some slumber party,* Kelsey thought.

"So, what shall we talk about? Donny Osmond?"

"Donny Osmond?"

"Yes, you know, that cute singer. Big teeth, though. Really should have those filed down. We'll talk about him. Oh, or David Cassidy. Now he's cute."

"I . . . I don't know what you want me to say."

Tammy's delighted expression darkened, and she glared at Kelsey. "I don't *want* you to say anything. We are just having a great conversation here, between friends. Remember? It's a slumber party." Her face darkened even more. "Don't fuck it up, Kelsey. You don't want to do that, trust me."

"Okay, tell me about you."

"Okay, well, I was born in Hollywood Hills, to very wealthy parents. My father was some sort of government official—I think CIA, but he would never admit it—and my mother was an actress."

Kelsey couldn't believe her ears. Had Tammy Rowe created a fantasy life for herself, along with the fantasy house?

"Anyway, mother used to take me to work with her on the set, and it was such fun. I met so many movie stars, like Rock Hudson, and James Garner, oh, and that cute guy from *Starsky and Hutch*. What was his name?"

"Tammy, what about Alisha? Was she with you?"

Again the woman's face darkened and her mouth became a thin line, her anger almost palpable.

"Never mind that," Tammy said, a scowl on her face. "Let's paint our nails, okay? Sound fun?" With a quick switch, the light and airy Slumber-Party Tammy was back.

"Why are you doing this?" Kelsey asked, her stomach aching, her fists clenched.

"Why am I doing what? Trying to get my guest to have a good time? I'm getting a little peeved with your questions, Kelsey. We're supposed to be having fun. It's a slumber party. Everyone has fun at slumber parties." Tammy jumped to her feet and walked away from the bed, stopping to pace in front of the door.

"I'm sorry, Tammy. I never went to slumber parties when I was a child," Kelsey said, quickly. "My father didn't allow it. I don't know what to do at one. I have no experience."

"Damn men," Tammy said, frowning even harder, her eyebrows furrowed together in anger. "Useless creatures. Useless. And they tried to say I was one of them! One of those belching, farting, butt-scratching reptiles that can't find the toilet, but instead spray the walls and everything around it with urine."

I think I better shut up, Kelsey thought, backing away a little.

"Do you know what *my* father did? Do you?" Tammy asked,

glowering in her direction.

"Made you act like a boy?" Kelsey asked, unsure what to say, not wanting to set Tammy off again.

"When he saw fit. The rest of the time, he would dress me up in Alisha's clothing and we'd do fashion shows. I thought it was fun. I thought he really loved me. Until he put his disgusting . . . thing in me. Disgusting."

"Your father sexually abused you?" Kelsey asked, shock growing as she pictured a poor young child, feeling like a girl, treated like a boy, forced to walk a tightrope between the two, never knowing where he—or she—belonged.

"Mother, of course, was no help at all," she went on, as though Kelsey hadn't spoken. "Give that woman a pint of vodka and Godzilla himself could have walked through our house and she wouldn't have noticed."

"I'm sorry. I'm sorry this happened to you."

"You really are, aren't you?" Tammy said, a soft smile curving her broad mouth, the anger dissipating from her eyes. She walked toward Kelsey. "But that was my other life, Kelsey. Don't worry. That's not the life I'm living now. This, all of this, my two homes, my job, everything is my fairy tale. Even back home in Santa Barbara, no one knows what I went through. No one. And no one ever will."

Kelsey's brain started to fire fear impulses and her breathing became sharp and rapid. She was here, in Tammy's make-believe world, but she knew the real Tammy. She knew the whole story, including what went on in Chapel Grace. Tammy wouldn't let her go. Tammy would never let her go.

She was going to die.

Chapter Sixty-Five

Detective Rita Jaramillo and Sheriff Dave Sparks tore Mary Telford's small motel unit apart, looking for clues that would indicate Alisha Telford or Tammy Rowe had been there.

The search dogs had honed in on a spot back at the scene of the accident and Alisha's getaway. Following the trail the officers had found tire tracks off a small dirt road. The getaway car had apparently been parked in a grove of trees just off the road.

Alisha Telford knew the area well.

The small room was barren of photographs or decoration, save for a small tarnished silver picture frame sitting on a dresser. Two small, but belligerent faces frowned at the camera, the black-and-white photo showing no joy of youth or pride. Everything else in the room was generic clutter and what others would regard as garbage.

Rita picked up the picture and examined it. Was Mary Telford a cold alcoholic mother, holding on to her trophy: the destruction of two young lives?

Both Alisha and Tammy, then Thomas, frowned, eyebrows knitted together, lips clenched tight. Alisha was a slightly shorter young blonde, with a thin ragged face. She appeared to be wearing something off the shoulder, too old for the child she was. Thomas was blank-faced, also tight-lipped, eyes vacuous and dark, although Rita knew they were blue. As she held it closer, she could see his eyes were not quite looking at the camera, but off somewhere in the distance? An escape?

Her ringing cell phone interrupted the examination.

"Jaramillo," Rita answered her cell phone, surprised to hear Quinn's voice.

"The DNA's in. The hair on Tessa Morrow's body was not Alisha's, but the lab said it was similar. We're at Rowe's now, gathering the evidence. Should find something to see if it's a match to her."

"Any sign of Kelsey? Anything?"

"No, nothing. It's like she didn't even live here. Immaculate, spotless, nothing to go on. Just cleaning up now."

"So, we know Alisha might not have been involved in the murders down there, but I saw her up here. And the fact Kelsey is missing says they were working together, and Tammy has her."

"What could possess two women, even two as horribly abused as these two were, to become so murderous?"

"I'm still working that. Lexi come up with anything?"

"No, but we're going to go back and brainstorm when we're done here. I just want to make sure we don't miss anything."

"We still don't have anything concrete tying Tammy Rowe to anything, Quinn. Alisha, well, that's a little easier. We have two murders to pin on her, and a cop murder at that. When we catch her, she's toast."

There was silence on the other end.

"She probably knows where Kelsey is," Quinn said after a minute. "I want her taken alive. No matter what."

"I know you do."

"She may be the only link we have to Kelsey."

"So, who's running the show here?" Quinn asked Lexi. "Which one of them is the mastermind, violent killer, and which one is the puppet?"

"Well, odds are if these two are the killers, and it sounds like at least Alisha is involved, then I would guess Tammy is running the show. But women rarely commit serial murder. I know, I know, I've said it a hundred times, and you're getting tired of hearing it, but it's true."

"Every one of these murders is connected to these two."

"Quinn, you need to realize the seriousness of this. If they have taken Kelsey, there's a good chance that . . ."

"That she's dead," he said flatly, finishing the sentence.

Chapter Sixty-Six

The silence, a wall of glass between them, separated Rita and Dave as they searched Mary Telford's small room at the end of the motel.

A job that shouldn't take long was made more difficult by the deceased woman's predilection to collect. Stacks of magazines were piled on both sides of the bed, with only a small entrance she must have crawled through at night to sleep. There were newspapers, old food wrappers, and hundreds of old copies of *TV Guide*.

The television was a small black-and-white model, balanced precariously on a cardboard box. The antenna was a coat hanger, and there was no on/off knob. A pair of pliers sat on the floor next to the TV, apparently the method she used to turn the TV on and off.

All the junk was impersonal: nothing told the life story of Mary Telford.

Dave pulled out several drawers in an old bureau and sifted through Mary Telford's stained, threadbare old-lady underwear.

"Yuck," he said, grimacing, his long, handsome face unhappy. "I feel like a perv."

"I'll let you play with my underwear when we're done," Rita said with a small smile, moving over to a tiny tri-corner desk.

Dave looked up and studied her face.

Rita didn't return the gaze, but continued to look through the contents of the desk.

She picked up some of the papers scattered across the desk and scanned them, then put them back and dropped to her hands and knees to pull out the wastebasket below the standard-issue hotel desk.

Inside the basket was a crumpled piece of paper and two dirty tissues. Rita reached her rubber-gloved hand in and pulled out the paper.

Smoothing it out, she read the writing, and then stood up.

"Well, here's somewhat of a tie. At least one that could explain Penny's connection."

"What?" Dave gratefully shut the underwear drawer and walked toward her.

The piece of paper had three names written on it—not the same three names Penny had written down on the paper she'd found in his desk earlier in the week, but three different names. Men's names.

"Charles Boudreaux, Clint Farrell, Leon Forbes."

"Ring a bell?" Dave asked.

"No. Not one tiny little peal. But look here, under the names. The phone number?"

"Yeah?"

"That's the SBPD number."

Rita pulled the cell phone out of her jacket pocket and dialed. "Yeah, Franklin? Jaramillo. I need you to run some names, okay? . . . What? . . . No, this is all related to our case, and it's a rush, so do it now. Quit bitching."

She gave him the names and hung up. "He's tired. Says he's overworked. Welcome to the club." Rita sighed and rubbed the back of her neck. "I'd kill for a bubble bath right now."

"I don't have bubble bath, but I have dish soap," Dave offered.

She narrowed her eyes at him. "What makes you think I'd be willing to step one foot in your house, huh?"

"Because I'm taking you to my house, whether you want to go or not."

"You can't boss me around, Dave. I'm not one of your backwoods little girlfriends. I can take care of myself. I always have."

"I like it when you talk tough, but here's the deal . . ." He grabbed her and pulled her to him, tightly, kissing her on the mouth, firmly at first and then softening, until her stomach quivered and her muscles felt like play dough. When he pulled away, they were both breathless. "I think I'm falling in love with you. I want to take care of you. If it makes you feel a little better, you can take care of me, too."

"Humph," Rita said, with all the dignity she could muster. "I'll think about it."

"Think long and hard."

"Long and hard. Yeah, I can do that," she said, with a suggestive look to his crotch.

"You better stop, or we won't get this done," Dave warned, a smile lighting his lips.

"Oh yes we will, because I am not doing anything here, in a dead woman's messy room."

"Later then," he said.

"Maybe."

Chapter Sixty-Seven

Rita sat at the small break table at the Redville County Sheriff's Department, poring over her notes. She'd checked in with Quinn after they left Mary Telford's motel room, and there was no news about Kelsey, or where Tammy Rowe had taken her.

When the cell phone rang again, she answered it expectantly, hoping for good news, or at least a break.

"You are not going to believe this, Jaramillo. Not fucking going to believe this."

"What, Franklin?"

"I ran those names. Guess what? They are all cops. Every last one of them."

"Cops?"

"Yep. Seems Ms. Telford did not come straight to Santa Barbara. One of the cops was on the SFPD. I spoke to Becker. He went back in the files. Charles Boudreaux was a career beat cop. Twenty years on the force. Died four years ago, of what appeared to be natural causes. Next of kin—Alisha Telford."

"Good God."

"Oh yeah. She collects a nice pension," Franklin said.

"Did he have life insurance?"

"I'm on it now, and trying to touch base with someone on the other two cops. Clint Farrell is from Sacramento, and Leon Forbes from San Jose. I have calls in to both places."

"Get on the horn and call them back. Tell them it's an emergency."

"Okay, will do."

"Holy shit," Rita said, her eyes wide, her brain trying to wrap around the information she had just learned. If Alisha Telford had hooked up with both other detectives, they might be dealing with a black widow. One with a taste for cops. Revenge.

She picked up her cell phone and called Quinn's number. "I think I'm getting a picture here," she said when he answered. "Franklin call you?"

"Yeah, he did," Quinn said, his exhaustion and stress communicating itself through the airwaves.

"Alisha Telford was married to a cop in San Francisco. He died of natural causes. Perhaps she was married to two other dead cops, cause of death unknown. She comes to SB and hooks up with another cop, Joe Malone, who is now dead. She's a black widow, Quinn!"

"Why all the other murders, though? Why the unrelated ones?"

"I don't know yet, but we know we have two killers. Maybe the only ones really connected to Alisha are the ones up here, and the cops. Her motives could be twofold—revenge and money. Mary Telford was in Santa Barbara not long ago. Did she really go to see Alisha and Tammy? Or did she know something about Alisha, something she was using to blackmail her."

"This gets more and more complicated every minute," Quinn said.

"Oh my God," Rita said, standing up suddenly. She looked over to see Dave standing in the doorway, watching her with concern. She must have raised her voice without realizing it. "Check the logs at the police station, Quinn. Have someone check them now. Maybe Mary Telford didn't come to see Alisha at all. Maybe she came down to blackmail her, and when she didn't succeed, she went to the cops.

"We need to find out if Joe Penny met with Mary Telford."

CHAPTER SIXTY-EIGHT

A wicked thunderstorm rolled into Southern California, causing waves to beat mercilessly against the surf and rain to pound on rooftops, as if tapping out an SOS message.

"There's really nothing here," Lexi said to Quinn as they sent the last of the uniforms and FBI agents back to the SBPD offices. Franklin was still researching the two cops who were listed on the paper, and also checking Penny's department logs, which should tell them whether or not he met with Mary Telford. If he did, that would also go a long way in explaining why he was killed.

"We're missing something. I'm going to go through her desk again."

"Quinn, you've already been through it four times."

He sighed deeply, and sat down in a burgundy rocker. They were in the office of Tammy Rowe's home.

"It's like a real person didn't even live here. She's like a figment of our imagination. Same with her office. And who tossed it? And why?"

"Her real life is somewhere else. We just have to find it."

"We need to search property records, see if she owns land or property anywhere else." Quinn stood up abruptly. "Let's go back to the office. Our answers aren't here."

They left the house under guard by two uniforms, and drove back to the office, both quiet and thinking.

When they entered the detective's squad room, Franklin

walked rapidly toward them, waving a sheet of paper.

"The day after Mary Telford showed up at the WAV meeting, a Mary Smith met with John Penny. My bet is that's Mary Telford."

"So Penny had his sights on Alisha, and stupidly went and let her know, without taking backup. How could he be so—"

"Stupid?" Lexi finished his sentence.

"Yeah, stupid."

"Penny was tired of being on the bottom rung," Franklin surmised. "Maybe he wanted the spotlight. Maybe he figured, she's just a small woman, he could handle her."

"And Penny let the information leak to Christy Frazier. After Penny died, maybe she put the pressure on Alisha, and ended up dead. Maybe she would have told me if I hadn't chased her off," Quinn said bitterly, cursing himself.

"You can't be everywhere and know everything," Lexi said, her arms crossed as she leaned back against a desk. "Penny made a mistake, and so did she. They miscalculated exactly what was going on here."

"What exactly is going on here? We still don't even know," Quinn reminded her. "Any more news on the other two cops?" he asked, turning to Franklin.

"So far, I've confirmed both died of what appeared to be a heart attack. Neither one was married, though. So the trail drops there."

"Maybe," Lexi said. "Maybe, unless she couldn't get them to marry her."

"Let's see if we can get the Sacramento and San Jose forces to give us a hand here. Have them talk to anyone who knew the two cops. See if there is a connection, see if she dated either one, or if we can find any records of her living there."

"Yeah, right, here I go. Mr. Data." Franklin saluted them and walked away.

Quinn looked up to see Lieutenant Bricker waving at him from the doorway of his office.

He left Lexi at Joe's old desk and sat down in the loo's office.

"Joe's funeral is tomorrow. His ex-wife and son and daughter are arriving today. They are the only family he has left. With Kelsey missing, and Joe's death, I think you need to take some time. You have plenty of sick leave and vacation accrued. You're just too close to this, Anderson."

"I'm not pulling off this, Loo. Please don't try to make me."

"Come on, Anderson, you've taken enough hits. You're one of my best. I don't want to lose you, but this is too personal."

"I'm fine," Quinn said tersely, feeling the tightening in his scalp and the scrape of his teeth as they met, grinding harshly.

Lieutenant Bricker shook his head and sat back in his chair, arms behind his head. "I'm telling you you're too close to this. You know the dangers of that."

Quinn fought for control, his stomach roiling and his heart pounding. He had to appear together or the loo would force him off the case.

"I'm fine. I'll let you know if I feel like I'm going to crack, okay?"

The lieutenant stared at him for a minute, then shook his head. "One misstep and you're off the case. I shouldn't be doing this."

Quinn sprang to his feet. "Thanks, Loo. You won't regret it."

"I better not," Bricker grumbled, and waved Quinn out of his office. "The funeral's at nine at the Leavitt Mortuary."

"I'll be there."

"I know."

Exhausted, Quinn and Lexi called it a night. She retired to her motel, and Quinn went home to his empty house.

Shades of Kelsey and Tia were everywhere, and they

underscored his fear and the fact that Kelsey was missing.

He'd called his mother and inquired after Tia, even speaking to her for a minute.

"It's so fun here, Quinn. Can we move here?"

"Well, I don't know, Punkin. We'll have to see."

"Okay, gotta go. We're watching movies again."

Tia sounded healthy and happy, a typical pre-teen. He couldn't tell her that her mother was missing. The knowledge would destroy her. What if something happened to Kelsey? What were the odds of him being appointed her guardian? What about her no-good deadbeat dad, who hadn't been seen or heard from in years?

"Stop thinking that way," he admonished himself, trying to shake off his black thoughts. The problem was, he knew the odds. He was all too familiar with the statistics about abductions. Was Kelsey already dead?

He moaned and stood up from the kitchen table, where he had been trying to force himself to eat a hamburger and fries from the local Jack in the Box. The food was cold and greasy, and he had no appetite.

He walked over to the file he'd brought home, and took it out to study it. Inside was Joe Malone's autopsy report. Quinn sat back down at the table and pushed the food away.

Cause of death appeared to be a massive coronary. Could Alisha have killed him? What drugs would make a death appear to be a heart attack? Would they show up in the standard tests the medical examiner ran?

Alisha was a registered nurse. She had access to drugs at the hospital. And yet she'd been surprised by Joe at the hospital. Or had she?

Quinn stood and walked out of the kitchen, entering the den where the computer was. He booted it up and sat down, logging on to the Internet and doing a Google search for drugs.

Using several different varieties of words, he stopped when he saw a familiar one: digoxin, or digitalis. There were hundreds of known cases of people dying from a digoxin overdose: some accidental, but most of them murder.

He raced back to the kitchen and grabbed Joe Malone's autopsy report, returning to the computer to compare the two.

The report noted Joe had elevated levels of digoxin in his system.

Quinn picked up the phone and dialed dispatch, asking them to find the medical examiner's home phone number.

He explained his concerns to Dr. Sloane, who had arrived back home from his Aspen vacation early, due to the crimes in Santa Barbara. Quinn knew the doctor wouldn't be happy.

Sloane sounded irritated and hurried when he answered.

"Look, Doc, it's Detective Anderson. Sorry to bother you at home. I've got some questions, though. You noted in Joe Malone's autopsy that he had elevated levels of digoxin in his body. Could that have killed him?"

"Well, technically, yes," Dr. Sloane said. "But Mr. Malone was a heart patient in the throes of a massive MI, Detective Anderson. They believed him to be in massive cardiac arrest, which could explain the digoxin. They gave it to him in the ER. It's in his chart."

"Could someone have been giving him digoxin on a regular basis? Enough so the little bit they gave him in the ER pushed him past the brink?"

"Possible, but not likely. The levels were elevated, but only slightly above normal."

"But it could have killed him?"

"Yes, technically, it could have killed him."

Quinn thanked the doctor and hung up. He studied the autopsy report carefully. First thing tomorrow morning, before

Joe's funeral, he would be making a call to the SFPD, to have Boudreaux's autopsy report sent to him.

Chapter Sixty-Nine

Rita closed her eyes on Dave Sparks' couch, just for a minute, and awoke several hours later with a pounding headache. She sat up and looked around. The room was dark. What had awakened her?

Dave had covered her with a blanket while she slept, and now it fell to the floor. She stood and picked up the blanket, tossing it on the couch, and then headed for the bathroom to relieve herself, wondering if Dave had gone to bed.

She pushed open the door to the bathroom to find it brightly lit with candles, the wax pooling around the stems. On the edge of the tub sat a bottle of wine and two glasses. The tub contained a few remaining bubbles, floating in random groups across the water, and one naked sheriff, who had fallen fast asleep with his head resting on the back of the tub. His loud snoring must have been what woke her up.

She giggled quietly, covering her mouth with her hand. The few remaining bubbles barely covered him, and she dipped a hand in the water to find it lukewarm. She looked down at his body, his firm chest, his muscled arms, and then lower, and she smiled.

Rita stood for a minute, her heart beating rapidly, all her earlier anger at him dissipating. She saw a container of Calgon on the counter, and knew he had made a special trip to the bath supplies aisle when they had stopped to grab some food to prepare for dinner.

She had been standoffish all evening, even after he made her a steak and salad, catering to her every whim.

On impulse, she stripped off her pants and shirt, removed her underwear and bra, and stepped into the tub, trying to avoid stepping on Dave.

As she sat down, her hand landed on a bar of soap that had apparently fallen into the tub and she pitched forward abruptly, landing on Dave's chest, causing him to open his eyes abruptly and gasp for air, letting out a loud "oomph."

She collapsed on his chest in giggles, unable to stop laughing.

"Well, hello. Guess you decided to join me, huh?"

"I didn't mean to land on you," she said, when she finally got control of her laughter. "This water is not very warm."

"I've been waiting a while. Guess I fell asleep."

He turned her around and settled her against his chest, and she reached up and turned on the hot water, swirling it around with her legs to spread it through the rest of the tub. Leaning against him, she could feel his burgeoning arousal, and she smiled.

"Good thing you have a big tub," she said, watching the water pour from the tap and hit the surface, creating more bubbles.

He didn't speak, instead grabbing the soap and washing her arms gently. He pushed her forward and scrubbed her back, massaging as he soaped her. He splashed the water on her back, and feeling the warmth, she turned the hot water off. Steam rose from the tub and smoked up the mirrors, and the candles made the whole scene incredibly romantic.

Dave pulled her back onto his chest, and began to wash her again, moving his hands and the soap around her breasts gently, in circles.

Rita sighed deeply, half-aroused and half-relaxed.

His hands moved slowly downward and her relaxation disappeared. "Oh, a girl could get used to this."

"That's what I intend," he replied.

Chapter Seventy

Kelsey stared at the ceiling of her prison, lying on the fluffy bedspread surrounded by stuffed animals. She had changed out of the baby-doll pajamas and back into her clothes after Tammy decided the slumber party was a bust and went to bed, locking Kelsey in.

After an hour had passed, she got up from the bed and quietly made her way to the window, pulling aside the frilly pink drapes to see that the window had been boarded over from the outside.

"Damn!" Tammy had obviously planned on a visitor, but was Kelsey the person the room had been set up for?

Kelsey began to pace in the small space on the side of the bed that wasn't taken up by childish toys or games. There was no way out of here that she could see. The only option would be to try to surprise Tammy when the woman entered the room next. That would mean being on the alert all night.

She looked around for a weapon, and picked up a heavy pink ceramic elephant bank. It was filled with money, she could tell, and if wielded correctly would do some damage.

Kelsey took up a post by the door, moving the chair from the vanity over to the side of it. Her only hope was to act quickly when Tammy opened the door. Since it was locked, that should give her the moment or two she needed to knock Tammy out, or at least stun her. She felt anger rise in her stomach and chest, percolating like hot coffee, ready to boil over. She waited.

"This better work. By God, it better work."

Chapter Seventy-One

Quinn opened his eyes in the empty bedroom, dawn peeking in at the windowsill letting stray beams of light filter through, but there were still plenty of shadows. It was still early morning.

His eyes were gritty and sore, and he knew he hadn't slept much. The particulars of this case, and wondering where Kelsey was, had kept the cogs of his brain operating well into the wee hours of the morning.

He remembered the first morning he and Kelsey had awakened together in this bed early then, too. They'd spent the night making love, and slept little.

"Shit!"

He rose from the bed and walked into the bathroom, turning on the shower and jumping inside. He had to find Kelsey today. Every day she was missing, the chance she would be found alive lessened.

The shower, hot and stinging, rained reminders of fear and desperation down his back, and he spent a long time under the spray, searching for answers to questions about life, career, and the future. What was he supposed to do? Where was Kelsey? Why did this happen.

Why didn't I see this coming? I'm a cop for God's sake. I should have seen the signs.

Joe's funeral was at nine a.m., and Quinn didn't feel prepared to see the casket, to confront death or mortality—not today.

He finally turned off the shower and stepped out, drying off with a towel. He heard the phone ring and glanced at the alarm clock as he picked up the phone—6:30 a.m.

"Anderson."

"Hello, Detective, hope it's not too early," Lexi said. "I'm still on East Coast time."

"I was up."

"Good. Well, we've done a search for property in Tammy Rowe's name, as well as Alisha Telford's, and nothing came up on either one. I'm sorry."

"It was a long shot," Quinn said, defeat filling his lungs like caustic acid.

"You'll be in after the funeral?" she asked him.

"Yes. As soon as I can get through. Follow through with the autopsy report on Boudreaux, please, and keep on Franklin to touch base with San Jose and Sacramento and see if anything turned up on Alisha Telford in those places."

"Will do," Lexi said.

After dressing, Quinn tried to force himself to eat a piece of toast, but it tasted like cardboard in his mouth and stuck in his throat. He choked about half of it down, washing it out of his throat with burning coffee, and then he gathered up the things he would need for the day.

He stood staring at himself in the full-length mirror hanging on the back of the bedroom door. He wore his dress blues and hat, the police uniform he rarely donned working as a detective. Only out of respect for a fallen officer did he wear them now.

Quinn wondered about John Penny and his funeral. When would it be? Would he have the same turnout as Joe Malone, a well-liked and respected long-time officer on the Santa Barbara police force?

He looked older in the mirror, changed, his dark hair showing more and more premature gray. His eyes looked shadowed, almost furtive, and his face was stern, somber, unyielding. It didn't show how he felt inside, which was something similar to a scrambled egg.

He'd lost a career partner when Joe Malone had died. Now his life partner, Kelsey, was missing, too. The job was wearing on him, eroding his buoyancy, dismantling his ability to bounce back.

Would he ever see Kelsey alive again? Did Alisha Telford kill Joe Malone? Was she responsible for all this?

His anger toward her rose, and he fought it back, like bitter bile, not wanting to let it overtake him and hinder his perception and ability to do the job quickly and fairly.

He would get Alisha Telford, but he'd do it the right way. Then maybe it would be time to settle down and concentrate on writing. He had some time off coming, and a great plot idea for a crime novel. Maybe he and Kelsey could buy a little place in the mountains of Colorado and . . .

If he ever saw Kelsey again.

He forced himself to stop his train of thought, and he glanced at his watch. It was eight a.m., time to leave for the funeral.

Please, let this be the only funeral I have to attend in the near future, aside from that of John Penny.

He would go to Penny's funeral, out of respect for the job, and what working as a police officer did to all of them—sometimes sucking the life right out of them. He might not have liked John Penny, or thought much of his police skills, but he was still part of the brotherhood, a fellow officer.

Quinn walked out of the house into bright sunlight. It was a glorious October day, no sign of rain or fog, as was so common on a coastal fall morning—a proper send-off for Joe Malone.

CHAPTER SEVENTY-TWO

Rita rose early, leaving Dave Sparks sleeping, and she wrapped the top blanket from the bed firmly around her and made her way to the kitchen to make coffee.

The sun already reached through the tall trees in Joe's backyard, and rays of sunlight darted into the green grass, a light breeze rippling it softly. She saw a deer nibbling on the edge of the lawn. It somehow sensed her presence, looking up abruptly and meeting her eyes, holding a solemn stare.

The moment became a contest—who would look away or move first. She held perfectly still and admired the deer's grayish coat and big brown eyes, the velvety-looking fur on its back, and white tail on its rump. It was a young buck, she could see, the beginnings of antlers growing out at the top of its head.

Life in the country; it seemed so peaceful. At least until Alisha Telford returned to this sleepy town.

The deer finally looked away and bounded off into the field, disappearing in a grove of trees. He stopped once, and turned to look at her again, making eye contact for a brief moment, almost curious, and then was gone.

Rita started as cold hands snaked into her blanket and grasped her breasts. She'd been so intent on watching the deer she hadn't heard Dave come up behind her.

"Morning," he mumbled into her ear, and she reached a hand back and rubbed it over his rough, stubbly chin. She arched into him and sighed contentedly.

"It seems so peaceful here," she said softly, still staring out the window. "I just watched a deer feeding in your back yard."

"Oh, yeah, that's my buddy. He comes here to hide out when the poachers are in the woods. He knows I don't hunt."

"Oh yeah, and how does he know that?"

"We have an understanding. I don't shoot living things unless they are shooting at me first."

"Sounds reasonable."

"I thought so."

Rita stopped for a minute as the sun grew brighter, and she remembered Quinn had told her today was Joe's funeral. He'd told her to stay there, that she was needed where she was until the two murderous women were caught. But she still felt guilty, missing the funeral of a fellow officer.

"I could use some help here, you know," Dave said, turning her around to face him.

"Oh, you don't need any help," she said with a purr.

"No, I mean it. I am going to need help here, in Redville and Chapel Grace. One of my deputies is dead. I need to hire a new one."

She stared at him, her mouth open, as his implication hit her head on.

"You mean me?"

"The pay isn't as good as it is in Santa Barbara, obviously, and it's not nearly as exciting, but as a bonus you can have me."

"You want me to come and work here?"

"Uh, yeah, that's what I said."

"Good God, I don't know, Dave. I mean . . ."

"It was just a thought," he said, dropping her arms and pulling away from her. "I know I don't have much excitement to offer."

"Whoa, slow down, cowboy. You just shocked me. That's all,"

Rita said, pulling him back to her. "I've never even considered leaving Santa Barbara or the force there."

"Well, think about it," Dave said roughly, his feelings obviously still hurt by her shock at his suggestion. "We better get ready for the day."

He turned and walked away from her, and she wrapped the blanket around her tightly. Leave the force and move to Northern California? Become a deputy in a Mayberry-like town with local characters? Why would she ever want to do that?

She could think of only one reason: Sheriff Dave Sparks.

"This is turning out to be a hell of a week," she whispered to herself.

Chapter Seventy-Three

Joe Malone's funeral was short and somber. His ex-wife and two teenaged children cried quietly by the graveside, surrounded by a sea of blue. Quinn stood next to Mary Malone, whom he'd spoken with briefly before the funeral. Joe's son fought back tears, rubbing at his eyes fiercely, his desire to be seen as a man at war with his desire to mourn the loss of his father. Joe's daughter was a beautiful teenage girl, with dark blue eyes and cupid-bow lips, and tears flowed down her cheeks freely, as the department chaplain said grace over the flag-draped coffin.

Quinn felt the sting of tears in his eyes as a bugler played the mournful "Taps."

He was relieved to leave the cemetery, after briefly consoling the children of Joe Malone, and return to the office. As he entered the building and walked into the detective's squad room, he spied Lexi at Joe's desk. No one looked right there. No one. It was Joe's desk.

He shook himself and walked forward, moving to his desk and nodding hello to the FBI agent.

"You look very sharp," Lexi said, a brief smile brightening her face, before it disappeared. The lines near her eyes and lips were visible, and she, too, looked older today, Quinn realized. The pressure of the case, the grisly murders, the unknown components were starting to weigh on all of them.

She got right down to business, sliding a copy of Charles Boudreaux's autopsy report across the desk to him.

As Quinn picked it up, he heard a murmuring disturbance travel through the room, a shift in the normal, caustic, hard-edged electricity that seemed to crackle just above them all the time.

Chief Eldon Hilliard, in one of his rare visits to the detective squad, glad-handed his way into the room, acknowledging people with a handshake or a mock salute, and a jovial grin.

His large, protruding stomach strained at the buttons of his uniform, which was rarely worn, as if to announce the arrival of a very important person.

Hilliard slowly made his way across the room to the bank of desks where Quinn, Lexi, and Franklin were.

"You must be Agent Richards," he boomed, eyeing Lexi with a wink and a large grin. He stuck a plump hand out to vigorously shake her more delicate one.

"You getting along here okay? These boys treating you right? You comfortable?"

"Yes, Chief Hilliard, I'm fine. Everything is going very well."

"Good, good. Well you let me know if you need anything. Anything at all."

He turned to Quinn and straightened out his broad smile, replacing it with a solemn, mournful one.

"Sad day today. Very sad. Lost one of our best detectives." Hilliard shook his head as if pondering the mysteries of life. "Two in one week. Unbelievable."

"Yes, sir," Quinn answered.

"We need to sit down, Detective. I need your advice. We are now two men short in the squad. We need to think about replacing them, not that they can ever be replaced, mind you."

Quinn's face hardened, and he tried not to glare at the man. "Carson Fletcher," he said grimly.

"Fletcher?"

"Put Fletcher back where he belongs. He's a good detective.

We need him here, not serving warrants."

"Well, I'll certainly take that under advisement," Chief Hilliard said, his tone a little less friendly than before.

"Put him with me. I'll vouch for him."

"We'll talk Monday," the chief said, nodding his head as though he agreed. "Come see me in my office. I want you to keep me posted on the M&M murders, please, Detective."

"Yes, Chief."

The large man left the office the same way he had entered, and Quinn shook his head.

Quinn picked Boudreaux's autopsy report up off the desk, and read, eyes skimming as he looked for drug readings. He found what he looked for halfway down the page. "Elevated levels of digoxin, otherwise known as digitalis."

"It's there. She's a black widow. I'd bet my life on it." He explained his theory about the digoxin to Lexi, and she took the autopsy report back and examined it, then asked for Joe Malone's report, and studied it too.

"I think you're right. But we have no proof."

Franklin walked into the office carrying coffee in a Styrofoam cup. He, too, was dressed in his blues, and he, too, looked much older today than he had the day before. Even the ever-present grin on his face was missing, and he was solemn, dark-eyed, and mournful.

"I left three messages with San Jose, yesterday," he said. "Sacramento called back last night, said they turned up nothing. Records search shows nothing. If she was there, it was under an assumed name."

"How long has Tammy Rowe been in Santa Barbara?" Lexi asked.

Quinn opened the folder and rummaged through papers until he came up with the information they had obtained from Santa Barbara Community Hospital.

"She's been with the hospital three years." Quinn picked up another piece of paper from the folder. "Alisha, same length of time."

"So, maybe we're not looking for just Alisha in San Jose and Sacramento. Maybe we're looking for both of them. Let's assume they've been together ever since they left Chapel Grace. Maybe they took turns picking up lonely police officers, and luring them into marriage, only to kill them off."

"Yeah, but in Sacramento and San Jose, there was no marriage."

"Okay, but perhaps the officers found them out, or got cold feet. So, they killed them anyway."

"We need autopsy reports on both officers," Quinn said, turning to Franklin. "And one more thing we need. Get me Alisha Telford and Tammy Rowe's bank account information. Alisha received the widow's benefits from Boudreaux. Where's the money? She had a nice apartment, but not showy. Tammy's house, on the other hand, is worth a bundle. Were they putting it into real estate? Hiding it? We need those bank records."

Franklin nodded and sat down at his phone to make some calls.

The thought hit Quinn so suddenly it almost knocked him off his feet.

"Good God," he said, turning to Lexi. "We need to search for property in the name of Charles Boudreaux. Alisha is his widow. It would have gone to her."

Chapter Seventy-Four

Kelsey started from a sound slumber to realize there was a noise in the keyhole. Cursing herself for falling asleep on guard, she swiftly pushed the ceramic elephant under the bed and jumped up on top of the covers, feigning sleep as Tammy Rowe pushed into the bedroom carrying a breakfast tray.

"Here you go. Wake up, sleepyhead," she called out cheerily, and Kelsey pretended to start and sat up slowly, rubbing at her eyes.

Tammy frowned, and set the tray down on the bed, as she saw Kelsey had changed back into her own clothes, and shook her head. She herself was dressed in silk pajamas that were casual and elegant, rather than the juvenile baby-doll gown she had been wearing when she left Kelsey for the night, locking her into the room.

"Why are you sleeping in your clothes? I told you to wear that," Tammy said, anger causing her voice to rise, as she pointed to the discarded gown on the floor near the closet.

"I . . . I . . . it was itchy. I had to take it off, because I was breaking out in a rash. I must be allergic to the material."

"Allergic? Humph," Tammy said. Her face was elegantly made-up, as usual, and her hair was immaculate, combed, hanging down long at her back.

"Well, let's have breakfast. You're going to get mighty tired of wearing the same thing, day in and day out. Soon enough you'll realize you have to change."

Day in and day out? How long was Tammy planning on keeping her here? Did that mean she wasn't planning to kill her?

Kelsey hesitated for a minute, then scooted toward the food on the tray. Her stomach had been rumbling, since the last food she ate had been on the plane the day before.

She was terribly hungry, but the food in front of her didn't look appetizing at all—burnt toast, runny eggs, and a half a grapefruit.

"Go ahead, eat it. I'm not much of a cook, and I already ate. But I'll keep you company."

Kelsey eyed the food suspiciously. Would it be poisoned?

"Don't worry," Tammy said, with a laugh. "It's safe. I'm not trying to kill you off. I'd be lonely while I'm waiting."

"Waiting?"

"Never mind that. Eat up."

With Tammy watching her, and keeping in mind her captor's mental status, Kelsey picked up a piece of toast and took a bite. Hard to poison toast, she thought. She hoped.

Kelsey watched in the vanity mirror as Tammy Rowe back-combed her hair, and curled it with a curling iron. She was wearing the baby-doll pajamas again, as Tammy had told her to change, pulling out the gun for emphasis.

She helplessly allowed Rowe's ministrations, watching for a chance to snatch the gun, which had been tightly belted in the sash of the robe Rowe had donned over her own pink-and-blue gown. The elegant-woman façade Tammy Rowe wore for the world seemed to disappear when she entered this room.

Now, they were preparing to play Miss America, a fake tiara sitting on the vanity, just waiting to be placed on Kelsey's head, the final touch. Her face was heavily painted, as was Tammy's.

At least it's not the swimsuit competition.

"Tammy?"

"Yes?" The woman hummed as she worked around Kelsey's head.

"Why did you kill those men?"

Tammy stopped for a moment, hesitant, her arms twitching in mid-air, holding a comb, and then she continued on, as though Kelsey never said a word. The humming began again.

"My mother," she said with a haughty air, "always said there are some things you just don't talk about in polite company."

Kelsey supposed this was the fantasy mother again, because from what she had learned of Tammy and Alisha's horrible childhood, their real mother would doubtless not have worried in the least about polite company.

She stared forward at her heavily made-up and artificial visage in the mirror, and thought back to her own tortured childhood. She, too, had been sexually abused by her father. The experience had not, however, turned her into a vicious killer. And what was Alisha's role in this?

She tried again.

"Does Alisha know about the murders? Does she know?"

Frustrated, Tammy pulled too hard at a stray piece of Kelsey's hair as she tried to smooth it into the mix. She threw the comb down on the table, and crossed her arms.

"Does Alisha know? No shit, Alisha knows. Alisha knows everything."

Chapter Seventy-Five

Franklin rushed to Quinn from across the room, waving a piece of paper. "I finally heard back from San Jose. An Alisha Boudreaux was dating Leon Forbes before his unfortunate demise. Cause of death is listed as heart attack. There was no autopsy, because he had been a heart patient for years."

"Did you run a search for Alisha Boudreaux?" Quinn asked.

"Yeah, and got nothing. But I talked to this guy's ex-partner, and he told me that Boudreaux, whom he described as a knockout with blond hair and blue eyes, was putting the press on Forbes to marry her. One day he just broke up with her. Never talked about it."

"So, she killed him anyway. She may be a black widow, but I have a feeling she has a very specific victim in mind. She's seeking revenge on cops. She killed Higgins for whatever he did, whether it was turning his head or what. She's been taking out that revenge ever since."

"Makes sense," Lexi said from across the desks, where she sat in Joe Malone's old place. She stood up and walked around to them. "The thing here is, I think we've been looking at Tammy as the lead here, the one running the show. She's a psychologist, right?"

Quinn dug Rowe's employment records out of the growing stack of papers on his desk, and read it carefully. "Says she graduated from the University of California, Irvine, with a doctoral degree. I'm going to call them and check. See if she really did attend college there."

He rummaged in the pile and pulled out Alisha's records, which also had her attending UC Irvine and graduating with a bachelor's degree in registered nursing.

He found the number and made the call, tapping his pencil on the desk as he was transferred several different times.

"Records," chirped a high-pitched female voice. "This is Amy."

"Amy, this is Detective Quinn Anderson, Santa Barbara Police Department." He explained to her what he needed, and she put him on hold while she checked with a supervisor.

"Okay, Detective, I can confirm for you a Tamara Rowe did attend college here, but only for one semester. She certainly didn't graduate, even with a bachelor's degree. Now, Alisha Telford, we have no record of her at all."

Quinn went with a hunch.

"Amy, can you check under another name? Alisha Boudreaux. B-o-u-d-r-e-a-u-x."

"Sure, just one minute, Detective."

After a moment, her cheerful voice came back on the line. "Yes, she did attend here for the four years, and also graduated. Summa cum laude, as a matter of fact. Top ten in her psychology class."

"Psychology?"

"Yes, it looks like she was a double major. Psychology and nursing."

He thanked her for her help and hung up the phone, shaking his head as Franklin and Lexi Richards watched. "Tammy Rowe never graduated. She's not a doctor. Doesn't even have a college degree. How did she pull this off? Alisha, on the other hand, did graduate, and at the top of her class. Two degrees, actually—nursing and psychology."

Lexi clucked her tongue as she considered what they had just learned.

"This changes things, Quinn. You realize that, don't you?"

"Oh yeah,, and somebody at the hospital is going to have a lot of explaining to do."

A records clerk walked quickly into the room and crossed to Quinn, handing him a piece of paper. "Found what you were looking for, Detective. You said to rush it. Charles Boudreaux has a small place out in the Santa Ynez Valley, about forty-five minutes from here."

Quinn grabbed the paper from the man, and Lexi and Franklin were on his heels as they left the building. He called in their information to dispatch, and hit the lights and sirens. The dispatcher called for backup and informed them that the Santa Barbara County Sheriff's Office was in the area and would secure the premises.

"Do not go in. Repeat, do not enter the premises. Suspect or suspects should be considered armed and dangerous."

Chapter Seventy-Six

Alisha Telford had been driving for hours, and her neck and back crackled with stiffness. Tussling with the female detective at Sheriff Higgins' house hadn't helped any, and she touched a sore spot on her cheekbone.

Things were not going well. Not well at all.

No one was supposed to know she was in Chapel Grace. How did they figure it out?

Now that she'd been seen there, she'd have to flee the country. Mexico had never appealed to her before, but it was close. She just had to get her money, tie up the loose ends, and head out.

Tammy was a liability now. Alisha had always known her mentally unbalanced sibling would have to be silenced at some point, but she'd hoped to avoid the inevitable as long as possible.

The finger of justice would have to point squarely at Tammy, in order for Alisha to come out clean.

Just before leaving Santa Barbara to tie up the loose ends in Chapel Grace, she'd given Tammy a note from their father, one he supposedly had written years before, where he called Tammy a stupid little boy. Alisha knew that would enrage her. After she destroyed the office, Alisha planted the scalpel used on John Penny.

Now, it was all for nothing. All her planning, down the drain.

Too late. You've been caught. Stupid! Just like they always said.

"I'm not stupid," she yelled, pounding her hand on the steering wheel. "I have more money than my stupid father made in his lifetime. I can live in the lap of luxury. He lived in squalor."

She just had to think; that was all. She just needed to put the pieces together.

Tammy hadn't answered her calls, either at her home or the office. Now Alisha was worried.

Where was she?

The money and the evidence was all safely tucked away in Santa Ynez. She just had to get there. Just twenty more miles to go.

Freedom was so close she could taste it.

Chapter Seventy-Seven

Quinn reached Santa Ynez in record time, and he radioed for directions to the property. The nearer they came, the more tense he grew, his muscles aching, his neck taut with frustration.

Green vineyards and long, snaking rows of grapes rolled past them as they traveled, contrasting sharply with the blue sky and white, fluffy clouds.

The car was silent, even Franklin closemouthed with the magnitude of the situation. Quinn reached the roadblock set up by the Santa Barbara Police Department, and the deputy waved him over, his hand placed on the gun strapped to his side.

Quinn had turned the lights off as they hit Santa Ynez, so the deputy hadn't seen them.

Quinn jumped out and flashed his badge, and said, "Detective Anderson, SBPD."

The deputy nodded his head and pointed out the property.

"It's about half a mile up that road. Neighbors say the owner is only here on occasional weekends, but Mrs. McAfree, who lives over there," he waved a hand to indicate a house on the other side of the road about half a mile away, "well, she's a widow. Guess she doesn't have much to do. She said a blue Volvo pulled in here yesterday. Hasn't seen anything since then."

"Volvo. Tammy Rowe."

Lexi and Franklin had exited the car and stood behind Quinn, listening to the conversation.

"Yeah, oddly enough, she said it wasn't the owner's car. She said she's seen the pretty blonde who lives here before, and she drives a small purple car."

"Purple?"

"That's what she said."

"We believe the one suspect, Alisha Telford, is traveling in a burgundy sedan of some sort. Small, four-door car, foreign model."

"You know how it is. One person's burgundy is another person's purple."

Quinn nodded. It could well be the car they were looking for.

"What's the coverage?"

"We've got three men down the road a piece, covering anyone trying to get in. SWAT is on the way, with a sharpshooter. They'll have to come in from behind on foot, because there isn't a road back there."

Two more sheriff's vehicles, lights flashing, pulled up as they were talking, and the deputy sheriffs exited their cars and joined the other officers. Behind them, a royal blue Ford pulled up, and a man in a suit got out and slowly walked up to the gathering group.

"Chief Hilliard," Quinn said, acknowledging the official head of the Santa Barbara Police Department with a nod.

"Anderson, Franklin. Agent Richards."

The chief rarely left his office, and his presence made Quinn even more uneasy than he already was.

"Serious situation we have here. Thanks for working with us, deputies."

The three deputies nodded their heads and looked from Quinn to Hilliard, unsure who was giving the orders.

Not waiting to find out if the chief was here to pull rank, and sure it was a political maneuver designed to cement his spot as the police chief, Quinn began mapping out a plan, one they would implement when the SWAT team arrived.

A large silver cargo truck arrived shortly after that, and the men in green piled out, the leader coming forward to get orders. Lieutenant Ron Shepard was a short, bulky man with an inscrutable face and large ears. The SWAT team stood as a group, grimly apart from the other officers, waiting for their assignments.

Quinn explained the terrain, as far as they knew it, and how the men would have to travel through thick trees and brambles behind the property.

The SWAT lieutenant listened closely, asked a few terse questions and then walked back to his men. After a brief conversation, the highly trained men set off to surround the house. Several more officers arrived, and soon the entire road swarmed with cars and flashing lights.

Because the house could not be seen from the road, Quinn hoped the spectacle taking place in the remote Santa Ynez canyon would not be sensed by Tammy Rowe. And Alisha Telford, he reminded himself, if she was there.

"Have you tried to establish communication with the occupants?" Chief Hilliard asked, looking at Quinn for an answer.

"No, we don't want to tip them off."

"There isn't a phone line in the house anyway," the deputy who had been first on the scene told them. "I checked with our office when I pulled up."

The SWAT team leader watched the last of his men disappear, and then walked back to the group. "We'll get somebody close, and try to get a visual into the house, without alerting the occupants we're there. If we can get a visual, we'll have a better idea of what we're dealing with. I don't think we want to storm in blind."

"A lot of people have died already," Quinn answered. "One or both of the murderers have someone in there now, and I don't want her hurt."

Ron Shepard's stony gaze told him he'd already been briefed on who they believed was inside the house with Tammy Rowe and possibly Alisha Telford.

"We'll do our best," he said, and walked away.

After a tense twenty minutes, the lieutenant returned to the small group watching the road that led to the house, and reported he had men close to the house, but they could not see inside.

"The windows are, for the most part, boarded over. The front window is heavily draped. We can't see any signs of life. I don't see we have any choice but to force entry."

Quinn sighed heavily, and looked skyward, before fixing his gaze on Ron Shepard. "I want to be there."

Chief Hilliard stepped forward and put a hand on his shoulder. "Let's allow SWAT to handle it, Detective Anderson.

Quinn shrugged the hand off his shoulder, and walked back to his vehicle, followed by Lexi. He could see several more cars pulling up that looked like the sedans favored by the FBI. They had plenty of reinforcements, but no way to gauge who was in the house, and how heavily armed they were.

"You pissed your chief off," Lexi said quietly, as she watched Quinn strip off his jacket and throw it into the back seat. He walked around to the trunk of the car and unlocked it, opening it up and pulling out a Kevlar vest.

"I'm going in," he said after he finished putting on the body armor. "I don't care what anyone says."

Franklin talked to an agitated Chief Hilliard, who gestured wildly with his arms and pointed his finger at the detective in a menacing, schoolteacher manner.

"I'll see if I can calm him down," Lexi said, a twinkle in her eye.

She walked over to Hilliard and said a few words. He stopped yelling at Franklin and turned to her in bewilderment.

Quinn wondered what she had said, but didn't have time to pursue it now. He walked back to the spot where the SWAT team leader stood, and asked, "You have a problem with me going in?"

"No," Ron Shephard replied, examining his weapon and not looking at Quinn. "Not as long as you aren't one of those pretty-boy, stupid-idiot cops."

"Never been accused of that," Quinn replied.

"Let's go."

Quinn followed Ron Shephard through the thick bramble on the west side of the Boudreaux property line. The going was slow, and stray grapevines overran the rich, fertile earth, evidently from an abandoned vineyard.

Perhaps Charles Boudreaux had dreamed of retiring from the force and becoming a premier vintner. God knows he wouldn't be the first to look for an out from the hard-line, tumultuous world of law enforcement.

Shephard stopped abruptly, pointed to his left, and Quinn saw the small, immaculate house. Shephard nodded at Quinn, and they began to cross toward the house, keeping to the side, where there were no windows. Quinn caught an occasional glimpse of men surrounding the property, although for the most part they stayed well hidden.

When they reached the side of the house, they stood with their backs to it, and Shephard spoke quietly into his shoulder mike. He then motioned to Quinn, and began to edge his way toward the front of the house. As they turned the corner, they saw two other officers coming in from the other side, and, ducking low in front of the curtained windows, they met on each side of the front door.

There was no screen on the oak door, and Shephard reached out a hand and checked the doorknob, moving it just a fraction.

He put his right hand up in the air, palm closed, and looked at all of them. They nodded, and he began to count to three with his fingers. As his ring finger on his right hand went up he grabbed the knob and threw open the door. They stormed into the house, other SWAT officers moving in from their camouflaged hiding places.

Swiftly, working on the art of surprise, they searched the small house, until one of the men yelled, "Got em!"

Quinn rushed to the room where the SWAT officer held two women at gunpoint.

Dressed in baby-doll pajamas and sitting in front of an Easy-Bake Oven, Quinn saw a shocked Kelsey and Tammy Rowe. Rowe had been in the act of pulling a small, round cake out of the light-bulb-operated oven, and had frozen in the act.

Quinn dashed forward and took her gun, which had been tucked into a tightly knotted sash. Kelsey jumped up and ran to him, as he handed the gun to another officer and pulled her out of the room.

"Wait, wait," she said, urgently, moving back into the doorway.

"Tammy, you need to stand up and put your hands up, okay? You need to surrender here."

The woman turned to her, dazed and confused, still holding the small, silver pan. "I don't know what to do. I don't know . . ."

"Put the pan down, Tammy, and put your hands up."

"But I—"

"Now!" Henderson moved toward her, his gun aimed directly at her. "Move. Hands in the air."

"You don't have to yell!" Tammy screamed back. "I heard you!"

Finally, she dropped the tin and stood slowly, her arms in the air, a defeated and confused look on her face.

"I don't know what to do now," she said, as they cuffed her and led her away. "I don't know what to do."

Quinn watched with puzzlement as she was escorted roughly from the house, and he turned back to Kelsey. "I don't get her reaction. It's not . . . It doesn't seem right."

"I don't think she planned any of it, Quinn," Kelsey said quietly, a tear rolling down her cheek. She was dressed in a baby-doll gown, bright pink fluffy material, and her face was covered in makeup, a faux tiara atop her blond hair, which had been curled and backcombed into a large cloud around her face.

"What do you mean? And what in the world were you doing?"

She looked down at herself and chuckled, the dark mascara starting to pool under her eyes as she helplessly shed tears. "We were playing Miss America. Then afterward, the winners had a tea party. Tammy won, of course. I was Miss Congeniality."

"Kelsey?"

"Always Miss Congeniality for me. You'd think for once I could be Miss America, but no—"

"Kelsey?"

"She didn't do it, Quinn. She's just a child, mentally ill. She was following instructions. Alisha's instructions."

"You mean she didn't kill any of those men?"

"No, I mean she never planned or did any of it without first being told what to do. The person you really want is Alisha. I can't believe it, but it's Alisha."

Chapter Seventy-Eight

Quinn allowed Kelsey to grab her own clothing and change quickly in the bathroom of the home, before he escorted her outside.

The formerly isolated property now swarmed with law enforcement officers. They searched the grounds, looking for clues, looking for bodies—looking for Alisha Telford.

Lexi walked up to Quinn and Kelsey, and put a hand on Kelsey's shoulder. "Every time I see you, you're in a bit of a pickle."

"Story of my life, I guess. I think I'm going to become a hermit. Safer that way."

"It's just a coincidence, Kelsey. You know that right?"

"Well, I don't think this is connected to what happened in Utah, if that's what you mean. But, man, how can I be so bad in picking friends? Maybe it's because I never really had any when I was young."

Lexi nodded her head sympathetically, and then began to question her methodically, taking notes as Kelsey answered.

Quinn made a call to Rita and confirmed there had been no sign of Alisha Telford. He brought her up to speed on developments.

"So I stay here until we have a read on where she might be?"

"For the time being, yeah."

"She's not here anymore, Quinn."

"Well, that's my hunch, too, but let's not take a chance."

He hung up the phone and it rang immediately, before he could place it back in his pocket.

"Anderson."

"It's Fletcher. Listen, I've been monkeying around with Alisha's name in the database all night, and I've found a burgundy Nissan Sentra, registered to one Alisha Boudreaux, but it's out of San Francisco."

"Good work, Fletcher. What's the license?"

He wrote it down as Fletcher spelled it.

"Personalized plate. VNGNCE."

"Vengeance."

"Yep, that's what I came up with. Weird, huh?"

"No, not anymore. I'll explain later. Good work, Fletch. I'm working on the chief. We need you back with the decs."

"Don't fuck with me, Anderson."

"Not fucking with you. I intend to get you back."

"You break this case, the bank is yours. Oh, speaking of that, no bank records. Can't find anything, not even a checking account for her under either name."

"Odd. Thanks for the good work. I'll get back to you."

Quinn disconnected from Fletcher and called dispatch to issue an alert on Alisha Telford/Boudreaux's vehicle.

Chapter Seventy-Nine

"Wanna ride out to the Johnson place with me?"

Sheriff Dave Sparks and Rita Jaramillo sat in Dave's office, Rita poring over the files of the M&M murders, antsy and feeling unfulfilled. It was coming down, and she knew it. Alisha Telford was no longer in Northern California. The entire thing would culminate in a huge climax and she wouldn't be there.

Rita wasn't a glory hog, but she had time invested in this case. And, honestly, it was personal. After her run-in with Telford, Rita wanted to face-off with her, see her get her comeuppance.

"Johnson place, as in the Johnson boys, county troublemakers?"

"Yep. Had another complaint they've been stealing tomatoes out of Mrs. Jefferson's garden."

"Well, we better get moving then."

"Hey, that may seem petty, but around here we take our gardening very seriously. The truth is, the Johnson boys are pretty harmless, until they get liquored up. Then it's a different story."

Rita laughed and stood up, following Sparks out of the office. Large Marge, as Rita had grown to think of her with slight affection, eyed them both and then hollered, "Don't be gone too long, Sheriff. And don't forget to check in with dispatch."

"Right, Marge," he hollered over his shoulder. "She thinks she's my mother," he said to Rita. "Mind if we stop in at the beauty parlor first?"

"The beauty parlor?"

"Yeah, I need to talk to Ramon. Won't take but a minute."

"Right."

They drove about halfway down the street, and Dave pulled up in front of Ramon's Cut and Curl.

"We could have walked," Rita said, feeling silly.

"It's on the way," he explained, and then got out, leaving her to follow him.

"Hey, Ramon, how's it hanging?" he asked as he entered the salon, the air smelling of permanent solution, caustic chemicals, and old-lady perfume.

"Now, Sheriff," said the Hispanic man standing in a station, working on an impossibly tall beehive of blue hair. He waggled a finger at the sheriff. "You shouldn't talk that way in front of my ladies. Should he, Thelma?"

The old lady under the pile of hair, tiny and shrunken, her weathered face shriveled up into prune-like texture, just giggled and waved at him coquettishly. "Go on with you, Sheriff."

"What can I do for you, Dave?" Ramon asked.

"Nancy Ellers asked me to deliver this to you. She fell and hurt her hip, so she couldn't get out and deliver it herself. It's for the drive."

Dave handed him the sack he had carried from the car, and Ramon put down his comb and hairspray, and opened the sack. "Oh, it's lovely! Look at it. The colors! It's lovely. It's going to be hard to give it away!"

"Lovely," echoed blue-hair.

"And who is your beautiful friend, by the way? No introductions, huh?" Ramon asked, turning to Rita. "I'm Ramon, as you probably already know. This lovely lady in the chair is Thelma, and over there somewhere," he waggled his hand in the general direction of the back of the salon, "is my useless and lazy partner, Pepper Angelo."

"I heard that," said a voice from the back room. A large, bulky, gray-haired man entered. "Well, hello. You are?"

"I'm Rita Jaramillo. Nice to meet you all."

"So, Rita," Pepper Angelo said, his bright, twinkling eyes fixed on her face. "Are you the woman who is finally going to land our elusive sheriff and make him happy?"

"Uh, I'm . . . uh . . ."

"Rita is a detective with the Santa Barbara Police Department. She's here working a case," Dave said, rescuing her, but also amused at her plight. He showed his amusement with a grin.

"Oh, well, we do hope you stick around," Ramon said. "Dave has been single waaaa-ayyy to long. He needs a woman."

"I'll keep that in mind."

"We have to go now," Dave said, a hand on Rita's elbow.

"Thanks for the delivery," Ramon said in a singsong voice.

"Goodbye," Thelma said.

As they stepped outside, Dave broke into laughter.

"Very funny," Rita said, stomping her foot, trying to keep from joining his gales of laughter. "You did that on purpose."

"No, I did not. I had to deliver the blanket. It's for the HIV drive Ramon and Pepper Angelo are spearheading."

She finally couldn't keep from smiling, even though she knew she blushed at the same time. "Let's go see the Johnson boys."

"Those two have been trying to set me up ever since they arrived. They came from San Francisco, just wanting to get away from the noise, the pollution, and the crime."

"And you don't have a lot of crime."

"No, not a lot, but enough."

"It's so quiet," Rita said, looking at the window as they drove out into the country.

"For the most part."

She knew instinctively that thoughts of his dead deputy filled his head.

"I lost a partner," he said after a moment.

"What?"

"I lost a partner in Los Angeles. That's what really made me come home. I was there, and couldn't do a thing to save him. Shot by a crackhead during a robbery."

"God, I'm sorry." Rita turned to watch him as he drove, a muscle in his cheek working in tension, as though he were clenching his jaw.

She reached out to stroke his face and he caught her hand, and pulled it to his chest.

He held it there the rest of the way to the Johnson place.

When Dave pulled up to a small, ramshackle house in the middle of two empty fields, Rita reluctantly pulled her hand away and surveyed the surroundings.

Tall trees stood directly on both sides of it, but the front yard was filled with stumps. There was no lawn to speak off, only weeds and pine needles, and tons of old junk—washing machines, the rusted-out frames of two or three cars, an old truck that sat up on cinderblocks.

"Nice," Rita said.

"Hey, we have our share of white trash, too. You city folk aren't the only ones."

"Dammit, would you stop calling me city folk, and acting like you're the local yokel sheriff? You're starting to piss me off."

"Sorry," he said, an unrepentant grin on his face.

"If this is the way you're going about trying to get me to stay, I'll let you in on something. It's not working."

"No, it's just my grating, obnoxious personality."

"You think I'm going to argue with that?"

He still chuckled after they exited the car and walked to the doorway. A screen door, useless because there was no netting where the screen should be, was the only thing barring their way. The inside door was wide open, and from inside they could hear loud music and some shouts.

Dave knocked sharply. There was no answer. He grabbed the door and stepped inside, Rita following closely. As the shouting got louder, she instinctively put a hand on the gun that was holstered to her side, hidden under a light jacket.

"No, you moron! I said Anaheim peppers! Those, over there, not jalapenos." As they entered the kitchen they saw three large men, shirtless, big bellies protruding. One of them stood stirring a large pot of red sauce, while the other two argued loudly at the counter about the vegetables they were chopping.

"Peppers, jalapenos, what's the damn difference. They're all the same."

"No, they are not. There is a very different flavor to the—"

"Jesus, Dewayne. I think Momma dropped you on your head when you was a baby or something."

"Hello, boys," Dave said, and the three men turned to face them.

"Oh, hi, Sheriff," the one stirring the pot said.

"Sheriff."

"Sheriff."

After acknowledging their visitors, the two brothers with the knives set back to arguing again. Along the counter were empty beer bottles, and Dave eyed them, then nodded to Rita.

"Boys, we need to talk."

"Can't it wait, Sheriff? We're making salsa," said the big-bellied brother who stirred the pot. "If those two idiots ever quit fighting, we can finish it up and get it in the jars before it's Christmas."

"Chuck, where did you get the tomatoes?"

"From the corner fruit stand."

"You have a receipt?"

"Hell, no, I don't have a receipt. I bought them from that Mex-i-can always sets up shop there. He don't even speak English, Sheriff."

"Chuck, see, I'm hearing you might have taken these tomatoes from someone's garden."

"Oh, that old bitch is saying we stole them tomatoes again? Dammit, Sheriff, we bought them."

The two brothers with knives were glaring at each other, and Rita watched them closely. They didn't seem to hear any of the conversation going on in the kitchen.

"I'm going to need some proof that you—"

"Loser!" screamed the one named Dewayne, as he lunged at his brother wielding the small, sharp chopping knife. Prepared for the attack, the other brother grabbed his wrist and jabbed his own knife, finding a target in the soft underbelly of his brother.

Rita moved quickly and pulled her gun, immediately placing it to the forehead of the attacker. Dewayne crumpled to the floor in a heap, sobbing, holding his side, and then pulling his hands away covered with blood.

Dave told Chuck to turn off the stove and move away from the pot, and he cuffed him. "Just for safety's sake."

He helped Rita turn the brother—whom she learned was called Bubba, no surprise—and they cuffed him, too.

Dave called for an ambulance and they stood surveying the scene, as Rita checked Dewayne's wounds. "It's a surface cut," she said. "He'll be okay."

"I think Momma dropped them both on their heads," Chuck said, shaking his head. "I just wanted to make some salsa."

"While I have your attention, Chuck," Dave said, "I wanted to ask you something."

"Yeah? What?"

"Your daddy ran with Jake Higgins and Sheriff Higgins, didn't he?"

"Yeah, the lazy no-good bastard. Left us for Momma to raise up, never gave her money or nothing. Came by to get laid and get Momma's hopes up, steal what little money she had, and then disappeared again."

"Well, did he ever mention anything about Carl Telford or Alisha Telford?"

"I went to school with Alisha. Pretty girl. Too quiet. Boring, almost."

"Did you ever hear anything about her with Sheriff Higgins?"

"Yeah, I heard something, but I sure didn't believe it."

"What did you hear?"

"Just drunk talk. One night Daddy was here, talking to Momma. I heard him telling her about the sheriff and his brother, about how they found Carl Telford growing reefer in his backyard. No big secret, really. Us boys use to steal it from him . . . Uh, anyway, guess Jake told his brother, and the sheriff came down hard on Carl, said he was gonna arrest him and put him away for a long time."

"What else," Dave asked.

"Daddy said Carl offered them something to get them to shut up and go away."

"And that was what?" Dave said, his voice betraying that he was tired of prodding Chuck along.

"Alisha."

"What?"

"Whenever and wherever they wanted her. Basically, he gave them a sex slave."

Chapter Eighty

"So, what's next?" Chief Hilliard said to Quinn and Lexi. He hadn't protested further after Lexi spoke with him, although Quinn hadn't given him much chance.

Quinn had sent a deputy back to Santa Barbara with Kelsey, giving him strict instructions not to leave her side. They would meet back up at the station to get her statement. For now, she wanted a shower and a nap.

"Well, Chief," Quinn said, "I think—"

Before he could finish his sentence, a shout arose from behind the house.

The radio Quinn held crackled to life, and one of the uniformed deputies summoned them to the shed behind the clapboard cottage.

"We had to break it down," a deputy told him, indicating the twisted door of the old, wooden shed. "It was locked up pretty tight. A deadbolt and key lock."

Quinn and Lexi pushed their way inside the small shed, Lexi stepping back instinctively and shivered.

"Oh, God."

Lining the walls were shelves, and on those shelves were jars filled with clear liquid. Each jar contained severed sexual organs, most likely from the M&M victims.

"Over here." One of the deputies inside motioned them to a corner. He pulled up a wooden slat, and they looked inside to see a briefcase. He pulled it out with his glove-covered hands, and tried to open it. It wouldn't budge.

Quinn pulled out his Swiss Army knife, and donned the gloves one of the techs handed him. He took the knife, quickly jimmied the lock, and it popped open.

Inside, neatly stacked, were hundreds of dollars, tens, twenties, and one hundred-dollar bills. "Guess there wasn't a bank account. Explains why we couldn't find it."

He stood up and turned to Lexi, as the other deputy began cataloguing the contents of the briefcase, getting ready to turn it over to the crime scene techs.

"She'll come back here," he said to Lexi.

"Yes. She will. She doesn't have a choice."

Chapter Eighty-One

The trap was set. All the obvious signs of law enforcement had been removed, as inside the house a bevy of agents and officers waited for Alisha Telford-Boudreaux to show up and claim her money.

The nearest neighbors were evacuated for safety reasons, and also to keep them from talking should Alisha become leery. Outside the house, in different positions, officers were also waiting, hoping it wouldn't be a long night.

Franklin had returned to the SBPD office to take Kelsey's statement. Quinn had called her several times to make sure she was okay.

"This guy will not leave me alone. I have to ask permission to go the bathroom," she told him with irritation.

"That's what I want," was his reply.

Now they waited.

Lexi Anderson watched a group of FBI agents as they played cards: poker with toothpicks for money.

Waiting.

Quinn stood up and walked into the room where they had found Kelsey, puzzling over the contents.

"She claims she didn't plan any of it," Franklin had told him, after he interviewed Tammy Rowe. "She says it was all Alisha's idea, and she was just doing what she was told."

"You get any more out of her than that?"

"No. She clams up when we ask where Alisha might be. The

department psych consultant met with her, too. She says Rowe is delusional. Switches between rational adult and confused child, but it's pretty clear that she was following a lead. She wouldn't have thought it up alone."

"Pretty whacked, isn't it?" Lexi said from the doorway, as he knelt and fingered the hair of a stuffed pink unicorn sitting on the floor.

"It wasn't ever about the serial killing, was it?" he said.

"Well, while I do believe Alisha Telford and Tammy Rowe had enough anger to do it, I think it was all set up by Alisha to cover her tracks."

"So, ultimately, the blame would all fall on Tammy."

"Yes. She's just too messed up to realize it. She thought they were on this big mission to clean up the world of victimizers, when in reality, Alisha was just covering her tracks so she could take the money and run."

"I sure hope she shows up soon."

"Me, too."

Chapter Eighty-Two

"Man, no wonder this chick is so fucked up," Rita said to Dave. They had driven back to the station house with the offending Johnson brother in the back of the car, then put him in the small cell, where he wailed and blubbered like a baby.

Chuck Johnson, who had been guilty of nothing but suspicion of stealing tomatoes, had been left behind, while Dewayne had been transported to the local clinic to be attended to.

They sat in Dave's office as nightfall reached the sleepy town, and the streets emptied. Rita had just hung up from sharing the information about the sheriff and Jake Higgins with Quinn.

"I'm worn out," Rita said, stretching.

"Me, too. Let's get out of here."

"What about Bubba?"

"Marge's husband is on duty." He motioned to the small, bald man who sat at Marge's desk eating a Baby Ruth candy bar and reading a magazine.

"He looks kind of . . . well, small."

"He is. If Marge ever sat on him, that would be it."

"Oh, you are so not funny."

They drove back to Dave's house, lights popping on in windows randomly as they passed, as though the car held some magic light switch that activated each one as they drove by.

"When I was little, I used to dream of living in the country," Rita said pensively, leaning against the window. "We'd have horses and chickens, and Mom would cook huge meals where the whole family would be in attendance. There'd be laughter and annoying aunts, uncles, and cousins, and I could run as far as I wanted and never see a sign of civilization."

"Used to be like that out here. Where did you grow up?"

She sat back from the window and turned to him. "A big mansion in Santa Barbara. Mom was the housekeeper. Most of the time the owner wasn't there. He was a big shot in Hollywood. I had the run of the place most of the time."

"Sounds nice."

"Not really. I mean, Mom and me were close, but then the media mogul's wife killed himself, and we had to clean it up. I saw firsthand what money can do. Then, a couple of years later Mr. Mogul went bankrupt and lost the place. He never came up anymore, anyway. Mom moved back to live with her sister in San Diego, and I stayed on and went to Santa Barbara State on scholarship. Joined the force after I graduated."

"You see your mom much?"

"Not as much as I like, but she and my *tia* Maria like to come visit and tour the wineries. They get tipsy. It's pretty funny."

"I bet. I miss my mom and dad. They were as country as you come. I was just a farm boy. Still am, I guess."

Rita leaned toward him and stared closely at his face.

"What are you looking at?" he asked.

"Hold still, I think I see a hayseed."

Dave laughed and swatted at her hand, and she sat back and leaned against the headrest, comfortable and drowsy.

Maybe she could get used to living here. Maybe.

Chapter Eighty-Three

Alisha Telford-Boudreaux stood on a hill high above her little hideaway. As dark settled in, she had watched the numerous headlights and flashing bars of the police cars leave from the area, and now it looked quiet and abandoned.

It wasn't.

Through her binoculars, before dusk settled in, she had watched several vehicles hide in a grove of trees not far from her property.

They were there, waiting in her house, waiting for her.

They already had Tammy. She'd intended to kill her brother/sister, because she'd worn out her usefulness. Now her dementia was just a liability. It had worked well before, when Alisha had engineered the murders. Everything had gone off without a hitch, Alisha laying out the plan and Tammy agreeing, although reluctantly at first.

But Tammy grew to love the game. So much, in fact, she had moved on Jake Higgins before Alisha was ready. So much, his death had set off an avalanche, resulting in Joe Malone's untimely death, before she could marry him and buy an insurance policy.

That little nest egg would have guaranteed she could disappear and never come back again. She still had enough money to get away, not comfortably, but that money was inaccessible, hidden below, or, if the cops weren't completely stupid, gone.

Now she was in trouble.
Surprisingly, she knew just what to do.

Chapter Eighty-Four

"You smell good," Rita said, cuddling up next to Dave's body, tucking her chin in the hollow of his neck.

"You taste good," he countered, and he reached over and pulled her on top of him. "Can we just stay here for a couple of months? I promise just to fuck you a couple of times a day, maybe six or seven."

"What? I was holding out for twelve. I'm outta here," she said, and pretended to move away from him, but he held her tight and she couldn't escape.

"Fine, then you better be ready to perform." She started to undulate her hips against him, and when she felt his reaction she smiled. Settling herself down on top of him, she watched his face as he closed his eyes and moved inside her, the expressions of passion stirring her own pleasure and whipping it up to a frenzy, until they were moving together in a steady rhythm, culminating in a heart-pounding climax.

She collapsed on top of him and then rolled off, both of them breathing hard with exertion.

After a moment, he turned to her and trailed a finger down her breast and around the nipple, then back up to her lips, where he traced their profile, then bent to kiss her.

"I love you."

She sat up, stunned. "What did you say?"

"I said I love you."

"I . . . it's a little quick, I mean. Oh, my God."

"That's not exactly the reaction I hoped for," he said.

"I'm sorry. I just didn't expect it, that's all."

"It's new, and it's growing, but it's still love. Getting stronger all the time. And I want the chance to let it grow. Even if I have to move to Santa Barbara."

"Are you serious?"

"Yes, I'm serious."

"Wow. Okay, I 'new love' you, too. I'm just not sure where it will end up."

"Why don't we just take it one day at a time."

"Okay, one day at a time."

She fell asleep in the crook of his arm, wondering about this "new love," and where it would take them, visions of small dark-haired children with hazel-green eyes dancing through her head.

Chapter Eighty-Five

Sometime around dawn, Dave awakened, his arm asleep as Rita rested comfortably on top of it. He gingerly pulled it out and stood up, stretching for a minute, then shuffled into the bathroom to empty his full bladder.

When he was done, he padded into the kitchen and took a glass from the cupboard, then walked to the fridge and opened it up, pouring himself a glass of ice water from the pitcher he kept stored inside.

"Well, well, well, who would have known little Davey Sparks would turn out so nice," a voice said from the kitchen table, and he turned in shock to see Alisha Telford, all grown up and ravishing, but still recognizable, sitting in his mother's high-backed dining chairs. Her gun was aimed directly at him.

"What are you doing, Alisha?" he said, trying to keep his voice calm. "Why are you here?"

"Because some friends of yours have something of mine, and I want it back. I figure they don't want to see another cop die, so they'll give me what they want."

"What friends?"

"Don't play dumb, Dave. It's just not cute, although I admit you are one fine specimen. I never would have known. Too bad I was so busy with the local boys, keeping my daddy out of trouble. I should have gotten to know you better. Maybe then I wouldn't be so damned angry."

Alisha stared directly at his crotch and he had to fight the urge to cover his nakedness with his hands. He couldn't play into her game.

"They'll never give it to you," he said.

"Sure they will. I just have to come up with a foolproof plan, that's all. I'm a little tired right now, but when I get my head on straight, I'll figure something out."

She watched him, her head cocked, a look of nostalgia spreading across her face. "You always protected me. When I didn't have anywhere else to go, I came to you and you protected me. How come you never tried anything?"

"You were hurt enough. You didn't need me making matters worse."

"You didn't find me attractive, Davey?"

"You've always been beautiful."

"But you never tried to fuck me."

Dave didn't answer for a minute, until finally he walked a few steps toward her. Alisha shook her head with a warning, and her lips tightened. They stared at each other, and Dave wondered what had happened to the frightened, birdlike girl who used to climb into his bed at night, heart beating like a small sparrow. She would curl up into a ball and press tightly against his back, seeking warmth.

"What did it, Alisha?"

"What are you talking about?"

"What finally pushed you over the edge?"

"I'm not over the edge, Davey. I just wised up, that's all."

"Something happened," he insisted. "Something happened to you. You stopped coming to see me at night, and avoided me during the day. Then you stopped coming to school. What happened."

"I said nothing happened!" Alisha's voice turned harsh, loud, and ragged. "Let it go, Dave. I don't want to hurt you. I don't give a shit about anyone else, but I really don't want to kill you." She lowered her voice again. "But please don't think I won't. Don't underestimate me."

"Did you kill them all, or was it Tammy?"

"I don't do that kind of dirty work. Not unless I have to. Tammy was hurt, too. They didn't know if she was a boy or a girl, so they raised her as a boy. But she insists she was always a girl. I studied it when I got my nursing degree. See, they gave her testosterone shots. Trying to make her into what they believed she was. Really drove her nutty. She mellowed out after a while, once we left, but when the time got close, I started giving it to her again. I needed her just slightly unbalanced."

"How could you do that to her?"

Alisha shook her head and gave him a look of disgust. "You want to know what happened, Davey-boy? You want to know what drove me over the edge?"

Dave was silent.

"Tammy decided she was a girl, and my father blew a gasket. Then Tammy told me the truth. Old Daddy had been sticking it to her for almost as long as me. The sick old fuck had been molesting us both.

"And Tammy? She thought she was in love with her own father. That's when I knew it had to stop. That's when we left."

"You killed your father."

"In a way, I suppose. The idiot was too drunk to get out after I set the house on fire. It was easy. He deserved it. They all did."

"Even the homeless guys? Or John Penny?"

"John Penny was snooping around. My loving mother came to get money from me, the old bitch, since she was in over her head at the Inn. Thought she could blackmail me. I didn't play along, told her to get lost, so she went to Penny and told him I was a murderer. He started digging around, and then told that stupid reporter about it. You can see why they both had to go.

"Now, let's go get your handcuffs. That's enough reminiscing." She stood up. "I need some sleep, and I certainly can't have you getting away from me."

"No!" Dave said forcefully, images of a sleeping Rita being shot by Alisha running through his head. "This won't work, Alisha. You have to stop now. What about Tammy? Are you just going to abandon her?"

"Don't move!" she said, emphasizing her point with a forceful thrust of the gun. "Surely you don't need to be convinced how easy it will be for me to kill you. Tammy was a liability. She was out of control. She started acting without me, before I was ready. If I leave now, they might just believe the murders were all committed by her."

"They won't believe it. They know you did some of them. You were seen."

"It doesn't matter," she said, anger flashing across her face. "I'll be long gone. But you are right about one thing. They won't believe it if I leave you alive to tell them the whole story. I'm really sorry, Dave. I do appreciate what you did for me so many years before."

She stood from the chair and put both hands on the gun, aiming for his chest.

"Drop the gun," Rita shouted from the kitchen doorway, and Alisha turned to her and jerked back, preparing to fire. Rita fired three rapid-fire shots into Alisha's body. She watched with a steely gaze as the woman opened her mouth, then dropped to the floor in a heap.

Dave rushed forward and took Alisha's gun, then trained it on the still body on the floor, but he knew she was close to death. He moved back to the phone and dialed 911, then walked over to Alisha, feeling her throat for a pulse.

"She's dead," he said, standing up.

"I know," Rita said, finally dropping the gun to her side. She had hurriedly put on a shirt and her underwear, but she wore no socks or shoes.

"I was worried she would find you. I was about to rush her."

"I heard a noise. I woke up and heard her voice."

She turned to him and he put his arms around her, as she moved into his chest and stayed there, still, for just a minute. She could hear his heart beating rapidly, and she knew hers did the same.

"Good thing you had your gun."

"Yeah, well, I thought you had another woman in here. I wasn't going to let you get away with that."

He smiled at her joke, and pushed away as he heard the wail of an ambulance.

"Marge's husband had to call out deputies from another county. We're a little short here in Redville."

"I think I know where you can find another one."

"Yeah?"

"Yeah."

Chapter Eighty-Six

"So, what was it you said to Hilliard," Quinn asked Lexi Richards as he and Kelsey sat with her at the Rusty Pitcher, sharing a pitcher of beer and a platter of buffalo wings.

"I told him the FBI was interested in you coming on board. We wanted to see how you perform under pressure. He backed right off. The man is a politician. There is always someone who ranks higher than he does."

"Like the federal government."

Lexi smiled, and wiped her mouth and hands off with a napkin. "These things are horribly greasy. I can feel them going straight to my thighs."

"Were you serious?" Kelsey asked her.

"About what?"

"About the FBI being interested in Quinn?"

"Yes," she said, raising her eyebrows, and then grabbing another hot wing and devouring it.

"I think I need a vacation," was Quinn's response.

"Take a long one, think about it. Always nice to know you have options."

"I have to go back to Utah," Kelsey announced, surprised there was no quiver in her voice. "My mother is stabilized. She's doing better, and they are ready to release her. But they can't let her go without someone to watch over her. That means me, I guess."

"Oh, I am not sure that's a good idea," Lexi said, her concern evident on her face. "Kelsey, you know some of Stone's men are still there, and after he called you, well . . ."

"Did you ever confirm it was him?"

"No, the call came from a pay phone, inside the prison. But we have no way of knowing for sure."

"It was him. He hasn't ever backed down on his claims, has he?"

"No. He still thinks he's divine, and God's army will be arriving any day to kill all his captors and set him free to carry out his father's prophecies."

"Well, I don't have a choice," Kelsey said, resignation coloring her voice a deep blue. "My mother has to be an outpatient for a while, so I'll be there at least three months."

"No," Quinn said, licking his fingers to remove the greasy orange residue from the wings.

"No? No what?"

"It's too dangerous. You can't."

"I don't have a choice. Did you miss that?"

"I can't let you."

"You can't stop me."

"Then I'm coming with you."

"For three months?"

"For as long as it takes."

"After you spent some time at Quantico you could work out of Salt Lake," Lexi offered helpfully, earning herself a nasty stare from Kelsey.

"I don't intend to stay there," Kelsey said with force. "And I sure don't want Quinn tromping all over the country chasing down the dregs of humanity."

"It's not your choice," Quinn said, with "so there" relish.

Kelsey lowered her head to her arms and covered her face, her body beginning to jerk.

"Damn, don't cry. I'm sorry," Quinn said, putting his arm on her. "Kelsey . . ."

She lifted her head and both Lexi and Quinn could see she was not crying, but laughing.

"I would say my life is like a bad movie, but there is never an end to it," she said through the laughter.

"More like a soap opera," Lexi said. "Those never do end."

"Hey, there are good parts," Quinn said. "What about me?"

"You, my love, and Tia, are the only things that keep me sane."

"Hey, what about me?" Lexi ad-libbed, and then smiled as they all laughed.

ABOUT THE AUTHOR

Natalie M. Roberts is the pseudonym for author Natalie R. Collins. Or is it the other way around? She'll never tell. She lives in Utah with her family.